Praise for

THE ROCK ORCHARD

"The Belles' influence is felt throughout Leaper's Fork, and just as inviting are the townspeople in Wall's wonderfully endearing story of love, life, and change, and Wall's extraordinary and original style is the icing on one very enticing cake."

—*Booklist*

"Paula Wall has written a delicious tale about quintessential southern belles with family ties so strong you could lace a corset with them. Authentic, romantic and beautifully told, this is a story to treasure."

—Adriana Trigiani, *New York Times* bestselling author
of *Queen of the Big Time*

"Fast, funny, and surprisingly fresh."

—*Kirkus Reviews*

"*The Rock Orchard* is endlessly clever and addictively fast-paced. To say that Wall . . . has a way with words is putting it mildly, and her storytelling is simultaneously sweet and sharp."

—*Bookpage*

The
ROCK
ORCHARD

A NOVEL

PAULA WALL

Washington Square Press

New York London Toronto Sydney

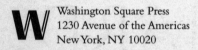

Washington Square Press
1230 Avenue of the Americas
New York, NY 10020

ISBN-13: 978-0-7434-9620-9
ISBN-10:   0-7434-9620-5
ISBN-13: 978-0-7434-9623-0 (Pbk)
ISBN-10:   0-7434-9623-X (Pbk)

First Washington Square Press trade paperback edition January 2006

10 9 8 7 6 5 4 3 2 1

WASHINGTON SQUARE PRESS and colophon are
registered trademarks of Simon & Schuster, Inc.

Manufactured in the United States of America

For information regarding special discounts for bulk purchases,
please contact Simon & Schuster Special Sales at 1-800-456-6798
or business@simonandschuster.com

FOR SHEILA, MY FRIEND, SISTER AND MUSE

ACKNOWLEDGMENTS

MANY THANKS to Aaron Priest, my Solomon; Emily Bestler, dream editor and true Southern Belle; Lucy Childs and Sarah Branham, my guardian angels; Deborah Lovett, if you didn't know the answer, I knew the question didn't matter; Nanette Noffsinger-Crowell, my common-sense compass; all the unsung heroes at Atria who actually sell the book; St. Paul's 7 A.M. Holy Eucharist, Coffee and Tall Tale Club; and Mother Wall, for giving me grit and my love for a good story.

And to Bill, thanks for the ride.

The
ROCK
ORCHARD

PREFACE

JUST BECAUSE a woman is good at something doesn't necessarily mean it's what she should do in life. If that were the case, most of the women in the Belle family would be hookers. It is common knowledge that Belle women make hard men melt like butter in a pan. They are equally adept at reversing the process.

The Belles live in a house that sits on a bluff overlooking the river. It has the look of a place whose owners grew bored with their money long ago. Honeysuckle vines wind around the columns like thread on a spool, and roses, wild as weeds, scratch at the paint like chiggers. It's a mystery where the lawn ends and the cemetery begins. The Belles are of the mind that dead people make the best neighbors.

Several years back, in an effort to turn our boring little town into a tourist trap, the historical society put up a brass plaque outside the Belles' gate declaring the old house an historic site.

Bellereve, the plaque reads, *was built in 1851 by Colonel Bedford Braxton Belle for his bride, Musette. During the War Between the States it was used as a hospital for soldiers of both armies who were wounded at the battle of Fort Donelson.*

History, of course, is never real. People either glorify it or horrify it. Or at the very least color it. What the sign doesn't say is that the fingerprints of slaves are baked into the brick and that when the rain sets in, no matter how many times they plaster and paint, the blood of soldiers seeps through the ceiling and watery red drops drip from the chandelier like tears.

Nor does the sign say that Musette was Cajun French and the second wife of Bedford Braxton Belle. The first Mrs. Belle was neither dead nor divorced, but Musette had a way about her that made a man forget his wife—and forget to breathe.

Musette had black hair and black eyes and could read the future better than most men could read the newspaper. And if she didn't like what she saw, she set out to change it.

"L'avenir n'est pas taillé dans la pierre," she'd say, as she slowly turned over the cards, *"seulement votre épitaphe."*

Loosely translated it means: "The future isn't carved in stone, only your epitaph."

They say Musette could dip her hand in the river and foretell the exact day it would freeze. She could lay her hand over a baby's heart and see his life as if he'd already lived it. Musette predicted fires, floods and tornadoes, and a month before Yankee soldiers marched across the Tennessee state line, she made the servants tear every sheet, petticoat, and pillowcase in the house into strips and roll them into bandages.

Despite her flawless track record, Bedford Braxton Belle wouldn't listen when she told him hard liquor would be the death of him. You can lead a horse to water, but a jackass takes his whiskey straight up. Musette lost her husband at the Battle of Franklin when a Union soldier shot him dead while he was drunkenly relieving himself under a persimmon tree. We rest easy knowing he didn't feel a thing.

Braxton Belle's life didn't bear enough fruit to fill a Dixie cup. But few men rise to the occasion. Most leave nothing more to show for their time on this earth than a stone to mark where their bones are buried. Musette wore black for the rest of her life, but then black was always her best color. And not a day passed that she didn't brush the leaves from Braxton's grave and kiss his granite marker. History may sweep aside the ordinary man, but women have a memory like flypaper.

Women love who they love, there is no rhyme or reason.

Musette never loved another man; however, she didn't object to men loving her. They say she welcomed more men into her harbor than the Statue of Liberty. Despite the fact that every wife, widow, and spinster in town prayed for her early demise, Musette lived to be an old woman and died in her sleep. They buried her body in the cemetery next to the house overlooking the river, but her spirit lingers like a lover's perfume.

Musette's grave is marked with a white marble likeness of her that is so real, if you stare too long, you'll swear her head turns your way and her stone breast rises and falls. Naked as a jaybird, she stares a man straight in the eyes with a look on her face that is far from pious. On either side of her, fully robed angels, hands folded in prayer, gaze longingly toward heaven as if to say, "Lord, help us."

One man's art is another man's ache, and Musette continues to be as big a pain in the ass dead as she was alive. For over a hundred years the aesthetically challenged have frigidly fought to have Musette removed—or at the very least, covered.

But money beats morality like paper beats rock. When an art professor from Nashville scrubbed the moss off the base and found "Rodin" carved into the stone, the balance of power shifted. The historical society immediately threw up a brass plaque declaring Musette an historic monument. Now scholars come from miles around to debate whether she is indeed an authentic Rodin of Paris, or an authentic Bodin from Memphis, whose family has been carving top-notch tombstones for as far back as anyone can remember.

Wherever the truth lies—and around these parts truth reclines on a regular basis—many a young man has familiarized himself with the female anatomy while studying the statue of Musette Belle, just as quite a few of their ancestors learned from studying the real thing. Even in death Musette continues to shock the good citizens of Leaper's Fork, and her descendants are doing their best to carry on her legacy.

Musette begat Solange, who begat Charlotte and Odette, who begat Angela, who begat Dixie. If there is one thing Belle women are fond of, it is begetting.

Some women barter their bodies like whores with wedding bands. Some use sex like a sword. But some women can touch a man and heal like Jesus. The man who sees sunrise from a Belle woman's bed will swear he's been born again.

CHAPTER 1

IN 1920 ODETTE BELLE'S hot-air balloon was struck by lightning and dropped out of the sky like a pigeon that had been shot. No one was surprised. God had been gunning for her for years. His feelings for the man she happened to be straddling at the time are pure speculation.

Spectators standing on the ground below said they could hear Odette laughing all the way down. It was more of a cackle, really—one of those laughs that promises a man he's missing the ride of his life.

The attorneys who handled Odette's affairs solemnly drew straws to see who would deliver her belongings to her next of kin. Fortified with a pint of moonshine, the lawyer who lost handed Odette's bastard baby to Charlotte Belle on a pillow—then ran for his life.

"Who in their right mind would give me a baby to raise?" Charlotte demanded incredulously.

Charlotte Belle had been turning heads and raising eyebrows for twenty-three years. It was commonly held that she was a cold-hearted vamp who thought nothing of stealing other women's husbands. The truth was she had no taste for domesticated men—except when the pickings were slim. Even then, she did not steal them. She merely took them for a joyride.

"People are always making messes for the rest of us to clean up," Charlotte said, slowly exhaling cigar smoke over the child.

Charlotte had no time for weak men or foolish women. She especially disliked tedious people. Since it had been her experience that most people were tedious, she disliked most people. Odette had fallen, as it were, into the foolish woman category.

Except for the canceled checks in their trust fund, Charlotte had not seen or heard from her half sister in years. Even by Belle standards, Odette had been a wild one. How she stayed in the missionary position long enough to get pregnant was a mystery.

"If this puppy is as foolish as her mother," Charlotte said, "we ought to do the world a favor and drop it in a pond."

Head tilted and hands folded on top of her apron, Charlotte's housekeeper studied the child critically. Perfectly content, the baby sucked on the corner of the pillowcase as if it had been dipped in caramel. Lettie had no doubt the child's taste for bed linen was a sign of things to come.

"She's a Belle, all right. Dropped out of the womb flirtin' with the doctor."

"Don't go getting yourself attached," Charlotte ordered firmly, as if wantonness was a universally sought after quality in a child. "She's just passing through."

Charlotte spent her nights at the Poor Man's Country Club and her days sleeping off her nights. She liked her whiskey straight up and her men gone in the morning. The last thing she wanted was a baby, be it hers or anyone else's.

It took nearly a month to find a relative who would take her niece.

"You're handing her over to Maude Meeks?" Lettie huffed incredulously. "Why, I wouldn't give that buzzard a rock to tend."

Dismissing the old woman with a wave of her hand, Charlotte set her jaw and scratched her signature on the check. Nothing hurt Charlotte more than parting with her hard-inherited cash.

Holding the baby tight to her shoulder, Lettie stared down at the check.

"It's absolutely amazing what the goodness of one's heart costs these days. It'd be cheaper to keep her."

"Old woman, don't start that mess," Charlotte said, as she

crammed the check into an envelope and ran her tongue along the seal. "We're not taking in every stray someone drops on the front porch."

"Well," Lettie said, laying the baby in Charlotte's arms before she could stop her, "at least hold her till I get her things."

"Je-sus Christ!" Charlotte fussed and fumbled with the pink flannel bundle as if her body were trying to reject it.

Arms crossed, Lettie stood at the door studying the two of them. One would assume they were mother and daughter, except Charlotte would most likely eat her young.

"You two was cut from the same cloth," Lettie said. "Trouble from start to finish."

"Hell," Charlotte said, head tilted down at the child, "this one's going to make me look like a saint."

"I reckon that Church of Christ cousin of yours will scare the spice out of her," Lettie sniffed, on her way out the door.

Lettie was a born-again Baptist. It had been Charlotte's observation that while the Baptists and the Church of Christ shared the same how-to manual, there was considerable brand loyalty.

As soon as Lettie was out of sight, Charlotte opened the top drawer of her desk, tossed out the contents, and dropped the baby in. Fist crammed in her mouth, the child looked up at Charlotte, black eyes wide as shot glasses.

"Nothing personal," Charlotte said, taking a long thin cigar out of the humidor. "It's strictly business."

Belle women were known for their skills in the bedroom and the boardroom. On a good day, the two merged. Dark velvet curtains draped the windows in Charlotte's office and fringed silk shawls muted the Tiffany lamps. Charlotte's mahogany desk was the size of a bed and it was not the least bit unusual for her to hold business meetings in silk pajamas. When a man walked into Charlotte's office, he felt an immediate urge to dicker.

For men, business is war. For Charlotte, business was like love-making. At the end of negotiations, all parties should walk away satisfied.

Scratching a match under the arm of her chair, Charlotte rolled her cigar in the flame. Shaking the match out, she leaned back and studied the baby in the drawer. As if sensing her fate was in the balance, the child lay perfectly still.

Charlotte did not have a maternal bone in her body. There was no tug in her heart for babies. She felt no sentimental urge to help the helpless. Charlotte was first and foremost a businesswoman. She looked down at the child and saw enormous start-up capital for an unpredictable return and a high probability of loss.

Still, there was the question of who would take over when she was gone. Charlotte had not turned her comfortable inheritance into an obscene fortune for freeloading relatives to fritter away.

"Well, ssshe-it!" Charlotte grumbled.

"Sssht," the baby spit back.

Eyebrows raised, Charlotte leaned over the drawer.

"What'd you say?"

Most likely it was just a sneeze or a sound babies make, but Charlotte took it as a sign. If ever there was a child to follow in her footsteps, it was one whose first attempt to communicate was a four-letter word.

"Lettie!" Charlotte's voice echoed through the old house as she tore up the check. "The damn thing is staying!"

Lettie couldn't hear her. She was in the attic dusting off the crib.

CHAPTER 2

I F THE BABY had a name, the lawyer who delivered her forgot to mention it as he ran to his Studebaker. He also forgot to bring diapers, which at the time seemed the greater oversight.

"How does the name Hope strike you?" Lettie asked, as she fed the baby her bottle.

Charlotte made every effort to ignore Lettie. Every afternoon, from one to three, Charlotte communed with her daybed. It was not a nap, she insisted. Just because a woman is flat on her back with her eyes closed doesn't mean she isn't working.

"Charity is a good name," Lettie chatted on. "But then I've always been partial to Faith." Living with Charlotte, Lettie was accustomed to carrying the full load of a conversation. "Then, of course, there's Patience."

Charlotte's eyebrows arched from the daybed. Actually, the name struck a chord with Charlotte, persistence being her favorite quality.

"Makes her sound like a Quaker," Charlotte finally decided.

"Chastity," Lettie countered.

Charlotte knew she'd better get involved before the child spent her life as a platitude.

"We'll call her Angela," she said decisively. "Angela Belle."

"Your great-grandmother's sister was named Angela." Lettie lifted the baby to her shoulder and patted her on the back. "She wore a chicken's claw around her neck and on full moons danced naked in the graveyard."

"You're not a blue-blooded Belle unless you're crazy as hell," Charlotte said with a touch of pride.

Lettie looked down at the baby siren she held in her arms. There was absolutely nothing angelic about the creature. Dark bedroom eyes and pouty lips puckered for kissing.

Lettie had been taking care of Belles for three generations. She was determined to turn at least one of them into a respectable lady before she died.

"Angela it is," Lettie said, and the deal was closed.

CHAPTER 3

CHARLOTTE subscribed to the free-range school of child rearing. She weaned her niece on Nehi grape juice and let her run around wild and half-naked with the handyman's boys.

"Angela Belle!" Lettie yelled from the porch, "You get in here right this minute and put a shirt on!"

"Boone Dickson ain't wearin' no shirt!" Angela hollered back.

"Well, she's got you there," Charlotte said from behind her newspaper.

Every day, Charlotte read the business section of the newspaper to her niece, and Angela listened as seriously as if she understood every word. People walking past the house on Sundays would see the two of them on the front porch and shake their heads. "She ought to have that child in church," they'd say. And they'd say it again when they walked home after Sunday night service.

The day Angela started school her freedom came to a screeching halt. Lettie scrubbed her black feet with pumice and a brush and somehow managed to force a pair of lace socks and patent leather shoes on her. Fussing and fighting, Angela cursed like a little demon sailor while Lettie pulled a comb through her hair.

"Ssshe-it!" Angela flinched, teeth gritted and tears running down her cheeks.

When Lettie finally got through with her, she was transformed.

"You look like a little lady," Lettie said, hands clasped in front of her. "Now, try and act like one."

All day Charlotte and Lettie watched the clock. When Angela

finally came strolling down the sidewalk, they were waiting at the gate.

"Where are your new shoes?" Lettie asked, staring down at her filthy bare feet.

"I gived the damn things away," Angela said, reaching under her dress and scratching at her lace underwear.

"Who did you give them to?" Charlotte demanded.

"KyAnn Merriweather."

"What did KyAnn Merriweather do to deserve your shoes?"

"Her feet wuz bleedin'."

"Why were they bleeding?"

"Stepped on a broken beer bottle with no shoes on."

"Well," Charlotte huffed, "that's what she gets for living in Stringtown."

If you came to Charlotte's door looking for a handout, she'd give you a broom. Charlotte was born rich and would die richer. For a woman who'd never done a real day's work in her life, she took a hard line on other people doing it.

"There's a reason why the rich are rich and the poor are poor," Charlotte said, "and money has absolutely nothing to do with it."

The only thing that irritated Charlotte more than the person looking for a handout was the person who gave it to him. Do-good-ers, she believed, were edging toward treason. The founding fathers, after all, did not write the Declaration of Dependence.

In capitalism, as in nature, survival of the fittest is the reigning principle. Do-gooders, by contrast, are committed to the survival of the weakest. If do-gooders had their way, Charlotte firmly believed, the American eagle would evolve into a pigeon cooing for crumbs. Needless to say, she thought she was getting dicked in the New Deal.

"What you tax, you get less of. What you subsidize, you get more of," Charlotte preached to her niece.

But nothing Charlotte said or did converted her niece to her theory of economic evolution. Every day Angela arrived home from school with less than she left with. She gave away her lunch, her book bag, and her hair bows. When she started giving away her dresses, Lettie put an end to it.

"No more nice clothes for you," Lettie said, stuffing the rag Angela had worn home into the ragbag.

That suited Angela just fine.

Oddly, Angela took to school like a bird to flight. She completed her homework almost before the teacher finished assigning it and read twice as many books as required. She had an understanding of history as if she'd lived it. Most surprising, she could stand in front of the classroom and read with the passion and clarity of a little southern Shakespearean thespian.

"*In the Churchyard at Cambridge,*" Angela read, standing bone straight and holding the book in front of her, "by Henry Wadsworth Longfellow."

> "*In the village churchyard she lies,*
> *Dust in her beautiful eyes,*
>   *No more she breathes, nor feels, nor stirs. . . .*
> *Was she a lady of high degree,*
> *So much in love with vanity*
>   *And foolish pomp of this world of ours . . .*
> *Hereafter?—And you think to look*
> *On the terrible pages of that Book*
>   *To find her failings, faults and errors?*
> *Ah, you will then have other cares,*
> *In your own shortcomings and despairs,*
>   *In your own secret sins and terrors!*"

"Yes." Teacher Hobbs sighed, hand to her heart. "That was simply beautiful. Now then, Angela, what can you tell us about this poem?"

Book tight to her chest, Angela's dark soulful eyes focused on a place the others could not see.

"That dead woman thought her shit don't stink," Angela said gravely. "But we cain't judge, 'cause in the end we wuz all born tuh die."

Despite Angela's being the best reader in the county, they sent Sue Ellen Parker to the State Speech Contest.

"While Angela is exceptionally bright and has a very good heart," Teacher Hobbs explained delicately, "we are very concerned about her . . . saucy nature."

"I know, I know," Charlotte said, taking a puff on her cigar. "We don't know where the hell she gets it."

While no one had the nerve to say it to Charlotte's face, most people blamed Angela's problems on the children she ran with. "Run with white trash and coloreds," they said, "and it's bound to rub off on you."

By colored, they meant KyAnn Merriweather.

After KyAnn's mama died, her daddy's new wife wanted no reminder of the old wife in her house, KyAnn being the most obvious of the dead woman's possessions. The result was that KyAnn spent more time at the Belles' house than her own.

"Children," Charlotte grumbled, "multiply like maggots."

Exactly who was rubbing off on whom was debatable. Both girls had the devil in them and in Lettie's mind there was only one thing that could save them—baked goods. Lettie firmly believed a woman who couldn't bake an angel food cake from memory had her picture hanging on hell's post office wall.

"We'll start with cornbread," Lettie said, lifting the two girls onto milk crates. "You got to crawl before you run."

Lettie tied dish towels around their waists and handed them each a wooden spoon. The dish towels struck KyAnn as a waste, being as they were much cleaner than the clothes they were wearing.

"The secret to good cornbread is," Lettie said, as she cracked an egg into the bowl, "you got to have your batter smooth and your grease hot."

Wrapping KyAnn's small brown fingers around the wooden spoon, Lettie moved her hand in a circle around the bowl.

"Stir," she said.

While KyAnn grasped the premise, the rationale escaped her entirely.

"Whats I need tuh know how tuh cook for?" she demanded.

"Women cook," Lettie said firmly. "Men eat."

Lettie had grossly underestimated the hand–eye coordination required to stir cornbread. One stiff stir and there was batter oozing down the cabinet and KyAnn's bowl sat spinning on the floor.

"You got to hold the bowl with one hand, while stirring with the other!" Lettie snapped at her.

"Well now, you didn't tell me that, did ya?" KyAnn snapped right back.

Three hours later the house was filled with smoke, grease dripped down the walls, and the backyard was covered with charred cornbread. Jumping and flinching, the girls swatted hot splattering grease with spatulas as if they were fighting off bees.

"Ssshe-it!" Angela hissed with every pop.

Finally, when each girl successfully flipped her first plate of hoecakes, there were tears in Lettie eyes. It was no less a miracle than when Helen Keller learned to sign "water."

CHAPTER 4

THERE WAS TALK of sending Angela away to school, but some-how Charlotte never got around to it. While the other little girls on the Bluff practiced which fork to use and how to dance the waltz, Angela spent her afternoons swimming in Lick Creek, and her evenings sprawled on the front porch listening to Lettie snore in her rocker and Charlotte argue with the evening newspaper.

"New Deal, my ass!" Charlotte huffed, as she read the headlines.

Sitting cross-legged on the floor, Angela and KyAnn scratched their chigger bites and studied the jacks spilled on the floor between them. Tossing the rubber ball into the air, KyAnn swept jacks up so fast Angela could barely see her fingers fly before the ball bounced.

"You should buy the Madison farm," Angela said out of the clear blue.

"And why should I do that?" Charlotte asked, from behind the newspaper.

"Miz Madison says if nobody don't buy it, Judge Lester at the bank's gonna take it."

"It's not my job to bail out the drowning," Charlotte said flatly.

Charlotte already owned half the county. She didn't need any more land.

"Besides, that land isn't good for anything."

Charlotte turned the page of the newspaper and cracked the spine.

"Too far out of town. Too hilly to farm."

The ball thumped quietly on the porch floor. Chin to her chest,

Lettie grumbled in her sleep. After a few minutes, the newspaper fell onto Charlotte's lap.

"Then again, it's on the river. And it's on the way to Nashville."

Staring off the porch, Charlotte took a long draw on her cigar.

"If it had a good road running through it—"

"If you owned it," Angela said, interrupting Charlotte's thoughts, "the Madisons could still live there."

Charlotte stared at her niece, completely baffled. Her niece's instinct for making money was completely canceled out by her inexplicable urge to give it away. It was as if she had been dropped on her head when she was a baby.

Shaking her cupped hands, Angela let the jacks spill onto the floor. And Charlotte went into her office to make the Madisons an offer on their land.

The summer Angela turned fourteen she took up canning. She and KyAnn bought baskets of vegetables and fruit at the farmer's market on the town square, hauled them back to the kitchen and proceeded to shuck, string, and snap.

Charlotte, who couldn't boil water in a teakettle, was flabbergasted.

"Where on earth does she get this?" she demanded, as they watched Angela stir a bubbling pot of thick blackberry jam with a wooden spoon.

"Musta got it from her daddy's side of the family," Lettie said, with her arms crossed.

"Odette always did aim low." Charlotte shook her head.

By the end of the summer you couldn't walk on the back porch for the rows of canned tomatoes, corn, and green beans. Cucumbers pickled in crocks and jars of jelly, jam, and preserves lined the windows like stained glass. Charlotte couldn't sleep a wink for the popping of jars sealing.

"That child is going to make a fine wife," Lettie said with satisfaction.

"I wouldn't bet on it," Charlotte said, as she sniffed a jar of jam appreciatively. "Pass the biscuits."

That winter, when Charlotte went searching through the pantry for a jar of jam, there wasn't one. Word finally got back to Charlotte that her niece and KyAnn Merriweather had been "borrowing" her car and passing out food to the poor folks in Stringtown.

Charlotte threw up her hands.

"There is no cure," she said, "for a bleeding heart."

CHAPTER 5

THE PEOPLE who sold Dr. Adam Montgomery the old Lester house didn't warn him about his neighbors until the deal was done. By that time he had seen Angela Belle standing on the widow's walk and was trapped like a fly in amber.

"The Belles are one of the oldest and wealthiest families in the county," Ann Lester said, as she sipped iced tea on Dr. Montgomery's porch.

"Money so old, you have to blow the dust off," her husband nodded.

"But they don't give a dime to church or charity."

"Sooner open a vein as open their pocketbook."

"And I would have to say their morals are . . ." Ann Lester twisted the pearl necklace at her throat " . . . less than sterling."

"They're white trash with money," Judge Lester declared.

The fact that Judge Lester was actually a banker never hindered him from rendering a verdict. One had to marvel at how prophetic his parents had been in naming him.

"It takes more than money to be old money," Ann Lester summed up neatly.

Dr. Adam Montgomery, whose money was so new the ink was still wet, knew exactly what she meant.

The house had belonged to Judge Lester's old bachelor uncle who passed away in his sleep with a smile on his face, his housekeeper in his bed and a fifth of Jack Daniel's on the nightstand. Fortunately, Judge found the bottle before the Sheriff got there and the

Lester name remained untarnished. Having evolved from a long line of ethically bankrupt men, Judge put great stock in discretion.

The Lesters sold the old place to the young doctor lock, stock, and liquor cabinet. The roof leaked, the floors creaked, and the musty rooms were dark as a tomb, but from a distance the old house looked grand. For Adam Montgomery a pretty façade always took precedence over a flawed foundation.

Adam Montgomery had blond hair and dusky blue eyes that passed for pensive. He had the perfect body to hang a tailored suit on and was the perfect height. With a slight lift of the chin, he looked down on most of the world.

He moved into the Lesters' house like a hermit crab, not changing a thing except for the letter *L* on the brass door knocker, and he didn't get around to that for almost a year.

When folks strolled past the old house and saw Dr. Montgomery sitting contentedly on the front porch, cigar wedged between his fingers and an open book in his lap, they shook their heads. Everyone thought it was bad luck for the young bachelor to buy the old bachelor's house. But whenever the joy of solitary living started taking hold of him, he popped open his pocket watch and stared at the picture of his refined fiancée until the euphoria passed.

The plan was for him to set up housekeeping, take over the lucrative medical practice from the old doctor who was retiring, and then his bride-to-be would join him. He was as inflexible with this plan as he was with his ambition. Adam's rudder was set in life. There would be no detours.

So, when he found Angela Belle lying flat on her back in his flower bed, knees spread and panting like a bird dog, he was caught completely off guard.

"My God," he said, falling to his knees, "you're having a baby!"

When Angela was seventeen years old, she found herself pregnant. Charlotte put the blame entirely on her philanthropic nature.

If there had been a war going on, Lettie could have stuck a ring on Angela's finger and told everyone that the father was off serving his country. Then, when the time was right, she'd kill him off. Maybe give him a medal. But there wasn't a war going on, at least not one that mattered in Leaper's Fork, so everyone knew that Angela Belle was in the family way—without a family.

How she got herself into this mess was not a mystery. Angela was as wild as a barn cat. *Who* was the twenty-dollar question. Regardless, one thing was for sure. She had nipped any possibility of respectability right in the bud—not that respectability had ever been a high priority for the Belles.

In those days a girl who got herself into trouble went away to have the baby, to another town, or if the family had real money, another continent. Maybe she and her mother would bring the baby back and tell everyone it was a new brother or sister. Maybe they wouldn't. But the fact was, a good family simply did not birth their bastards at home, especially in a flower bed.

A pain catching her breath, Angela drove her fingers into the dirt like roots. Throwing back her head, she laughed like a mad woman. Along with loose morals, Angela had inherited the Belle cackle. If Satan's mistress had a sense of humor, she would cackle like a Belle. Dr. Montgomery simply stared at her. Since they hadn't studied demonic possession at Harvard, he was at a loss.

"Do somethin'!" she hissed at him.

Pulling off his coat, he carefully laid it over her bare knees. Angela looked up at him as if he had lost his mind. Granted, she had never given birth to a baby before, but she suspected there was more to it than that.

He had only caught glimpses of her before, but even at a distance she put him to the test. Dark hair, sloe eyes, and a mouth he could not look away from. Adam was a man who worshipped the modern holy trinity—church, country and class. But at that moment, kneeling in the dirt, conviction faded. His eyes moved over her and a heat began to rise from him. He wanted this woman, to take her fully, to have her as his and his alone.

"I thought you was a doctor," she panted, snapping him out of his fog.

Honestly, he had forgotten.

"I'll go get my bag," he muttered, starting to stand.

"What in hell's bells is in the damn bag?"

The answer, frankly, was his courage. But now did not seem the best time to reveal this.

Medicine did not come naturally to Adam. He had no instinct for it. He had been in Leaper's Fork for over a month, but still had not seen a single patient without the old doctor standing by his side. The smell of iodine made him nauseous, blood made his knees weak, and in emergencies he froze stiff as a corpse. In a nutshell, the sick made him sick.

Adam became a doctor for the same reasons he did everything in life—upward mobility. The fact that he had not been born into the upper class annoyed him immensely. While his stepfather was from money, his mother was not. He had never met his real father, and didn't feel guilty about being relieved that he was dead. If he had lived, Adam Montgomery would have been grinding sausage the day Angela Belle's water broke in his flower bed.

A butcher's son has four ways of climbing out of the slaughter-house—business, law, medicine, or marriage. Adam did not have the teeth for law or the backbone for business. Medicine and marriage were his only way up. He had no problem using human suffering as his ladder. He just wished it wasn't so messy.

But Angela Belle had very little tolerance for the observers in life, even when she wasn't giving birth to a zeppelin. Reaching up with her muddy fingers, she grabbed him by the front of his starched white shirt and pulled him down into her face.

"You can do this!" she said through gritted teeth. "I know you can do this!"

And so, filled with the faith of a woman, Adam rolled up his sleeves and pretended to be a man.

"Push!" he ordered, when the time came.

"I can't!" she cried, shaking her head back and forth in his lilies of the valley.

"Of course you can!" he thundered.

There was no doubt in Adam Montgomery's mind that Angela Belle could knock the moon off its orbit if she put her mind to it. She was, after all, the pushiest woman he had ever met.

CHAPTER 6

Angela's baby had chocolate brown eyes and soft black curls. She was the color of toasted almond and smelled like a candy bar. When Angela held her, the child melted into her arms. It was all Angela could do to keep from licking her.

Despite everyone's concerns, mothering came as natural to Angela as breathing. She hauled the baby around with her wherever she went, and thought nothing of plopping a breast out and feeding it on the courthouse steps.

Watching Angela feed her baby was as close to veneration as most men in town would ever get, but the women viewed it from a different angle. Ann Lester called an emergency session of the Christian Women's Charity to discuss the blasphemy over finger sandwiches and fruit tea.

"The cats are gathering at the Dumpster," Charlotte noted, as she and Lettie watched the line of cars pull into the Lesters' driveway from the front porch.

Whenever two or more Christian women came together in a huddle, Charlotte lost what little religion she had.

"Nothing wrong with Christianity that getting rid of the Christians wouldn't fix," Charlotte grumbled into her newspaper.

"Don't throw the baby out with the bathwater," Lettie told her.

Then turning her eyes to heaven, Lettie said a silent prayer for Charlotte's heathen soul, with a footnote regarding getting struck by lightning by proximity.

Despite the Christian Women's Charity trying their darnedest to have breast-feeding banned in public, not one city councilman could bring himself to say the word "breast" at the public hearing. Since they couldn't outlaw "feeding," the issue was dropped.

CHAPTER 7

THE DAY ADAM finally took over the old doctor's practice, he inherited his ivy-covered brick building, his patients, his nurse, and his nurse's African violets. Adam had a problem with the violets.

The low-lying little flowers lined every windowsill in the otherwise spartan office. White violets filled the examination room window and purple ones stared at Adam while he stood at the toilet. Adam pictured himself more a tasteful palm or a split-leaf philodendron kind of doctor. African violets were simply not part of his self-image.

"They certainly are messy," he said, staring at the dead blossoms on the floor and the watermarks on the windowsills.

"All living things are messy," Nurse Marshall informed him brusquely.

Nurse Marshall had been the school nurse for a while, but the job was too cushy. She was meant for the front line. A day without blood was a waste of her talents.

Nurse Marshall ran her office like a military campaign. The waiting room had four ladder-back chairs and a brass spittoon. There were no pictures on the plaster walls and the only magazine was a *Farmer's Almanac*. She did not intend for people to wait in her waiting room.

Nurse Marshall's only passion besides medicine was her violets. And she cared for them with surprising tenderness, pinching their wayward leaves and fertilizing them like clockwork.

In Adam's mind violets were a badge of the blue-collar. Every middle-class home in Leaper's Fork had one blooming in the kitchen window. Adam couldn't bring himself to admit this, and didn't have the gumption to order Nurse Marshall to get rid of them.

He had no choice but to kill them.

Every Friday afternoon, Nurse Marshall filled two large pickle jars with tap water and fertilizer and left them on the kitchen counter to set over the weekend. Every Friday evening, after Nurse Marshall left for the day, Dr. Montgomery doctored the water.

The declining health of the violets became a major concern for the citizens of Leaper's Fork. Every patient who walked through the door lifted a limp leaf, drove their finger into the dirt, and called out their diagnosis. "Too much sun. Too little sun. Too much water. Too little water. Too much fertilizer. Too little fertilizer." Some patients took to waiting on the porch, fearing whatever was killing Nurse Marshall's violets was contagious.

Her inability to heal her violets hit Nurse Marshall hard. She treated for mites and mealy bugs. She changed fertilizers and used a thermometer to check for drafts. She quietly talked to them as she turned them on the sill. But no matter how much of herself she poured into their recovery, the violets steadily declined.

As Nurse Marshall watched the life fade from her flowers, something faded from her. She had always felt that being a nurse was more than her profession. It was her calling. She believed that she was as important to the cure as any pill or procedure. But now, she began to doubt herself. If she couldn't save her beloved plants, what hope did she have against the suffering of the world?

"Angela," the receptionist called from the window, "Doctor Montgomery will see you now."

Baby propped on her hip, Angela padded barefoot behind Nurse Marshall down the hall to the examination room. As they walked past his office, Adam posed in front of his desk, forehead furled over a five-pound medical book randomly opened to jungle rot.

Standing in front of the mirror, Adam combed his blond hair and studied his reflection for a full five minutes before he finally walked down the hall. When he opened the door, Angela Belle was sitting on his three-legged stool, barefooted and knees spread like a nutcracker.

"It's time for her six-month checkup," she said, handing him her baby. "There ain't nuthin' wrong with her."

"*Isn't*," he corrected firmly. "There *isn't* anything wrong with her."

"There *isn't* nuthin' wrong with her," Angela echoed.

And she said it in a way that made Adam feel as if he were the one who needed correcting.

While he listened to her baby's heart, Angela played with his medical instruments. Pressing her tongue down with a wooden tongue depressor, she studied her throat in the reflection of the metal Q-tip canister lid. Shaking down a thermometer, she took her temperature. Then picking up his rubber mallet, she tapped it against her knee.

"You look like you're runnin' a fever," she said, as her long bare leg kicked into the air.

"It's just the heat," he said, as he moved the stethoscope on her baby's chest.

Adam felt Angela's black eyes slowly scrutinize his vest and tie under his white doctor's coat.

"You'd be a whole lot cooler if you'd strip off some of them clothes," she said.

Adam opened his mouth, but nothing came out.

Picking up his tuning fork, Angela tinged it against the counter, then ran the cool vibrating metal over her lips and down her throat. As it hummed past the missing button on her dress into her cleavage, she shivered.

"Ghost musta stepped on my grave," she said, chill bumps on her arms and nipples perked hard as diamonds.

Swinging around, Adam bent over her baby's chart, squeezed his eyes shut, and panted like a dog.

After nearly an hour of examining Angela's baby, while trying to avoid examining Angela, Adam finally conceded.

"She's in perfect health," he said, as he scrubbed his hands at the sink.

"I told you so," Angela said, hopping off the stool.

Leaning over the examination table, Angela kissed her baby's bare belly.

"What a good girl you were," she said, shaking her soft hair all over the child. "And we know what good girls get—a kiss for every day of the week."

The baby kicked and squealed as Angela covered her with kisses. The sight of them together squeezed Adam's heart until it hurt. Angela blurred into a woman at that moment and it made him want her even more. He wanted to press her against the wall and smash his face into hers. He wanted to tear her dress away and squeeze her swollen breasts. . . .

"What about our suckers?" Angela demanded.

Digging into his coat pocket, he pulled out two.

Snatching the candy, Angela left him standing there with his hand hanging in the air. She was halfway across the waiting room when Nurse Marshall called her back.

"It happened all at once," the nurse said, staring down at her dying violets.

Passing her baby to the nurse, Angela popped the cherry sucker out of her mouth and placed it on the *Farmer's Almanac* on the coffee table. While Adam watched from the receptionist's window, Angela picked up a pot, closed her eyes, and held the withered leaves against her cheek as though they wanted to whisper something to her.

When she looked up, Angela's black eyes stared straight at Adam.

Adam stopped breathing.

"Take them home," Angela said, lifting her baby from Nurse Marshall's arms. "Change the dirt and water them with rainwater. They'll come 'round in 'bout a month."

"I've been growing violets in this office for fifteen years." Nurse Marshall shook her head. "They've always loved it here."

"What we love and what loves us," Angela said, *"isn't* always one and the same."

Then, pulling her sticky sucker off the magazine cover, Angela popped it back into her mouth and padded barefoot out the door with her baby on her hip.

Adam had three more patients to see after Angela left—a sore throat, a high blood pressure, and an infected arm. Under normal circumstances he would have breezed through them in an hour, barely taking the time to look at the names on the files, much less their faces. His job was to fix what was broken. Medicine, Adam felt, would be the perfect profession if only a patient could drop his illness off for repair.

But that day the essence of Angela lingered in his office. Twice he thought he caught a glimpse of her straddling the three-legged stool next to the examination table, watching him. The thought of her, knees spread and licking her sucker, had a profound effect on his bedside manner.

He took a swab of Booker Earhart's sore throat, just to make sure it wasn't the strep. He laid his hand over Hattie Taylor's when he broke the news to her that her blood pressure was a little high, and she'd have to give up bacon. The infected arm belonged to Leroy Stinson. Somehow, Leroy had managed to hook himself instead of a crappie while he was night fishing under the bridge. Leroy wasn't sure if it was the hook or the rusty fish knife he used to cut it out with that had made his arm swell up like Popeye's.

"If it gives you any more trouble," Adam told Leroy, as he walked him to the door, "give me a call at home."

Nurse Marshall and the receptionist raised their eyebrows at each other.

That afternoon, Adam fell asleep at his desk, head on his arm and drooling on Booker Earhart's chart. All that compassion had drained him dry. The courthouse clock chiming jerked him awake. Combing his fingers through his hair, he cursed Angela Belle. Even when she wasn't in the room, he felt her pushing him in a direction he didn't want to go.

CHAPTER 8

WHEN DR. MONTGOMERY'S fiancée looked out the window at the Leaper's Fork train station, she almost didn't get off the train.

"Chin up," Mrs. Jackson said, gripping her daughter's hand bravely. "We knew it wouldn't be Boston."

Lydia Jackson was a cameo come to life. Her skin was porcelain. Her hair spun platinum. Men stared at her as though she were a work of art. Her placid expression seldom betrayed her thoughts, and she held herself very still, as though any sudden movement might disturb the admirer's viewing experience.

"What is that hideous smell?" Mrs. Jackson asked.

The man sitting across from them tilted his nose up and sniffed.

"Well, now," he said, "I reckon that would be the renderin' plant."

He knew Mrs. Jackson couldn't possibly be talking about the chewing tobacco or snuff plant, which, from his point of view, was perfume for the nose.

"It's simply awful," Mrs. Jackson muttered, pulling a scented hand-kerchief out of her pocketbook and holding it to her nose.

"Wait til summer." The man nodded knowingly. "You ain't smelt awful till you get a whiff of them pig heads afloatin' down the Red River in August."

Expressionless, Mrs. Jackson stared at the man.

" 'Course," he added, making a little sucking noise between the gap in his teeth, "nuthin' grows them catfish like pig parts."

Mrs. Jackson had warned Lydia on the train ride down to expect that the surroundings might have caused some amount of deterioration in Adam.

"Men always veer off the track when you turn them loose," she said knowingly.

But Adam's decline was not so much a slight detour as an expedition. Lydia's eyes passed over him twice before recognizing the unkempt man standing with his hat in his hand on the train platform. His shirt was wrinkled, his shoes scuffed, and his hair looked as if it had been combed with a rake.

Adam sensed her disapproval immediately.

"Forgive me," he apologized, self-consciously combing his fingers through his hair. "I've been up all night delivering the Wallace baby."

Lydia stared at him blankly. Somehow, she had placed "Doctor" in the same category as Earl or Count. It had never occurred to her that Adam would actually have to do something.

To say Lydia and Mrs. Jackson had expected a more formal welcome would be an understatement. But they were aware that people were watching them, smiling and whispering behind their hands, and so, said nothing.

"It was touch and go," Adam said, picking up their bags. "A breech. But Louise Wallace is a fighter."

Without so much as a hello, Adam dove into the details of his night. Half of what he said sounded like a foreign language to Lydia and her mother. The other half was so repulsively graphic he could have been describing some pagan native ritual. They couldn't believe he would tell them such things.

"When she started to hemorrhage, we held our breath," Adam went on, oblivious to the fact that all color had drained from Lydia's already porcelain white face and that her lips had formed a thin seamless line.

The qualities Lydia had admired most in her fiancé, his dapper appearance, aloof demeanor, and cool detachment to anything non-material, had been replaced with a passion for his profession.

"Being a doctor is so much more than I thought it would be," he said, eyes shining. "It is beyond words."

Lydia certainly couldn't think of any. It had been almost a year since he'd seen her. She had been jarred to death on a train for what seemed like weeks. She was standing in a noisy train station in a smelly small town, and the man she was supposed to marry looked as though he should be standing in a soup line.

But none of these things were what caused the shadow to fall over Lydia's face. Lydia was simply one of those women who could not tolerate two suns in a man's universe. For Dr. Montgomery to enjoy his work was one thing. Having it eclipse her was quite another.

"Lydia is very happy for you," Mrs. Jackson said, gripping Lydia's arm so tightly it cut off the circulation. "Aren't you, dear?"

Slowly, Lydia smiled. She was a woman who understood delayed gratification perfectly. Adam noted that she looked a little like a baby with colic.

A town is like a woman, either she knows what she's worth or she doesn't. Since the Belles had always owned half the county, Leaper's Fork did not sell herself cheap.

It was Musette Belle's observation, as she entertained both Yankee and Rebel officers, that in good times or bad the one thing a man was sure to reach for was a cigar. The result was that while the cities around her crawled into the backseat with any filthy factory or foundry that flashed a little cash, Leaper's Fork became the pampered mistress of tobacco. Granted, she didn't grow like her industrious sister cities, but she didn't age like them either.

Buyers, sellers, and growers from all over the world came to do a little business, bringing their money with them. By the turn of the century, you couldn't skip a rock without hitting a white-columned mansion. Tennessee walking horses pranced on velvet pastures and slept in barns nicer than anything a Chicago factory worker reared his children in.

Pull a sheet off a clothesline in Chattanooga and it was dirtier than before you washed it. Drink a glass of water in Nashville and you were playing typhoid roulette. But in Leaper's Fork a woman's dress was still white when she got home from church on Easter Sunday, and a preacher could dip a sinner into the river without poisoning him before the baptism took.

The stock market went up and the stock market went down, but just as Musette had predicted, men kept lighting up. And Leaper's Fork had money to burn. Unfortunately, the prosperity only trickled across the river. When the privileged felt like slumming, they took the ferry over to Stringtown for whiskey and to listen to the river blues. In that regard, nothing much had changed the day Dr. Adam Montgomery took his fiancée on a tour of the town.

Five tree-lined streets named for dead presidents fed into the courthouse square. Twice, Mayor Pegram, a contractor by trade and a developer's pimp at heart, tried to cut down the trees to widen the streets. Both times Charlotte Belle swore she'd widen the gap between his rear end if he did.

Everyone set their watch by the courthouse clock, which always ran a little slow. And everyone knew everyone else's business, usually before they knew it themselves. Old men lined the courthouse benches in the shade, spitting tobacco, and whittling away at the truth and the stick of maple in their hands. There was a church on every corner, steeples pointing the way to heaven. Each had the new doctor on its prayer list, ostensibly for his work with the sick, but in truth to save his Catholic soul.

On the glass storefronts were carefully painted signs for Harrington's Hardware, Mason's Barber Shop, McHenry's Florist, the First National Bank, the Feed Store, the Kandy Kitchen, which was owned by the Greeks, the Dime Store, and Winningham's Drug Store. There were two funeral homes in town. If you needed a hospital you had to drive fifty miles to Nashville, but Leaper's Fork could bury its dead with the best of them.

"But where are the dress shops?" Mrs. Jackson asked, turning her head from side to side.

Adam slowed the car to a stop in front of Mademoiselle's, the town's best dress shop. Velma Bellamy was dressing a mannequin in the front window while Hattie Taylor stood outside nodding her approval or shaking her head. An ornate Victorian birdcage sat by the door on the sidewalk.

"They keep blackbirds at the dress shop?" Mrs. Jackson frowned.

"It's a mynah bird," Adam explained. "Robert E. Lee."

"She's a big girl!" the bird squawked and whistled. "She's a big girl!"

"Filthy creature," Mrs. Jackson muttered.

Adam quickly threw the car into gear and drove on.

Once around the square and you'd seen all there was to see. The speed you took a visitor around depended on your objective. Adam drove so slowly Mrs. Jackson could see liver spots forming on the tops of her hands.

In truth, Adam's goal was not so much to sightsee as to be seen. People strolling on the sidewalk stopped to watch as they drove past. Men leaned against the barbershop door, and women pressed their faces against the window at the Kandy Kitchen.

Adam had no doubt they were looking at Lydia. He glanced at her in the seat beside him. Her platinum hair gleamed in the sunlight and her pale profile was regal. He was glad he had put the top down. He was glad the pale yellow color of her dress matched his pale yellow convertible.

"Wait until you see the post office," he said, sensing the women's deteriorating mood.

They rounded the courthouse and he downshifted to a stop beside the feed store so they could get the full frontal view of the architectural wonder. Rome has the Coliseum. France, the Eiffel Tower. Leaper's Fork has its post office.

"The architect was a political prisoner in China for ten years," Adam explained, summarizing the historical society's brass plaque on the front of the building for them. "When he was released, our government compensated him by commissioning the post office."

The architect's stay in an Oriental prison had a profound influence on his art. The streaked copper roof sloped like a pagan temple. Giant beaked gargoyles with clawed feet glared down at pedestrians from the arched corners, and the dark deep-set windows looked like black eyes daring patrons to enter. The architectural highlight of Leaper's Fork was the most grotesque structure Mrs. Jackson had ever laid eyes on.

"Imagine spending the best years of your life staring out a tiny window at the same landscape day after day," Adam said, as they stared at the building.

Lydia had been in Leaper's Fork less than two hours, but knew exactly how the architect must have felt.

CHAPTER 9

LYDIA AND HER MOTHER had expected a small gathering of the town's elite for their first public appearance. Lydia bought a new dress specifically for the occasion. Instead, without taking them to change out of their travel clothes, Adam drove straight to Dot's Diner, known for its meat and three. He ordered "specials all around" before the ladies even sat down.

The front of the diner faced the courthouse. The back looked out over the river. But it was the points of view being argued in between that really got your attention. Men huddled around coffee cups and argued everything from politics to religion to the life span of a lightning bug trapped in a jar.

A varnished large-mouth bass stared down from over the cash register. And, compliments of the cigarette vending machine salesman, a giant red, white, and blue poster of Uncle Sam waving an American flag with one hand while smoking a cigarette with the other covered the back wall.

Under normal circumstances Mrs. Jackson would not have set foot in a place like this. But it was an hour past her mealtime and she was getting irritable. Judging by the looks of her, she hadn't missed that many meals.

"Do you eat here often?" Mrs. Jackson asked, glancing around the diner.

Adam ate two meals a day at the diner. Sometimes three.

"From time to time," he said.

"Who does the cooking at the house?"

"Mrs. Meeks."

"But I thought she was the housekeeper."

Along with the furniture, Dr. Montgomery inherited the old Mr. Lester's housekeeper.

"She manages both nicely," he said.

The truth was Mrs. Meeks's idea of a light dinner was country ham and biscuits with hot grease gravy. She wasn't that fond of cleaning either.

While Mrs. Jackson held her fork to the light and Lydia ran a gloved finger across the table, the other patrons sipped their coffee, chewed their pie, and stared at them.

"How's that arm doing?" Adam called out to a man sitting on a stool at the counter.

"Doc, she's jest 'bout healed," Leroy Stinson said, holding up his bandage. "That med'cine you give me done dried the oozin' right up."

Mrs. Jackson was still trying to recover from the oozing, when Dot appeared at the table and announced the catch of the day. "Coleslaw, hushpuppies, white beans, and fried catfish straight off the trot line," Dot said proudly, as she dropped their plates on the table in front of them. "Willie threw on an extra cat as a welcome."

The purpose of Lydia and her mother's visit was to start the renovations on Dr. Montgomery's house before the wedding. By the end of the meal, it was painfully obvious to both of them that this would not be necessary. This was not an easy decision for Mrs. Jackson. A lot of time and money had been invested in the merger between her daughter and Adam Montgomery.

The Jacksons' fortune was fading fast. Any day they would be old money without the money. Lydia's great-great-grandfather arrived in this country with the clothes on his back and the conviction to do whatever it took to never be anyone's lackey again. But like a print, each generation of Jacksons had faded a little from the original. Now all that remained was a genius for spending money without the slightest idea of how to produce it. Mrs. Jackson maintained their lifestyle by chipping off bits of her late husband's assets and selling them to the highest bidder. She had fried her golden goose and was selling it by the piece. Lydia was the breast and thigh.

Lydia Jackson was as cultured as a pearl. She had grown up with nothing but the best. She knew this because people told her so. But Lydia depended on the good taste of others to get her by. She was the last person to applaud at the opera, she never offered her opinion at the theater because she didn't have one, and she wouldn't know good wine from cough syrup.

Lydia measured herself by the envy of others. And nothing gave her greater pleasure than possessing things other people wanted, even if she herself had no use for them. In truth, that was why she was engaged to Dr. Adam Montgomery. Good looks, a Harvard degree, and the trust fund from his stepfather made Adam one of the most sought after bachelors in Boston. Naturally, Lydia set out to do whatever it took to reel him in.

But now, away from civilization, Adam's value had depreciated considerably. What good is money if you live in a place where you can't spend it? Holding her daughter's eyes, Mrs. Jackson solemnly nodded, signaling Lydia to do what must be done.

"Adam. . . ." Lydia began.

Adam eagerly turned to his fiancée.

Another woman might hesitate at breaking a man's heart. That thought never crossed Lydia's mind.

She thought about the dreary train ride, days of staring at nothing but pastures and hills. She thought about how selfish it was of Adam to move her to this backwater void. She thought about the time she had wasted on the engagement, and all the potential husbands who had slipped through her fingers during that time. She thought about Egan Mercer, whose family was one of the oldest and wealthiest in Boston. If she were engaged to Egan, she'd be sitting on the front porch of his winter home on Banyan Island instead of staring into the glassy eyes of a mounted fish.

By the time Lydia stopped thinking, breaking the engagement seemed kind compared to what she really wanted to do, which was shove Adam's face into the puddle of grease floating on her plate.

"Adam," she said firmly, "there is something we must discuss."

But as Lydia was about to break the news, Adam's eyes drifted away from her across the restaurant to the front door. His posture straightened and a heat rose from him that Lydia could feel from across the table.

Turning, Lydia followed his stare to a girl with a baby plopped on her hip like a basket of dirty laundry.

"Good heavens!" Mrs. Jackson squinted across the room. "Is she wearing shoes?"

Angela's bare feet were so dirty they looked like penny loafers. But that was the least of her problems. Several of the buttons on her dress were missing and her hair was such a tangled mess one expected bats to come flying out.

Brushing a wild strand off her forehead with the back of her hand, Angela scanned the room. Lydia couldn't help but notice that every man's head turned to her like needles pointing north. Spotting Adam, Angela wove her way through the tables toward him, in his fiancée's mind, like a snake in the grass. Instinctively, the hair on the back of Lydia's neck bristled.

"Mama and baby is doin' just fine," Angela announced when she arrived at their table, "but Daddy Wallace is lookin' a little green around the gills."

Belle women had been visiting newborns for as far back as anyone could remember. Many a mother held her breath until a Belle leaned over her baby's crib, laid her hand on the baby's chest and spoke her mind. Everyone was relieved when Angela inherited the job, since most of what was on Charlotte's mind was unspeakable.

"Is the baby eating all right?" Adam asked.

"Jumped on the teat like a duck on a June bug," Angela said.

It was not the words that passed between Adam and the girl that made Lydia and her mother glance at each other across the table.

"Adam," Lydia said sternly.

Turning to Lydia, Adam seemed to go blank, blinking as though he had not only forgotten she was sitting there, but who on earth she was.

Shifting the baby from one hip to the other, Angela held out her hand.

"Angela Belle," she said, "Dr. Montgomery's neighbor."

In all his letters to Lydia, not once had Adam mentioned this girl.

"Lydia Jackson," Lydia said, laying her thin hand lightly in Angela's, "the future Mrs. Adam Montgomery."

When Dot Wyatt came around to take their pie order, she was surprised to see that not a bite of food had passed between Dr. Montgomery's fiancée's lips.

"Is sumpthin' wrong?" Dot asked, staring at Lydia's untouched plate.

"I don't eat freshwater fish," Lydia said, in a way that made everyone around her stop chewing.

"Well," Dot said, jerking the plate off the table, "I'm not sure you could call this river 'freshwater,' but I'll ask around."

Lydia smiled.

Frankly, Dot thought she looked a little constipated.

People dropped their heads as Dot stomped past them on her way back to the kitchen.

"Well?" Willie asked, wiping his hands on his apron as he peeked through the service window.

"Butter wouldn't melt in her mouth," Dot muttered, as she banged Lydia's plate into the trash.

The Jackson-Montgomery wedding was scheduled for the following Easter, but under the circumstances Mrs. Jackson decided the date should be moved up.

"Thanksgiving?" Adam nearly spit his drink across his living room. "But that's less than two months away."

"Lydia simply cannot bear to be separated from you a minute longer," Mrs. Jackson explained, sitting next to Lydia like her translator.

And so, when Adam put Lydia and her mother back on the train, it was with the understanding that he would join them in Boston in four weeks.

"Do you think it's safe to leave him here alone?" Lydia asked, as she waved good-bye through the train window.

"It is *never* safe to leave them alone," Mrs. Jackson said, as she pulled off a glove.

"Perhaps you should stay."

Mrs. Jackson glanced out the train window at Adam standing obediently on the platform.

"Oh, let him have his last hurrah," she said, smiling as she waved. "Nothing makes a man more manageable than a little guilt."

CHAPTER 10

"Mornin', Dr. Montgomery," the man said, as they passed on the street.

Ed Binkley tipped his hat while his young wife, Mary Louise, tucked her cheek into her shoulder like a dove and blushed a smile.

Adam touched the rim of his hat and bowed his head slightly, not so much as a greeting, but a blessing. He had no idea who these people were, but the fact that they knew him and greeted him with respect, even awe, made him swell. Their deference settled on him like 24-karat dew. This was why he left Boston and came to Leaper's Fork—instant esteem. Those who frown on being a big fish in a small pond have never swum with the sharks.

In Boston, Adam was a man who had everything, but was nothing. In Leaper's Fork, he was the man he always wanted to be. Here, Adam believed, his life would be ideal. As long as no one ever truly got to know him.

Lydia's visit was like a splash of ice water. Suddenly, Adam saw himself, the town, and Angela Belle through Lydia's eyes. Lydia's visit healed him of his temporary insanity over Angela Belle. It reminded him of where he came from and where he was going. Next to Angela, Lydia was like a pearl among hogs. What had he been thinking?

His fiancée was everything he wanted in a wife. She was beautiful, refined, and well connected. They made a handsome couple and would have handsome children. Adam could be sure Lydia would never do anything to embarrass him.

Angela Belle, on the other hand, was humiliation incarnate. Her morals were beyond tarnished; they were eroded and pocked. She was crude, vulgar, and rough as a corncob. She wore dresses his housekeeper wouldn't use for rags, had a mouth like a sewer, and a laugh that clawed his skin like dirty fingernails. She had absolutely no refinement and he withered at the thought of being seen with her in public. Of course, it was the thought of being alone with her that haunted him.

The night before he was to leave for Boston, Adam sat on his back porch smoking a cigar. He told his housekeeper he liked to watch the moon rise over the river, but Mrs. Meeks knew the only thing Adam Montgomery was mooning over was Angela Belle.

Cigar wedged between his fingers, Adam swirled brandy in a glass. What he really wanted was a beer. But even alone on his own back porch, Adam kept up appearances.

Falling autumn leaves gave the air an amber hue as though seen through a jar of honey. Across the river, smoke rose from Leroy Stinson's tobacco barn, and bales of hay bound with twine lay scattered on the fields. When Adam heard the courthouse clock bell, he turned to the Belle house. Just as surely as the sun set every evening, Angela Belle would be there to watch it.

The French doors on the second floor eased open and she strolled out onto the widow's walk. Arching her back, she stretched like a cat. Then leaning against the rail, she slowly ran a bare foot up and down the back of her leg, stroking herself. Most red-blooded men would have looked up at Angela Belle's long tanned legs and breasts hanging over the balcony and thanked Jesus. Adam could not help but notice that she didn't cover her mouth when she yawned.

The sun was molten red. "Blood on the sun," the old timers say, "means a storm is on the way." As the sun slipped into the river, it set the world ablaze. The windows of the Belle house seemed to burst into flames, and Angela appeared to be standing in a house on fire. For a brief moment, Adam had the overwhelming urge to rescue her.

He didn't notice the wall of rain moving in until he heard it on the roof above his head. As he watched the shower move across his lawn, he assumed Angela would run inside. She didn't. Standing on the balcony, she watched it come as though she had willed it.

Tilting her head back, she opened her mouth and let the drops fall on her tongue. Rain ran down her face and throat, and her hair streamed down her back like spilled black paint. Dress clinging to her, she slowly began to sway.

Adam glanced from side to side, his face burning. He found no consolation in the fact that he was the only Peeping Tom witnessing this woman's wantonness.

The harder it rained, the harder she danced, shoulders rolling, arms stretched above her head. When it started to thunder, she unbuttoned her dress and let it fall. Only by the grace of God did Adam keep from sucking the cigar down his throat.

Eyes closed and hips rocking, she slowly ran her hands down her slick silk slip. Adam leaned forward in his chair like a puppet being pulled to life by his strings. As she slid the straps off her shoulders, all Adam's plans and promises slipped away. When the slip fell to her feet, Adam came out of the chair like a horse out of the gate.

Running down the porch steps, he tripped and slipped across the muddy yard. Unable to find the path through the privet hedge between their houses, he tore a new one. Lightning cracked the sky wide open and thunder rattled the windows, but Adam kept running through the rain like a man desperate to catch the last train to paradise.

He was taking the front steps of the Belle house three at a time when he heard it. A baby was crying. Angela Belle's bastard baby. The sound stopped him like a brick wall. Head bowed, he stood perfectly still. Rain ran down his face and dripped from his lips and chin. Slowly, Adam backed down the steps.

Five weeks later Adam was married. It was a large wedding, even by Boston standards. Lydia wore a white satin gown from Paris that made her look long and slender, like one of the white calla lilies she carried.

Julia Mercer, Egan Mercer's sister, was the maid of honor. Crone Sewell was the best man. Crone and Adam were not close friends. The truth was, Adam didn't even care for him that much. But as Lydia pointed out, Crone was the same height as Adam and from one of the oldest families in Boston.

There was a stained glass window of the Nativity behind the altar in the cathedral. As the priest droned on about the sanctity of marriage, Adam found himself staring at the Virgin Mary and thinking of Angela Belle. He could see her lying in his flower bed, black hair strewn around her face, and her knees spread.

"You can do this," she said, pulling him down to her. "I know you can do this."

In the cool dark cathedral, Adam's face flushed, and sweat beaded on his lip.

It was the silence that brought him back.

"What?" Adam blinked at the priest.

"Do you take this woman to be your lawfully wedded wife?" the priest repeated.

As if confused, Adam turned to his groomsmen. Collis Taylor nodded encouragingly and Crone Sewell glanced at his watch. Adam glanced back at the stone-faced people shifting uncomfortably in the pews. It occurred to him that he knew hardly any of them.

Then he turned to Lydia. Her skin was the color of frost.

"Adam?"

"Yes?"

The priest, taking this to be Adam's answer, continued with the ceremony. When Lydia slipped the ring on Adam's finger, she thought the tears in his eyes were for her.

Adam and Lydia honeymooned in Italy. In Naples, Adam rented a convertible and drove Lydia around the Piazza Municipio, with the Mediterranean blue harbor on one side and the medieval monastery Certosa di San Martino on the other.

"Many believe the monastery is the finest example of Neapolitan Baroque architecture in the world," Adam quoted from memory.

At the Castel dell'Ova they looked out at Mount Vesuvius and the islands of Procida and Ischias. At the foot of the hill of Posillipo, fishing boats and yachts bobbed in the inlet. In the Gothic church of San Domenico Magiore, they strolled past fourteenth-century frescoes and the masterpieces of Caravaggio and Giordano.

"The apse of the church was built in 1289 and there are 27 chapels," Adam read, as they stood in front of the *Annunciation* by Titian.

"Yes," Lydia said. Sighing, she turned to face him. "But where are the dress shops?"

In the evenings, while Lydia soaked in the tub with the bathroom door locked, Adam sat on the balcony of their hotel room watching the sunset and aching for Angela Belle.

They were scheduled to spend three warm months in southern Italy. After six frigid weeks with Lydia, Adam cut the honeymoon short.

"Are you coming down with something?" Lydia asked, as she sipped her tea.

"Hypothermia," Adam said, motioning for the waiter to remove his untouched breakfast.

Cup suspended in the air, Lydia stared across the table at him. For a split second, Adam thought he saw concern cross her face.

"Is it contagious?"

"Apparently," Adam said.

Lydia moved to Leaper's Fork with the conviction and self-sacrifice of a missionary's wife following her husband into the jungle. As luck would have it, she discovered a small tribe of old moneyed natives living there. Granted, it was southern old money, but what they lacked in East Coast sophistication, they more than made up for in liquid assets.

Rolling up her sleeves, she set out to civilize the southern rednecked savages. If she couldn't convince Adam to return to Boston, then, by God, she would bring a little of Boston to Leaper's Fork.

Among the wedding gifts was a package from Egan Mercer, the man Lydia didn't marry. Shoving all the other gifts aside—silver, crystal, china, and linen—Lydia stared at the brown package tied with string, lightly brushing her finger over the name on the return address.

Slowly, carefully, she peeled the packing paper away as if picking the petals off a daisy. He loves me. He loves me not. When she lifted the top off the silver foil box, her hand went to her mouth. Nestled on the silk lining of the box was a delicate Herend porcelain swan, hand painted, fragile as an eggshell, and small enough to fit in her palm.

Since it was from Egan, she knew it must be valuable. Lydia loved it immediately.

"Oh," she sighed.

Adam looked up from his book, didn't see the point, and resumed reading.

"It's from Egan."

Jealousy stabbed Adam in the chest, but it had almost nothing to do with Lydia. Hearing the name Egan Mercer always put a knot in his stomach.

Cradling the swan in both hands, Lydia walked across the study and placed it on the fireplace mantel like a sacrifice. Adam could never again enter the room without seeing it. A constant reminder of the life she gave up for him. A constant reminder of the man Adam wasn't.

CHAPTER 11

On SUNDAYS, Charlotte rested. From Lettie's point of view, it was completely indistinguishable from the other six days of the week.

Hands wrapped around a coffee cup, she sat on the front porch staring at a spider's web. Spanning from the eave of the porch to the Boston fern to the rail, it was an architectural wonder. Fragile as frosty breath, yet tough as fishing line. It was cruel by necessity, yet the dew beaded on the silk threads like pearls on lace. Charlotte was mesmerized by the beauty, humbled by the design, and challenged by the contradiction. But mostly, she was in awe of the architect.

Every night the spider wove the web. And every morning Lettie knocked it down with a broom. Against all odds, Charlotte always held out a little hope that the spider would win. On Sundays, Charlotte stared at a spider weaving a web and saw the face of God. That, in a nutshell, was Charlotte's religion.

"Sally Colston is expecting again," Lettie announced, as she pushed herself up the porch steps. "That'll make seven. Doc says one more baby and her bladder's going to fall out."

On Sundays, Lettie went to church. As far as Charlotte could tell, God had absolutely nothing to do with it.

"John Bellamy is back on the bottle, weaving and staggering all over the place." Lettie clucked her tongue as she slowly lowered her stiff bones into her rocker. "Man could barely carry the collection plate."

Finally situated, she turned her attention to Charlotte. The day was half over and Charlotte was still lounging on the front porch in her pajamas, hair like a rat's nest and makeup smudged around her eyes.

"Those flimsy pajamas are indecent," Lettie said.

"You should have seen me before I put them on," Charlotte said into her coffee cup.

Sighing, Lettie turned her scrutiny to the lawn where Angela was playing with her baby. Kneeling on the grass, Angela reached her arms out in front of her as she gently coaxed the child to come to her. As she wobbled precariously toward her mother, she squealed with delight. Like all Belle women, she was immune to the fear of falling.

"Angela ought to have that baby in church," Lettie said.

"Can't think of a better place for a child to develop a mind that's not her own," Charlotte replied.

Ignoring her, Lettie dove into her real mission.

"Today's sermon was from Nehemiah," she said, tugging her gloves off a finger at a time. "The public confession of sin. It's all well and good to confess your sins to God, but since God knows everything anyway, it ain't news to him. No, sir, Reverend Lyle says you have to lay those transgressions on the altar. Public humiliation is a small price to pay to be saved from an eternity of hell's fire. Wash that dirty linen in public, Reverend Lyle says, and you're not likely to roll in the mud again."

Snapping open her patent leather pocketbook, Lettie took out a handkerchief and patted her forehead. Taking a deep breath, she preached on.

"Reverend Lyle says if we had to wear a sign around our neck announcing our sins, there'd be a lot less sinnin' goin' on in this town."

She turned her eyes toward Charlotte.

"Some of us," she said, "would have to wear a billboard."

"How is it," Charlotte asked, "that every Sunday it takes you four hours to summarize a one-hour sermon?"

"Reverend Lyle only preached fifty minutes today," Lettie said, pulling a hatpin from her hat. "He's coming down with the flu."

"God is a just god," Charlotte said into her coffee cup.

The war between Charlotte and Reverend Lyle was common knowledge. Nothing irritated the Reverend more than a happy sinner. And there was no happier sinner than Charlotte Belle.

"A good woman does not drink, curse, or dance!" he preached from the pulpit. "She does not smoke or wear pants like a man!"

At least once a month, Reverend Lyle gave a blistering sermon on what a good woman was not.

"A good woman does not spend her nights at the Poor Man's Country Club! She does not hoard her money from the church and the needy!"

There was no doubt in anyone's mind who he spent most of his sermons referring to. Short of calling out Charlotte's name and address, the description of wanton woman fit her to a *T*.

"If you heard the sermon yourself," Lettie said, "I wouldn't have to tell you about it."

"Jesus Christ couldn't sit through that fool's sermons."

"*But I say unto you,*" Lettie recited, "*whosoever says, 'You fool!' shall be liable to the hell of fire.*"

"Old woman, you don't thump the Bible at me—you beat it like a drum."

"That's because along with being hardheaded, you are apparently hard of hearing."

Charlotte pushed off her rocker so hard it slammed against the wall. Nothing irritated her more than having religion shoved down her throat. And no one carried a bigger shovel than Lettie.

"Baptists are like fleas!" Charlotte flared. "Impossible to get rid of and irritating as hell!"

"On Judgment Day," Lettie said smugly, "I have no doubt the burn will take your mind off the itch."

Cursing under her breath, Charlotte stomped off the porch and headed across the lawn. Lettie, spotting the spider's web, reached for her broom.

Mr. Bennett, the caretaker, was accustomed to seeing Charlotte Belle wander through the cemetery at all hours of the day and night.

"It's where she does her thinking," he explained to his assistant, Digger.

Leaning against his pick in the half-dug grave, Digger watched Charlotte slowly stroll among the tombstones in her white silk pajamas.

"Most women got bats flyin' in their head," Mr. Bennett said, tapping his temple. "That Charlotte Belle's got a man's mind."

"I bet thinkin' ain't all she be good at," Digger said, as he drove his shovel into the dirt.

Mr. Bennett grew reverent as he reflected on the time he caught Charlotte Belle offering her condolences to the widower Jack Briley on top of his late wife's tombstone. Most women were seduced by sweet talk and promises. The smell of funeral wreaths and tombstones brought Charlotte to her knees. The woman never missed a funeral.

CHAPTER 12

"I SWEAR, I BEEN so tired here lately," Reba Earhart said, rubbing her hands together on the kitchen table, "it's all I kin do to throw scratch to the chickins."

When a woman needed a second opinion, she came to the Belles. No one doubted Dr. Montgomery could analyze piss with the best of them. (It was his ability to pour it out of a boot that gave them pause.)

"You got four boys," Charlotte said bluntly. "Why aren't their lazy butts out feeding the chickens?"

The Belles' kitchen was not your average woman's altar. When you gathered for communion at the Belles' table, you were not served solace.

"What'd Dr. Montgomery tell you?" Angela asked, as she refilled Reba's coffee.

"He give me these here pills," Reba said, pulling a bottle out of her pocketbook.

Wiping her hands on her dress, Angela took the bottle and studied the label.

"Take them with a saltine soda cracker," she said, handing the bottle back, "or they'll make you sick as a dog."

They say the more money you have, the less you're compelled to flaunt it. At the Belles, Baccarat crystal collected dust in the china cabinet and the lace linens never left the cedar chest. A bottle of Louisiana Red Hot sat in the middle of the kitchen table and a pot of

55

white beans simmered on the stove. Glass wind chimes clinked on the back porch and the breeze blew through the screen door into the kitchen like warm baby's breath.

Taking a tea cake off the plate, Reba nibbled on it. She had one tooth giving her trouble and several already gone, but her sweet tooth was still hanging in there.

"You sleeping all right?" Angela asked, breaking a tea cake in two and handing half to her baby playing on a quilt on the floor.

"Cain't hold my eyes open in daylight," Reba admitted. "Cain't close um at dark."

Poor women grow old fast, but Reba was speeding toward the finish line faster than most. Hair dull as pewter. Forehead creased like a Japanese fan. She was the same age as Charlotte, but to look at her you'd guess she was ten years older. Head tucked, shoulders slumped, she carried herself like a whipped dog.

Women like Reba were a mystery to Charlotte. She'd walk a mile to save a penny on a pound of bacon, but tossed the years of her life away like scraps to the dogs.

"Charlie says if we don't get rain soon, we'll be feedin' the corn to the hogs," Reba said, staring out the kitchen window.

Charlotte huffed. "Charlie Earhart can barely tell time, much less predict the weather."

Reba's daddy's farm had been the pride of the county, before Charlie got his hands on it. River bottom so rich you could spit and grow teeth. Now, if you sent a soil sample off to the agriculture office, the analysis would come back saying, "add dirt."

Charlie was a man with more pride than sense. If Reba said go left, he'd go right. If she said it was going to snow, he'd put on a short-sleeve shirt. It was Charlotte's theory that every wrinkle on Reba's face would melt away if Charlie Earhart choked to death on the chew of tobacco he kept stuffed in his smug cheek.

"I been waitin' on Charlie's daddy hand and foot," Reba sighed. "Thought that stroke woulda slowed him down, but I swear he gets meaner every day."

Reba rubbed a bruise on her arm the color of eggplant.

"And I guess you heered my oldest done got it in his head to move up to Dee-troit. Wants to work in that car factory."

Hands wrapped around her coffee, Reba stared at the cup as if she might find hope at the bottom.

"They say Dee-troit's a mighty mean place."

"Earl's moving to Detroit?" Charlotte shook her head. "Lord, I sure feel sorry for those Yankees."

Reba chuckled behind her hand to cover her missing tooth. Her laugh was as close to crying as a plum to a prune.

"Ain't it the truth," she said, shaking her head. "Ain't it the truth."

Angela glanced across the table at Charlotte, and Charlotte nodded. Disappearing into the pantry, Angela came back carrying a small brown bottle.

"Pour a capful of this into Charlie's daddy's coffee in the morning," she said, handing the bottle to Reba. "It'll improve his disposition."

"It won't kill him, will it?" Reba whispered, staring at the bottle.

"Not unless you force it down his throat with a shotgun," Charlotte said from behind her coffee cup.

Reba's face burned. A woman had to watch her thoughts when she was around the Belle women.

"Now," Charlotte said, striking a match under her chair and rolling a cigar over it, "have you seen what Garner is charging for a smoked ham at the grocery?"

Shaking the match out, Charlotte leaned back in her chair.

"What do you say you keep a dozen or so of those piglets Charlie is planning to give away at market, fatten them up, and hang them in that old smokehouse behind the barn? Why, folks used to drive all the way from Nashville for one of your daddy's smoked hams."

Then they talked a little business, because in Charlotte's mind the woman who doesn't control her own economics can never be saved.

CHAPTER 13

WHEN THE GYPSIES came to town to bury their dead, the town slept with one eye open. They locked their doors, nailed down everything that could be nailed down, and leaned a shotgun next to the bed. Of course, the travelers still robbed them blind.

"Locking your door against a Gypsy is like putting up a picket fence to keep the wind out," Lettie said, jerking damp clothes off the clothesline as though any minute a traveler was going to swoop down and snatch her billowing bloomers.

Anything that turned up missing, the town blamed it on the travelers. If the stolen watch or pocketknife then turned up on the floorboard of the truck or under the couch cushion a month later, the good citizens reasoned the Gypsies would have taken it if it hadn't been lost in the first place.

The Gypsies set up camp on the edge of Stringtown, downwind of the dump. It was a traveler's paradise. A spring gushed out of the bluff, the tin dipper still nailed to the tree from the year before, dry limbs for firewood lay on the ground as if they'd spilled out of a truck, and the dump was like a giant five-and-dime store without the cash registers. Bandanas tied over their nose and mouth, the children picked through the smoldering heaps, scavenging scrap metal, hubcaps, and anything else they could barter, sell, or use. The older men set up shop by the road, where they did metalwork and horseshoeing. And the women took off for town to sell trinkets and wander door-to-door asking for odd jobs.

By the end of the week, they covered the town like migrant birds. A fiddler played while his daughter danced on the sidewalk. Men threw dice behind the feed store. And children too small to snatch candy off the Kandy Kitchen countertop stole roses from the Garden Club's grounds and sold them on the courthouse steps.

When word got out that the old fortune-teller was back reading cards in the alterations room of Mademoiselle's Dress Shop, every woman in town suddenly needed a new dress.

The year before, the old Gypsy had told Dot Wyatt she would "find what she had lost." The very next day Dot found a twenty-dollar bill wedged in the seat of a booth at the diner. Despite the fact that Dot could not exactly recall when she'd lost the twenty, there was no doubt in anyone's mind that the fortune-teller was the real McCoy.

The fortune-teller also told Mary Louise Binkley that her eldest son was going to die. Well, Mary Louise didn't have a son—or a daughter either, for that matter.

"*Bibaxt*," the *drabaripé* said, patting Mary Louise's hand. "Bad luck comes even to good people."

Four months later, Mary Louise miscarried and the baby was a boy.

Knowing the old Gypsy's cards dealt not only fortune but also misfortune gave one pause. Still, the line of women willing to gamble with their fate snaked all the way around the dress shop.

"Going to the devil! Going to the devil!" Robert E. Lee cawed, running back and forth on his perch, as the women filed past his cage.

To ease their trepidation as they waited, the women shopped. It was inevitable that, given enough time, they would find a pair of earrings, a purse, or a hat that they simply could not live without. Business at the dress shop always doubled when the travelers were in town.

As soon as Clara Bowen, the mayor's secretary, sat down at the alteration table, Hattie Taylor rushed over to the door. Pretending to straighten the rack of hair barrettes, Hattie tilted her head toward the crack in the curtain.

Clara was a gaunt, lonely, wasted woman. Even fat didn't like hanging around with her. When she typed, you could hear bone hitting metal. On the outside, Clara was as neat as a pin. On the inside, she was pure nasty. If you had business at the courthouse, you had to pass through Clara—and Clara made sure the trip was as difficult and drawn out as possible. A couple could drive to Kentucky, get married, go on their honeymoon, and have a baby in the oven before Clara would approve a marriage license. If you bought a piece of land on the Red River, you'd have better luck moving the river than having the deed transferred. There wasn't a man or woman in town Clara hadn't pissed off at one time or another.

What goes around comes around. When Clara brought groceries home, the bag always broke before she made it into the kitchen. When she got her hair fixed at the Beauty Barn, it was sure to rain, and she couldn't pull a new pair of silk stockings out of the package without snagging them. Nothing came easy for Clara, and that made her even harder.

"I want you to know, I don't believe in this nonsense," Clara told the fortune-teller sharply. "I think it's pure hogwash."

Shuffling the worn cards, the old *drabaripé* ignored her. Clara was not a woman who liked being ignored.

"I only have ten minutes for this." Clara brushed an imaginary fleck of lint off her tailored suit to establish the hierarchy in the room. "I have to get back to the courthouse."

The fortune-teller slapped the deck on the table and Clara cut the cards.

"Your work . . . ," the old Gypsy began, as she slowly turned over a card, "it is very important."

Clara leaned imperceptibly forward in her chair.

"*Kon khakhavel o balo wi leste si I shuri,*" the Gypsy said.

"What does that mean?" Clara demanded.

The actual translation was, "The one who feeds the pig also holds the knife over it when it is fattened." But a gifted fortune-teller always distills the cards into a more palatable form.

"The sacrifice you make," the Gypsy said, shaking her head sympathetically, "no one knows."

Clara's chin lifted lightly, pulling her flat chest up with it.

"Your man boss . . . he is a fool."

Clara's thin lips drew into a colorless pucker like snapped rubber bands.

There was no doubt in Clara's mind she would make a better mayor than the man who held the office. There was no doubt in her mind that she was too good for every man who thought he was too good for her. There was no doubt in Clara's mind about anything— and that's what made men leery. Nothing puts a man off like a woman who whittles on his masculinity.

"You do work. He get glory."

Clara fell back in the chair.

"I do the work. He gets the credit?" Clara huffed bitterly. "Tell me something I don't know!"

The fortune-teller wanted to tell Clara she was a bitch, but figured that wouldn't be news to her either.

The town was evenly divided about the Gypsies, the pros being the people who made money off them, the cons being the ones who were conned. In Charlotte Belle's mind, it was probably a wash. She'd never seen people work so hard for the freedom to do nothing. Still, she'd take a Gypsy over a lazy loafer waiting for a handout any day.

Charlotte was working at her desk when she glanced up and saw the Gypsy running across her lawn, skirt jangling with Judge Lester's silverware. Crouching behind the hydrangeas, she bobbed up to see if the coast was clear. Then flying up the porch steps, she darted through the open French doors into Charlotte's office, and flattened her body against the wallpaper.

Breathing hard, the Gypsy watched anxiously to see if she was being followed. Then sensing she wasn't alone in the dark room, she slowly turned her head. At first all she could make out was the glowing tip of a cigar. When her eye finally focused on Charlotte, she sucked in a breath and froze. She was wearing a blood-red skirt, five pounds of fake gold bracelets, and had a wolf's tooth hanging around her neck, but apparently, she thought if she didn't blink, Charlotte wouldn't notice her.

"You stole from Judge Lester?" Charlotte asked, staring at the teaspoon sticking out of her hem.

"What he expect?" The Gypsy shrugged. "You step on a snake, you surprised it bites you?"

Across the street, they could hear doors slamming and Judge Lester yelling at the housekeeper. Charlotte calmly took a draw on her cigar. In her mind there was nothing lower than a thief. Under normal circumstances she would have had the woman tarred and feathered. But somehow a Gypsy robbing a banker struck her as heavenly accounting.

"*Vitsa,*" the Gypsy said, as though she had read Charlotte's mind, "we cut from the same cloth."

"Steal from me," Charlotte said, through a cloud of smoke, "and you'll never steal again."

Lifting the wolf tooth to her lips, the Gypsy kissed it.

Her eyes were smudged with charcoal liner and her wrists were green from the cheap bracelets dangling on them. Her blouse hung off a shoulder and her cheeks were so hollow, they looked bruised. Her name was Radmila, Mila for short, and as thieves went, she was highly industrious.

Hands on her hips, Mila wandered around the room appraising Charlotte's office, then Charlotte.

"You marry money?" she asked, her fingers skimming over the silk shawl draped over the couch.

Charlotte huffed.

"Ah," Mila curled her lip, "you born with gold spoon on tongue."

"I could give you this house and every penny to my name," Charlotte said flatly. "In five years, I'd be the richest person in the county and you'd be back stealing gold spoons."

"Money," Mila shrugged, "she is a curse."

"Only," Charlotte said, "to those who don't have it."

Cautiously leaning forward, Mila peeked out the door toward the Lesters'. Then she looked back at Charlotte. Since Charlotte hadn't snitched on her, she was in debt to her. To not pay one's debts was *prikasa,* very bad luck. Reeking of Ann Lester's perfume, she jangled across the room.

"Kintala," she said, jerking Charlotte's hand up. "A favor for a favor."

Turning Charlotte's hand over, the Gypsy traced the lines with one of Judge Lester's butter knives. Charlotte couldn't help but notice that there was a *W* engraved on the Lesters' silverware. One could only assume that Judge Lester, being the idiot that he was, couldn't spell his own name.

"Many men want you," Mila said, head bowed over Charlotte's hand, "but you want only one."

Mila's face was so close Charlotte could feel her hot breath.

"I see him!" she suddenly said in amazement. "I see him right here!"

"What does he look like?" Charlotte demanded.

"He save people in the water," Mila said very slowly, as she searched Charlotte's hand.

"The love of my life is a lifeguard," Charlotte scoffed.

When it came to men, Charlotte didn't have a discriminating bone in her body. But it'd be a cold day in hell before she loved a man with a job that was seasonal.

"Tell me who it is!" Charlotte ordered.

Mila turned her dark eyes up to Charlotte and knew she had her. Grabbing Charlotte's wrist, she held her roughly.

"Give me your magic," she hissed, digging her dirty fingernails into Charlotte's skin, "the magic that gave you all this! You have enough. You don't need any more."

Charlotte's breathing slowed and her eyes narrowed to black lethal slits. Dropping Charlotte's hand, Mila drew back as if she'd been holding a rattlesnake.

"*Never* threaten me during negotiations," Charlotte said, in a voice so low it came from the grave.

"You give me what I want." Mila shrugged sheepishly. "I give you what you want."

"I thought you said money was a curse."

"Only," Mila said, "to those who don't have it."

Charlotte liked a quick study. Finding the conditions of the deal acceptable, she uncoiled.

"If money's all you're looking for, you'll never be rich."

Mila waved her hand impatiently in the air. She didn't have time for philosophy.

"Tell me how to make the *love* come to me," she demanded.

The Romani word for money is "love." If there is a word for love, Mila did not need it. Charlotte didn't speak Romani, but she knew exactly what Mila meant. The language of money is universal.

"I can tell you how to draw money like a magnet," Charlotte said quietly, as though it were a seduction. "The secret to being rich is this. . . ."

Lips parted and breathless, the Gypsy leaned toward her.

"You are what you are, until you decide to be different."

Eyes narrowed, Mila jerked back. Glaring at Charlotte, she spit on the Oriental rug.

"Chor! O xonxano baro! You are a liar and a thief!"

"I never dick a partner in a deal," Charlotte said, leaning back in her chair. "If you want to be rich, I've told you all you need to know."

Grudgingly, Mila grabbed Charlotte's hand again and stared at her palm. But just as she opened her mouth to tell Charlotte what she wanted to know, her head jerked away. Charlotte turned to see what had spooked her. Running across the yard waving a shotgun, was Judge Lester, the Sheriff right behind him.

"Thief! Thief!" Judge yelled.

And when Charlotte turned back, the Gypsy was gone.

The travelers buried their dead in the pauper's graveyard next to the city cemetery. It was a pitiful place. Ragweed grew as high as the markers and flowers rotted in broken pots. A wrought iron fence surrounded the plot, the rusty bars bent and bowed as though the dead had tried to beat their way back to the living.

What the Romani lacked in real estate, they more than made up for in ceremony. Nobody threw a funeral like the Gypsies. More important, they paid in cash. They shipped Emil Mazursky's body to a holding vault at Foster's Funeral Home, where two of his wife's brothers stood guard until the rest of the tribe could assemble.

"I promise you," Mr. Foster assured them, as the two men poured a line of salt around the casket, "your brother-in-law is perfectly safe with us."

Despite all of Mr. Foster's assurances, the brothers refused to leave Emil's side. They were not guarding the dead from the living. Emil had treated his dog better than his wife. He beat her, took other women in her bed, and humiliated her every way a man can. His wife was a small dark woman of few words, the most lethal kind of woman. No one was surprised when Emil and his dog died suddenly and simultaneously.

The Romani believe the dead return to haunt the living. So the question was, who should the tribe fear more, the ghost of Emil Mazursky—or the woman who killed him?

"A man fit as a stallion falls dead—it happens," they shrugged.

Until Emil was safely buried, his wife hid. Her face covered with a scarf, she sat in a circle of burning candles tying the *Mulengi dori*— the dead man's string—to protect her. As soon as one began to flicker, she lit another. Back and forth she rocked, kissing her *treshul* and frantically muttering words of protection. *"Bolde tut doshman,"* she whispered. *"Desrobireja."*

Even after her brothers sewed Emil's lips together and plugged his ears and nostrils with beeswax to keep his soul from slipping from his body, no one called her name for fear Emil would find her.

The widow's brothers hired the Negro band at the Poor Man's Country Club to lead the funeral procession. Since they didn't know any Gypsy music, the band played "Just a Closer Walk with Thee" as the Gypsies walked behind Emil's casket through town, wailing and sobbing. People pulled their cars to the side of the road until the procession passed and pedestrians took off their hats and rested them on their chests. At the cemetery, four Romani stood guard at the entrance so only their own could enter.

Red McHenry, the florist's son, had decorated the "empty chair" for the deceased. He wound satin ribbon up the legs and arms, and covered the cane in carnations and chrysanthemums. It was a beauty, everyone said. Red had a flair for funerals, like a true craftsman for the dead.

One by one, the Gypsies stood in front of the coffin, making last amends with Emil. Then came the Pomana. They sang and danced and ate and drank. They threw coins onto the coffin and tossed Emil's personal belongings onto the bonfire until you could see the flames from across the river. When they lowered Emil into the ground, they jumped down onto the coffin and danced on the dead.

That night Charlotte dreamed she was in the graveyard dancing with the Gypsies. Clapping and stomping the ground, they twirled around the fire. The Gypsy from her front porch was there, the wolf tooth swinging at her cleavage.

"Drink," Mila said, shoving a bottle at Charlotte.

Turning the bottle up, Charlotte kept drinking until the Gypsy jerked it away from her. Charlotte's eyes closed and her head fell back. Grabbing her hand, Mila pulled her to the edge of the fire.

"There," she said, pointing into the flames, "there he is. The man who will own you."

While the Gypsies danced around her, Charlotte searched the fire. She could see the outline of a man wavering in the heat, but she couldn't make out his face. Every time she stepped close enough to see him, the flames forced her away.

"*Kintala,*" Mila said. "I have told you all you need to know."

Then the Gypsy threw back her head and laughed.

At dawn, the travelers were gone. The fire was nothing but embers, and the grave of Emil Mazursky was covered with pins, needles, and nails. Broken bottles were planted around the perimeter, shard up, and *treshuls* hung on the tombstone to keep the soul buried.

Charlotte woke up with the worst hangover she'd ever had in her life. She dragged herself into Dot's Diner and waved away her usual plate of sausage and eggs. Feeling her way to the end of the counter, she climbed up onto a stool and rubbed her temples as Dot poured her coffee.

"Wonder what those Gypsies did with the dog?" Ben Harring-ton asked.

"What dog?" Willie asked, leaning through the service window.

"The one she poisoned with her husband."

"They buried it on top of the casket," Charlotte said, from the end of the counter.

CHAPTER 14

T HE DAY LYDIA JACKSON married Adam Montgomery she was as pure as pasteurized milk. Before they were married, whenever Adam's kisses got a little too passionate or his hand slid a little too high, Lydia quickly pushed him away.

"Stop," she said firmly.

It made Adam want her all the more.

But when he went to kiss his bride on their wedding night, he realized what Charlotte Belle had known about Lydia the first time she laid eyes on her. Lydia was so cold you could make ice cubes in her mouth.

At first, Adam thought it would be a simple matter of reeducating Lydia. After devoting so much time and energy to saving herself for marriage, naturally it was going to take a while to thaw her out. What Adam didn't consider was that a woman who can effortlessly shun passion for twenty-four years might not be resisting it—but avoiding it.

"Adam," Lydia grimaced, as she peeled his fingers off of her, "must you cling to me like a burr?"

Being a man of great reason, and at that moment, very little action, Adam considered every possible cause for his situation. Maybe there was something physically wrong with Lydia. Maybe she had been traumatized as a child. Or maybe he was to blame. Surely, if he were more of a man, he could bring the woman out in Lydia.

The thought of this last possibility sucked the life right out of Adam. If he couldn't satisfy Lydia, a woman with no experience, what hope did he have with Angela Belle? Not that it was a possibility, he quickly reminded himself. But a man doesn't become a doctor without suffering from the preexisting condition of enlarged ego. And so, taking a deep breath, Adam blew the notion of his own inadequacy away and put the blame on Lydia.

In public, Adam was an envied man. In private, he was sleeping with a marble statue. When he leaned to kiss her, she turned her head. When he held her, he could almost hear her counting the seconds she felt obligated to stay in his arms before pulling away.

"Really, Adam," she'd patronize when he begged. "Pull yourself together."

Their marriage evolved into a simple barter system. When Lydia wanted something, she let Adam have his way. Even then, making love to Lydia was as close to playing solitaire as a man could get.

Meanwhile, as Adam slowly froze to death, Angela Belle simmered next door like a pot of red-hot jambalaya. Angela wasn't yet twenty years old, but her thermostat was already set on Steam. If she had been alluring as a girl, womanhood was turning her into a smoldering siren.

Every night young men would "just happen to be in the neighborhood." On Saturday nights automobiles lined the driveway beyond the gate and onto the street. Adam could handle the parties. Sometimes, he even built up the courage to crash them. It was the single strange car parked in front of Angela's house that burned a hole in him. The thought of Angela alone with another man sent Adam into a seething frenzy. The fact that he had these feelings as his wife slept peacefully beside him was irrelevant.

"Why doesn't he just pee around the perimeter of our yard?" Charlotte asked, as they watched Adam cut through the hedgerow between their houses.

"Why don't you like him?" Angela mused, arms draped around the porch column as if she were part of the vine growing on it.

"He's never done anything to like."

"Maybe he will someday."

"I wouldn't put any money on it," Charlotte said.

Adam was a man torn in two. From the neck up, he wanted Lydia. But the rest of him wanted Angela. Standing next to Angela made his heart race and his body burn. Lying in bed next to Lydia, he was afraid to go to sleep at night for fear he'd wake up with his balls banded.

In Lydia's mind sex was a filthy, crude business, and women who liked it were no better than squalling cats in the night. A woman of class and breeding was above the desire and devoid of the need. Since Angela Belle lacked both conditions, Lydia could only reach one conclusion. She was a slut.

And so you can imagine Lydia's horror the first time she found her houseguests from Boston lounging on the Belles' front porch.

"Now, now, dear," Mrs. Jackson said, patting her daughter's hand, "don't throw a hissy."

"A *hissy?*" Lydia hissed, knowing the only place her mother could have possibly picked up such a term was Charlotte Belle's front porch.

Lydia had devoted herself—and her husband's money—toward making their home a "destination." She fancied herself floating through a houseful of the East Coast elite, dazzling them with continental cuisine, priceless art and antiques, and a perfectly stocked wine cellar. They would tour her gardens and marvel at her ability to create such a cultural oasis in the southern desert.

In reality, every evening Lydia watched her guests meander across her yard to the Belles', where they delighted in such southern delicacies as moonshine in Mason jars, bawdy conversation, and shoofly pie.

The more frustrated Lydia became, the meaner she got. The meaner she got, the scarcer Adam became. He would leave home early and work late. The only time they saw each other was passing in the hall, where Adam dropped his eyes and pressed against the wall to avoid touching her for fear she'd claw his eyes out.

It's funny the things a woman's mind will cook up when she's left alone to stew. Day after day Lydia wandered through her empty house noting every speck of dust Mrs. Meeks missed and every wilted petal the gardener neglected. She moved her porcelain swan from the left side of Adam's mantel to the right, stepped back and studied it, then put it right back where it was to begin with. She stared at her reflection in her dressing mirror for so long she could see herself aging, the corners of her mouth dropping, the muscles in her neck tightening like catgut on a violin.

From her front porch, Lydia could hear the Belles and their guests laughing. She knew they were laughing at her, or worse, pitying her. When she caught her husband staring longingly toward the Belle house, Lydia really began to sour. Granted, she had never been that sweet to begin with, but now she was turning to vinegar.

It was already dark when Adam joined the gathering on the Belles' front porch. Fringed silk scarves had been tossed over the lamps inside the house—cobalt blue, lipstick red, pumpkin gold—so that the wavy old windows looked like stained glass. Half a dozen young men and women draped themselves on the porch, ice clinking in their glasses and the tips of their cigarettes glowing like red lightning bugs. A few lawn torches had been lit, just enough to keep a person from falling off the porch, and a bar had been set up so they could help themselves.

A young good-looking man was well into a story when Adam joined them. His accent was high southern, the syllables sustained, slow and smooth, but with an occasional lick Adam couldn't quite put his finger on.

"And fa-ther said, 'I am sor-ry, but we simply do not allow dogs in the . . .'"

Adam realized he was the funeral director's son, home from college for the spring break. He was a Harvard man, like Adam.

The young man stopped mid-sentence, lips still parted for the word that had failed to materialize. The others followed his stare back to a woman walking across the yard. Silver satin poured over her as though she were dressed in moonlight. She seemed suspended in the night, immune to gravity and the earthly laws that weighted the rest of them down. Sensing they were watching, her head turned their way. Even from that distance her eyes drew them in, caught the young men's breath and held it.

"Charlotte!" one of them called out. "Come join us!"

Seeing the looks on their young faces, she laughed. It was a laugh that let them all know how little they knew about anything, but how exciting it would be to find out. Someone cleared his throat and the young man who'd been telling the story looked around disoriented.

"I'm sorry," Foster said, throwing his hands up hopelessly. "I completely forgot what I was talking about."

And everyone burst out laughing.

"But what happened to the dog?" someone finally asked.

"Oh, they buried him with the corpse." Taking a drink, Foster continued to watch Charlotte's progress across the yard. "They buried it on top of the casket."

CHAPTER 15

"EASY, DOC!" Boone Dickson sat on Adam's examination table. There was blood splattered on the front of his white T-shirt and his knuckles were raw. It was going to take at least twelve stitches to close the gash over his eyebrow.

"Beer bottle," Boone answered when asked. "Ol' Danny Baker thought I was makin' a pass at his wife."

"Were you?" Adam asked, as he tossed another bloody cotton ball into the tray.

Boone gave Adam a weary look that let him know the absurdity of the question. He did not make passes at women. But they sure as hell made passes at him. Having women throw themselves at him was one of the hazards of being Boone Dickson. The men called him "Easy" for the way he had with women. And while most of them would give their right nut to be in his shoes, or more specifically the front seat of his pickup truck, Boone had grown jaded by the inevitable. Which of course made women want him even more.

Adam was flabbergasted by the phenomenon. Even his no-nonsense nurse, in her white orthopedic shoes and horn-rimmed glasses, suddenly found reasons to straighten the *Life* magazines or water the split-leaf palm when Boone Dickson was in the waiting room.

From Adam's point of view, Boone lacked every quality a woman should want. He slouched on the examination table as though the weight of his massive chest and arms was more than his backbone could carry, and his thick black hair spent more time in his eyes than in a part. If he said ten words at a time it was a miracle. And his grin had the devil in it.

But for women, his threat was his temptation. Boone could melt a girl's resolve simply by leaning against his truck and smoking a cigarette. Even good women found themselves running their fingers down their neckline, licking their lips, and rubbing their legs together like crickets in his presence. His sisters-in-law brought him fried chicken still warm from the skillet and fresh grated coconut cakes. Mrs. Lyle, the minister's wife, pieced quilts for him with Bible verses cross-stitched along the hem. Boone's appeal was nonpartisan and ecumenical.

"For a white boy," KyAnn Merriweather would say when Boone stopped by to pick up a plate of barbecue, "youse shore is tasty."

KyAnn had blazed her way into womanhood. Like the pepper she was named for, she made a man's skin burn. She was tall and black with amber eyes. A man heard drums when he looked at her. She wore next to nothing under her sauce-stained apron, and you got the impression she could smoke ribs just by blowing on them.

As a rule, KyAnn had no use for white men, but even she had a taste for Boone. He was the first white man to eat at Poor Man's Country Club. And where Boone Dickson went, other men followed.

Dipping a long black finger into the hot sauce, she'd reach across the counter and smear it on Boone's lips.

"Sugar, you be thinkin' that burns," she'd purr, "come 'round and see KyAnn some night."

"Woman," Boone would answer, eyeing the roomful of black men watching him over their pork ribs, "you're gonna get me killed."

Then KyAnn would smile. There was nothing she enjoyed more than making a man uneasy.

Men who knew Boone knew it wasn't his fault when their girl-friends rubbed up against him at the bar, or hung their arms around his neck and whispered drunkenly into his ear. A smart man even knew how to use it to his advantage. Boone was like a teaser bull. Fifteen minutes near Boone and a woman's legs just fell open.

But men who didn't know Boone, or were a little insecure about their way with women to begin with, didn't take it that well. Boone had been defending himself against grown men since he was fourteen, when the next door neighbor came home early after working the night shift at the meatpacking plant and found Boone fidgeting with his wife's zipper in their bedroom. Boone learned right then and there that the last thing anyone wants to hear is that the woman started it.

The result of all of this was that Adam saw Boone on a regular basis.

"They need to close the Poor Man's Country Club before someone gets killed," Adam said, as he pulled a stitch.

"Ain't the window's fault when a bird flies into it," Boone said.

Boone never said anything that wasn't obvious, but usually it wasn't obvious until he said it.

"Just the same," Adam said, "my medical advice to you is stay away from the place."

Adam gave Dickson a stern stare, and Boone met it straight on. Boone's eyes were black bottomless pools that many a woman had drowned in. When he met a man's gaze, he didn't so much look at him, as into him. One suspected Boone could see through bullshit like glass. Not a comfortable situation for a man who devoted a great deal of time and energy to his façade.

Like someone who'd just lost a game of chicken, Adam looked away. Pulling the last stitch, he tied the knot and snipped the thread.

"How much I owe you, Doc?" Boone asked, as Adam dropped the scissors onto the tray.

Boone made his living fixing other men's mistakes, a leaking roof, a bad electric plug the electrician had given up on, a washing machine that had stopped washing. When the clock in the city courthouse stopped,

Boone was the one who got it working again. It took him two weeks, but he did it. Boone would climb church steeples to secure a tilting cross or belly crawl with the snakes under the parsonage to reinforce its sagging foundation. When Reba Earhart turned on the tap water one morning and crickets poured out, she called Boone. He could barely keep up with all the repair work on the slipshod houses Joe Pegram threw up. Bad wiring, bad plumbing, mold growing in the closets. A man could learn everything he needed to know about the construction business watching Boone redo what Pegram had half-done.

"When I lit the fireplace last night," Adam said, as he scrubbed his hands under the faucet, "more smoke billowed into the library than up the chimney."

"Probably the damper," Boone said, easing off the table. "When you look up the chimney, can you see light?"

Blank as a blackboard, Doc stared at Boone. Most poor men would have used this opportunity to put a rich man in his place.

"I'll take care of it," Boone said, as he pulled off his torn, bloody T-shirt, wadded it into a ball and tossed it into the trash.

Boone stood in front of Doc half naked. Soft black hair ran down his chest, disappearing below his belt. He had arms that made a woman feel light as a scarf, a stomach flat enough to iron on, and an attitude set on smolder. A normal man would have taken one look at Boone Dickson and locked his wife in the attic. The thought never crossed Adam's mind.

Lydia took the news that Boone would be fixing the fireplace with the same enthusiasm she felt when the housekeeper bought a new flyswatter.

"Tell him to use the back door," she told Mrs. Meeks, even though Boone was standing right in front of her, "and make him take his boots off on the porch."

As soon as Lydia left the room, Boone promptly walked out the front door to get his toolbox from the truck. On his way back in, he made it a point to clean his work boots on the Oriental rug.

Knowing women the way he did, Boone had Lydia pegged the instant he saw her. She had beauty that would blind a man, and the disposition of a broken beer bottle. He felt sorry for Doc. A man in love with a woman like Lydia was doomed.

Boone had worked on all the old houses in town, but he knew the Montgomerys' like the back of his hand. He had reinforced the floor in the downstairs bathroom after one of the clawed legs on the tub burst through the rotten wood. He'd patched over two dozen leaks in the slate roof and secured the leaning three-story kitchen chimney back to the exterior wall, anchoring it with thick steel rods.

As he walked through the entrance hall, he studied the cantilevered curving stairway. For decades it had been pulling away from the wall. The previous owner had been too cheap to fix it right. He hired a carpenter to cut a piece of four-inch molding to cover the gap. Now, even the molding was pulling away from the wall.

From the street, the Montgomery house looked solid. Up close, even the columns were cracking. The original owner spent everything on the façade. Now the old mansion was crumbling from the foundation up.

Boone made a mental note to mention the stairway to Doc.

In Adam's study, he set his toolbox down and knelt in front of the fireplace. Pulling a cigarette from behind his ear, he ran his tongue down the side, then hung it on his lip. Lighting a match with his thumbnail, he took a deep draw and exhaled into the chimney. The smoke curled and twisted right back into the room. The cracks around the old windows drew a better draft than the chimney. Reaching up inside, Boone pulled the damper. The lever broke off in his hand, and a brick fell out with it.

Opening his pocketknife, Boone ran the blunt side of the blade down the brick mortar. It crumbled like sand. Cleaning the knife on his pants, Boone shook his head. The only thing holding the Montgomery house together was money. One day, a strong wind was going to blow her to the ground.

After banging around in the fireplace for over an hour, Boone went in search of Lydia. He found her on her hands and knees in her flower garden. The gardener had taken care of the grounds for over twenty years. But the day after Lydia arrived in Leaper's Fork, she announced she would be staking off a small plot to call her own. Every day she dug, pampered, and watered. While all around her lilacs bloomed, ferns unfurled, and lilies rose from the ground like trumpets, Lydia's flower bed looked like someone had poured gasoline on it and struck a match. A brittle clematis vine withered on the iron trellis and sparse clumps of spindly, anemic annuals drooped in their row. Lydia was a woman who was used to getting her way. The fact that the more attention she gave a plant, the quicker it tried to leave this earth infuriated her to no end.

"It's the damper," Boone said, holding out an unidentifiable piece of rusty metal.

Shielding her eyes with a gloved hand, Lydia glared up at him. From where Boone was standing, he could see all the way down her blouse straight to the Promised Land.

"Buy a new one," she ordered, wondering why on earth he was bothering her with this.

The Montgomerys' house was over one hundred years old. Chances were, a local blacksmith had made the damper, but Boone didn't see any need of wasting words on Lydia.

"I'll make a new one and bring it by tomorrow."

Most women would have been impressed that a man could make something from nothing with his bare hands, or at least they would feign feminine appreciation. Lydia went back to trying to raise a dead plant back to life.

"Queen Anne's lace," Boone said, nodding at the limp stalk in her hands.

Lydia frowned. She could have sworn she planted dahlias.

"Woman," he said, "it's a weed."

Jerking her head up, Lydia flashed a glare at him like a cotton-mouth ready to strike. Shrugging, he turned and walked away.

At his truck, Boone tossed the old damper into the bed. Climbing behind the wheel, he slipped the key out from under the seat, gave her a little choke, and pumped the gas pedal three times before grinding the ignition.

"The woman couldn't grow mold on loaf bread," he muttered, as he threw the truck into gear.

When Lydia heard Boone's truck rattle down the road, she jerked the weed out of the ground, ripped it into pieces and threw the shredded remains into the wheelbarrow.

The next day, as Boone Dickson pulled into the driveway, Lydia pulled out. When she got to the street, she put her foot on the brake and sat there. It wasn't easy for someone, whose only interest was buying things, to kill time in Leaper's Fork.

When the housekeeper announced Lydia Montgomery was waiting in her living room, Ann Lester's day took a dive. Nothing perturbs a snooty woman more than being outsnooted. When Lydia Montgomery sniffed her way into town, Ann dropped to runner-up and she'd been smarting from it ever since.

Ann could repeat every single put-down Lydia had slung at her, and she made a habit of reviewing the list daily just to keep her claws sharp.

"That dress was very popular in Boston . . . *last year.*" "A single string of pearls is so . . . *understated.*" "A log lake home is so . . . *quaint.*"

"Should I tell her you're feelin' puny?" the Lesters' housekeeper whispered.

What Ann really wanted to tell Lydia was to go straight to hell, but a southern lady would never insult a guest. If Satan himself dropped by unexpected, a southern lady would whip up a devil's food cake and invite him to stay for supper.

"What a pleasant surprise!" Ann Lester said, sweeping into the living room with a smile on her face like half a ring of pineapple floating in congealed peach Jell-O.

"I just happened to be in the neighborhood," Lydia said, bending down to study Ann Lester's porcelain egg collection in the curio cabinet, "and thought I would drop in."

The Montgomerys lived a stone's throw from the Lesters. You could practically stand at Ann's bedroom window and shoot the lights out on Lydia's front porch, which Ann Lester had seriously considered on several occasions.

Lydia had never *stopped by* before, much less been invited.

"You collect eggs?" Ann Lester asked, as she lifted a jeweled orb from its stand.

Gently opening the egg, she held it up for Lydia to envy.

The majority of Ann Lesters' eggs, like the majority of the Lester's wealth, had been "acquired" during the Depression. Unknown to the Daughters of the Confederacy, the first Lesters to set foot in the New World were pirates. When they were finally run out of North Carolina, they migrated to Tennessee. Landlocked, they turned to banking. It had been a natural evolution.

"Is it Fabergé?" Lydia asked, staring at the egg.

"Well . . . no."

Sighing, Lydia turned away and Ann Lester's most precious possession was reduced to dust.

Teacup in hand, Lydia wandered apathetically from a painting to some porcelain birds. She stared blandly at Ann Lester's choice in curtain fabric, covered a yawn at the wallpaper, and lifted an eyebrow at the signed bronze Remington. But when she glanced at the vase of calla lilies on the mantel a second time, Ann Lester knew she had her.

"I don't know how many times I've told that housekeeper of mine that I want these thrown out daily," Ann Lester fussed.

"Thrown out?" Lydia echoed.

Grabbing the perfectly beautiful flowers by the stems, Ann Lester tossed them into the fireplace.

"I like my flowers cut fresh every morning," she said, dusting her hands.

"Cut fresh?"

"From the garden."

"You grow lilies?"

"Like weeds," Ann Lester said, with a drop of the wrist. "They're absolutely taking over the place. As Mama used to say, 'Only a heart that's chilly can't grow a lily.'"

The two women smiled at each other.

"Well, dear," Ann Lester said, standing, "I am sorry to have to cut this lovely visit short, but I have a committee meeting."

"A committee meeting?" Lydia took a sip of tea.

"The Christian Women's Charity. We're planning our Annual Christmas Bazaar."

"Bazaar?"

"To raise money for the poor."

Lydia's expression was as blank as a sleeping cat's. Ann Lester couldn't tell if she disapproved of money changing in the church, or didn't know what poor people were.

"I'm in charge of the refreshments."

"Refreshments?"

"Finger sandwiches—chicken salad with pecans, with the crust cut off."

Ann twisted her single strand of pearls. She wished to God she'd had the cook use almonds instead of pecans.

Lydia's eyes turned to the window. Boone Dickson's truck was still parked in her driveway.

"Well," Lydia said, setting her cup down, "I'll serve the tea."

Ann Lester held her breath for a full fifteen seconds.

"Actually," Ann finally said, "it's fruit punch with orange sherbet ice cream."

Lydia arched an eyebrow and Ann Lester had a small stroke.

"Well," Lydia said, pulling on a glove, "I can serve that, too."

When Lydia arrived home from the Christian Women's Charity that evening, Adam had a fire roaring in the fireplace. It was the middle of June and his office was sweltering. But for Adam, a fire in the fireplace was not about heat.

"The new damper," he announced proudly, as he poked a log, "works perfectly!"

Lydia was struck by the fact that Adam saw no distinction between paying to have something fixed and fixing it himself. For some reason this irritated her enormously, but she wasn't sure why.

CHAPTER 16

"Easy, doc!" Boone flinched.

It had been almost a month since Adam had last seen Boone, which was probably some kind of record.

"Barstool," Boone said, when asked.

"I'm guessing it's cracked, but not broken," Adam said, as he gently pressed against Boone's black and purple ribs. "I'm going to X-ray just to make sure."

"Would that X-ray make me feel better?"

"Can't say that it would."

"Then what d'yu say you just tape her up and save me the time and money?"

Adam had to marvel at Boone's body. The blow would have put a normal man in the hospital. But Boone Dickson was built like a tank.

"No heavy lifting for a couple of weeks," Adam said, as he finished taping the bandage around Boone's ribs, "and stay out of the Poor Man's Country Club."

Grimacing, Boone slowly slid off the examination table.

"How much I owe you, Doc?"

"Yesterday," Adam said, as he washed his hands, "when I flipped the light switch on in the bedroom, sparks flew out like the Fourth of July."

"Sounds to me like you need an electrician," Boone said, flinching as he pulled his shirt on.

"It caught the wallpaper on fire."

"What do you say I just pay you the money outright?"

"Fine," Adam said, drying his hands, "then after you fix the electric switch, I can hand it right back to you."

"I think you need to call Danny Baker. Best electrician in the tri-counties."

"I've already had Danny Baker look at the wiring and things are still burning up."

Hands on his hips, Boone stared at the floor.

"It's just a little wiring job," Adam said, irritated that Boone was making such a fuss. "It's not like I'm sending you off to war."

Lydia was still in bed when she heard the brass door-knocker banging on the front door. Rolling her head on the satin pillow, she looked at the clock. It was the housekeeper's day off, which meant no one was going to answer it. The cook only cooked. The gardener only gardened. And she had no idea what all the other people loitering around the house did. She wasn't even sure if they were on the payroll. What she did know was she did not answer doors. Staring at the ceiling, she waited for the banging to stop.

It didn't.

If Boone was surprised when Lydia threw open the door in her nightgown, he didn't give her the satisfaction of showing it.

"It's six forty-five," she said icily.

"I start work at seven," he informed her, pushing roughly past.

Lydia stood motionless in the doorway like an ice sculpture in chiffon frost. Chin up, back arched, she squinted at him through half open eyes as though he was so far beneath her she could barely make him out.

If a man tried to kiss the frigid bitch, Boone thought, his mouth would freeze to her skin.

"Well," she finally said, "as long as you're here."

Closing the door with her fingertips, she floated up the long curving stairway leading Boone to the burned out light switch in her bedroom.

A blind man could have closed his eyes and followed the trail of Lydia's perfume. Boone was not blind. Sunlight poured through the beveled glass window on the landing, passing through Lydia's gown like a movie projector light through film. Boone had never considered himself a man of great imagination. In this instance, he didn't need to be.

On the landing, Lydia turned to see why Boone had stopped. The look on his face said it all.

"You filthy animal," she hissed.

Pulling back her arm, Lydia hit him as hard as she could. Under normal circumstances it would have been equivalent to getting pinged by a pea. But when it came to hitting people where it hurt, Lydia had perfect aim. Her fist finished off what the barstool started and Boone's cracked rib snapped like a twig.

"Jesus!" he bellowed, bending double.

When Lydia pulled back to punch him again, Boone grabbed her wrists and pinned her to the wall.

"Let go of me!" She twisted and squirmed.

Jerking her away from the wall, Boone threw her down onto the landing. Scooting backward, Lydia tucked herself into the corner. Jaw set and breathing hard, Boone glared down at her. The fact that he wasn't moving scared them both.

"When I get back," he finally said hoarsely, "I want you gone."

Gripping his side, Boone bent down, picked up his toolbox and left.

When she heard the door slam, Lydia wrapped her arms around her knees and rocked back and forth. She imagined all the things he could have done to her. He could have ripped her gown off and run his hands all over her body. He could have forced himself on top of her and had his way, and there was absolutely nothing she could have done to stop him. By the time Lydia got through reviewing all the things Boone Dickson could have done to her, her silk panties were drenched.

CHAPTER 17

THE WOMEN in Leaper's Fork knew all about Boone Dickson.

"Daddy died when he was just a boy," Mrs. Meeks said, as she tucked the sheets in on Lydia's bed. "Tractor rolled over on him. Left his poor mama with four boys to raise. Then his mama up and got the TB."

Mrs. Meeks shook her head sadly. "That boy took care of her right up to the end. Cooked. Cleaned. Fed her like a baby."

"Did he marry a local girl?" Lydia asked nonchalantly, as she brushed her hair at her dresser.

"Marry?" Mrs. Meeks huffed, as she plumped a pillow. "I doubt a team of wild horses could drag Boone Dickson down the aisle. Although many a girl's pulled out all the ropes."

This was all well and good, but it was not the kind of information Lydia was looking for.

"Boone Dickson," Judge Lester said, as Lydia poured him a cup of tea. "Ann went to school with the boy, that is, until he quit. Believe his mother got ill or something."

"Tuberculosis," Ann Lester said.

"Always wondered why they didn't ship her off to the sanitarium."

"The family couldn't afford it," Ann Lester explained to Lydia.

"The Dicksons have always been poor as dirt." Stirring his tea,

Judge tinged his spoon against the china. "Four boys in the family and all of them scratch out a living like chickens."

"They work very hard," Ann said quietly into her cup.

"Whenever anything needs work around the house, Ann uses Dickson. Don't you, dear?"

Ann Lester twisted her pearl necklace.

"He's quite the ladies' man, although why escapes me. Crude fellow. Arms like a gorilla."

This prompted Judge to study his gold cuff links.

"Why, just last year the mayor's wife made an absolute fool out of herself at the church potluck supper," he said absently. "Something about Patsy Wood stealing her seat next to Boone Dickson."

Determining one cuff extended beyond his coat sleeve farther than the other, he made the appropriate adjustment.

"Dear, remember that night Rufus Edwards's wife got drunk and climbed into Dickson's truck at the Poor Man's and wouldn't get out?" Judge chuckled at the woman's humiliation. "Rufus had to peel her fingers off the steering wheel."

As Judge rambled on, Ann's eyes wandered off the porch and the vaguest of smiles rose on her lips.

"Ann? Ann!"

Startled, Ann Lester blinked at her husband.

"I said, even perfectly decent women seem to lose all reason when it comes to Dickson."

"So I've heard," Ann said, turning her wedding ring round and round on her finger.

"Personally, I've always wondered why Dickson and Angela Belle didn't get together." Judge sniffed. "Two pigs in a blanket, if you ask me."

One of the first things Lydia did when she moved into Adam Montgomery's house was convert the sewing room that was adjacent to the bedroom into a walk-in closet. It was the logical thing to do. Not knowing which end of a needle to thread, she didn't plan to do much needlepoint.

This was where Boone found her when he came to finish the wiring. Lydia stood in full daylight wrapped in nothing but a silk sheet.

"Woman," Boone said quietly, "don't start something you can't finish."

Lydia let the sheet slide to the floor.

"Close the door," Boone told her.

And she did.

Normally, Boone held a woman after. It was the rule of repeat business.

"Don't run till her mouth stops running," his oldest brother always said.

"Get off of me!" Lydia hissed, pushing him away.

There was no play in Lydia, fore or after.

Rolling onto his back on the floor beside her, Boone stared up at the ceiling. He noted the watery brown spot in the corner and wondered if the leak was old or new.

"This is never going to happen again," Lydia insisted.

Jerking his jeans out from under her, Boone pulled them on a leg at a time.

"Never," she informed him, as she wrapped the sheet around her.

Finding his screwdriver, Boone hung it back on his tool belt. Then he searched the closet for anything else that might have fallen out of his pants.

" . . . Never . . . Never. . . . ," Lydia said adamantly.

Standing in the doorway, Boone looked down at Lydia. Her hair was mussed every which way, her lips were a bruised blur. Her porcelain skin blushed like a plum. A woman was never more beautiful than just after.

"Woman," Boone said, "you are a spider."

On that note, Lydia hurled a high heel at him.

The next day Boone came to finish the job he never got around to the day before.

"If you tell anyone what happened," Lydia said, "I'll swear you raped me."

While Lydia talked to herself, Boone unscrewed the light-switch plate.

"No one would believe I would willingly do *that* with *you.*"

Boone was pretty sure no one would believe Lydia would do *that* with *anyone.*

Pulling the plate off the wall, he studied the tangle of charred wiring.

"Hand me those needle-nose pliers," he said, nodding at his tool-box.

Lydia stared at him blankly.

"Looks like a heron's beak," he said.

She looked down at the toolbox and had no idea what she was looking at. But then, she didn't know what a heron's beak looked like either. When she reached for the adjustable wrench, Boone shook his head. Hand hovering over the needle-nose pliers, she glanced at him. He nodded.

Lifting the pliers out of the toolbox, she continued to absolve herself.

"We both know you took advantage of me," she said, mindlessly tracing the edges of the pliers with her fingertips. "There was absolutely nothing I could do about it."

"You begged for it like a two-dollar whore," Boone said.

As the pliers flew toward his head, he grabbed her wrist. And the next thing they both knew, they were at it again.

Every day for the next two weeks, Lydia found a fixture or appliance that was in urgent need of repair. And they did it in the basement, the attic, the bathroom, and the pantry.

"I had no idea the furnace used coal," she mused, as she rode him like a pogo stick.

"It's a-b-bout to go!" he said, meaning the furnace.

You really couldn't call what Lydia did to Boone making love. It was more like two cats fighting in a bag. Slamming up and down, she scratched and bit, while Boone gritted his teeth and held on.

They were rattling the bottles in the wine cellar one afternoon, when in the midst of it all, Lydia suddenly sucked in a breath. Her body went rigid and her eyes went wide with surprise.

"Let go of me!" she cried, fighting him. "Let go!"

But Boone held tight, forcing himself up in her as far as he could go.

"Easy," he soothed, holding her to him, barely rocking her. "Easy."

Breath short and quick, she stared at him like a terrified child.

"Come for me, woman," he whispered, when he felt her womb grip him. "Come just for me."

As the contractions moved up her body, Lydia's head fell back and her body went boneless. When she was most vulnerable, Boone swung her under him.

"Say you want it," he said, petting her breast, kissing her mouth. "Say it."

"Yes," she agreed. She would have agreed to anything. "Yes, I want it."

"Say you want me."

Lydia looked up at him. His eyes were black bottomless pools that she could easily drown in.

"Yes," she said. "I want you."

Then he moved very slowly, until tears ran down her face and their skin became seamless.

CHAPTER 18

WHEN THEY STARTED worrying about Boone's truck being parked at Lydia's house, they began to meet anywhere and everywhere. They met at Yellow Creek where Boone threw a tarp on the bank, then made love again while standing in the creek. They met at the cemetery, where Boone picked the lock on the Manns' mausoleum and pounded Lydia so hard against the granite slab it burned the letter *M* onto her butt like a brand. They met at Stinson's tobacco barn, so that for days after, her hair smelled like hickory smoke and dark fired tobacco. They met in his truck in the rain, Boone steering with his knee, freeing his right hand to caress her.

Secret lovers are like children who believe that if they hold their hands over their eyes no one else can see them. Even if the Sheriff hadn't seen Lydia's car parked next to Boone's truck down at the river, or Ben Harrington hadn't caught them slipping into Stinson's tobacco barn while he was dove hunting, people would have figured it out.

"Haven't seen you down at the Poor Man's in a while," Ben said, as he filled a bag with the copper fittings Boone was buying to fix Stinson's well-house pump.

"Haven't been there in a while," Boone said.

All the men passing the time in the hardware store grinned at each other.

You couldn't wipe the smile off Boone Dickson's face. He didn't need whiskey. He was drunk on Lydia Montgomery.

Everyone in town knew about Boone and Lydia. Everyone, except for Dr. Adam Montgomery.

A dreamy softness came over Lydia. Her cheeks blushed like wild roses and wisps of hair fell around her face. Her lips were always a little parted now, and she had to consciously remind herself to hold her knees together. It was all Lydia could do to put clothes on in the morning, living only for the moment when Boone would take them off of her.

Love is contagious, and Boone and Lydia seemed to infect the whole town.

Willie was counting cans of corn in the stockroom of the diner when Dot came up behind him. She whispered in his ear and he put down his clipboard.

"What do you suppose people would think if they knew what these cans knew?" he asked, as he unbuttoned his shirt.

Leg hiked up on a lard can, Dot unhooked her garter.

"I think we'd get a dollar more for a plate lunch."

CHAPTER 19

MAYBE IT WAS the passion that made her womb more hospitable. Or maybe, unconsciously, she willed it to happen. Regardless, when Lydia was late that month, she had no doubt she was carrying Boone Dickson's child.

To her own surprise a warm contentment came over her, a peace she had never known. She could be a wife to Boone and a mother to his child. She would learn to cook and sew and clean his house. She would live to love him, and he in turn would make her feel safe and satisfied. These were the things Lydia intended to tell Boone when she turned her car down the gravel road to Stringtown, not giving a damn who saw her.

Stringtown wasn't a place found on any map, but its borders were clearly defined by the residents of Leaper's Fork. It was a convenient location, if you had business at the dump, the train tracks, or the river. The very qualities that made the land beautiful, the rocky bluffs weeping with springs and covered in ferns and moss, were also the qualities that made the residents poor as church mice. A goat couldn't stand up straight on most of the land, and what dirt managed to cling to the sheer shale slopes, was so poor even the weeds seemed distressed.

If a refrigerator bumped out of the truck before it made it to the dump, or a broken chair, or an old tire, the good citizens of Leaper's Fork saw it as charity. Leaper's Fork trash was a treasure in Stringtown.

But Lydia didn't see any of this as she dodged the potholes in the red clay road. She didn't see the smoke rising off the dump or the abandoned cars, stripped and rusting on the side of the road. She didn't see the barefoot dirty-faced children staring at her like field mice in faded overalls and hand-me-down dresses. A woman in love is like a racehorse with blinders.

When Lydia saw "Dickson" scrawled on the mailbox, she turned her car down the narrow lane. The gravel turned to dirt. The dirt turned into a field. And when Boone's house finally came into view, Lydia's blinders began to slip.

The old house was smaller than her garage. There was no sidewalk, just a worn path in the grass. As Lydia cautiously climbed the front steps, a chicken flew off the porch.

When she knocked on the front door, no one answered. When she tried the handle, it wasn't locked.

The smell of poverty hit Lydia as she opened the door, decades of white beans, boiled cabbage, and sweat. She had never smelled it before, but she instinctively knew. She slowly walked through the house as though taking inventory. Yellowed crocheted doilies on threadbare chairs. A wood box of split kindling beside a cookstove in the kitchen. On the back porch, a rusty wringer washer, a mottled mirror on a nail, and a white enamel wash pan under the water pump. Twenty feet from the porch, an outhouse. A chenille bedspread so thin Lydia could see the patchwork quilt underneath. In the closet, one suit, one tie. Boone's shoes, two pairs, sat at the bottom.

Family photographs in dime-store frames hung along the hall wall. The wedding picture. Boone's daddy, dark and serious. Boone's mother, an ethereal beauty, eyes shining like mercury. Boone's baby picture, black hair, black eyes. The children, four boys, stacked like blocks. The family photo with Boone's father. The family photo without. Boone's mother, hair gray, face drawn, eyes dead as dust.

Lydia backed away from the wall. She saw nothing as she made her way through the small house. When she stepped out onto the front porch, it was raining, the dirt dissolved to red mud. She was halfway down the porch steps when she stopped. Head bowed, she stood perfectly still. Rain ran down her face and dripped from her lips and chin. She could hear the rain tapping on the rusty tin roof. Slowly, she raised her head and her shoulders straightened. All emotion had drained from her face and her eyes were frosty gray. She did not look back as she walked to her car.

When Lydia arrived home from Stringtown, she was surprised to find Julia Mercer from Boston sitting on her front porch.

"Truly, I didn't know I was coming myself." Julia leaned back in the white wicker chair as if she was the mistress of the house, and Lydia was the visitor. "A nasty storm hit Banyan and Father insisted I go see about the house."

Julia was not a beautiful woman, but she dared you to think otherwise. She always dressed as if on expedition, white linen shirt open at the collar, khaki slacks, and a smug expression as though she found your life utterly amusing—even if you were not.

Lydia, over the past few months, had taken on the style of an unmade bed. Hair soft, lipstick blurred, and legs bare. She stopped wearing jewelry because it got in the way. Her dress was plain white cotton, something she'd picked up in town because it was cool and loose and easy to get out of.

Taking a sip of her drink, Julia looked her up and down. Suddenly, Lydia saw herself through Julia's eyes and her face burned.

"I'm a mess." Lydia laughed, awkwardly touching her hair.

Actually, Julia thought Lydia had never looked more beautiful. Of course, she was not the kind of woman to say so.

Suddenly, Julia grew alert, the pupils of her eyes drawing to a point like a hawk spotting a mouse.

"My. My," she said, head tilted. "What have we here?"

Lydia swung around to find Boone standing behind her. And her lips parted and her body opened the way it always did when she looked at him.

"Aren't you going to introduce us?" Julia finally asked.

Julia's eyes moved over Boone appraising him the way she would a horse for build, stamina, and speed. But Boone's eyes were on Lydia. She looked nervous, cornered. He lifted his hand as though to soothe her and she took a step back.

"I thought I'd made it clear," Lydia said fiercely. "Workmen use the back door!"

Her voice hung in the air like the echo of a rifle. Lydia would never forget the look on Boone's face, like a wounded animal that couldn't understand why she'd shot him. Backing away from her, Boone turned and walked down the front steps.

"He's just the handyman," Lydia said, as they watched him walk to his truck.

"Handy indeed," Julia said, smiling into her glass.

That night Lydia went to her husband.

"Wait. Wait," Adam whispered, pulling away from her so that he could hang his coat over the chair.

Adam started a slow waltz. His kisses polite, his touch choreographed with no room for improvisation, self-conscious, as though being judged on style and presentation. Lydia stared at the ceiling.

When Boone made love to Lydia he didn't notice the sun burning his back. When Boone had Lydia under him, he couldn't feel the rocks digging into his knee. When Boone was inside Lydia, he was oblivious to everything outside of her. When Adam made love to Lydia, he was oblivious to Lydia.

"Sorry," he muttered, when his elbow caught her hair. Apologizing for the technical error, not for having pulled a wisp of her hair.

As Adam danced on without her, Lydia drifted to another place and another partner. She closed her eyes and Boone was above her, sweaty and on fire, his black hair hanging around his face.

"Woman, do you want it?" Boone whispered.

"Yes," Lydia whispered.

"Do you want me?"

"I want you."

Climbing onto Adam, Lydia rode him like the wind. Stunned, Adam lasted approximately forty-five seconds. When it was over, they rolled apart. Turning her back to him, Lydia stared at the wall. Adam, who considered the event a complete success, didn't so much fall asleep, as fall into a smiling coma.

At sunrise, when Adam reached for Lydia, she was gone. He found her outside standing on the bluff, looking out at the river. As he walked toward his wife, he was overwhelmed with hope. She had come to him. She wanted him. Now everything would be different.

"You're shivering," Adam said, laying his coat over her bare shoulders.

Swinging around, Lydia slapped him so hard he stumbled backward and fell to the ground. Hand to his face, Adam lay on the grass looking up at her, horrified. Lydia glared down at him with so much disgust and revulsion it drew him into a ball.

Everything Lydia had once admired about Adam, his sophistication and civility, now seemed prissy and weak. His hands were soft, and he touched her as though she were made of glass. Adam's passion had been polished away. All that remained was the ritual. He was a man who hung his coat up before making love, and she hated him for it.

Pushing himself to a stand, Adam looked at Lydia. Then he turned away and walked back to the house.

CHAPTER 20

"WELL, I 'SPECT Boone Dickson won't be fixin' nothin' 'round the house anytime soon," Mrs. Meeks said, as she fluffed the pillow on the bed.

"Why is that?" Lydia asked casually, as she tightened the screw on her earring at her dressing table.

"He done got off to war," Mrs. Meeks said, smoothing the bedspread.

"War," Lydia whispered.

"Gonna be a whole lotta women mighty sad over losin' that one," Mrs. Meeks said, as she gathered up the dirty linens.

Mrs. Meeks pulled the door closed behind her. Alone at her dressing table, Lydia stared at her reflection. Lifting her hand, she brushed her fingers over her lips and let them slide down her neck, but she felt nothing. The only touch her body would answer to was Boone's.

CHAPTER 21

EVERY WEDNESDAY Angela Belle came to town. And every Wednesday Dr. Montgomery "accidentally" ran into her. That Doc sat by the diner window for thirty minutes picking at a piece of pie until she rounded the corner did not go unnoticed.

"Never seen a man so whupped," the Sheriff said, rolling a toothpick from one side of his mouth to the other.

"Got him by the short hairs," Willie concurred.

Naturally, every man in town thought Doc was getting some. Naturally, every woman in town knew better.

"A dog don't dance for a bone he's already chewed," Dot said, sliding Ben Harrington's plate lunch in front of him.

"Depends on the bone," the Sheriff said, as they watched Doc run across the street to catch up with Angela.

"Depends on the dog," Dot countered, giving Willie a look that made his face burn.

It was hard to believe that the wild, barefooted hellion Angela Belle had been as a girl had transformed into the twenty-year-old standing on the sidewalk. Her eyes were dark and promising, and she had a way about her that was far too certain for a woman so young. One could only imagine the seductive things Angela whispered that made Doc stare at her mouth as though he could taste it.

"You ought to build a hospital," Angela said, as they walked past the Kandy Kitchen.

"A hospital?"

"Nearest one is fifty miles away."

Adam thought about buying her ice cream, but they had ice cream the week before and he was afraid people might talk.

"At the end of Madison Street, on the old Madison farm," Angela said, still thinking about hospitals.

It had never crossed Adam's mind to build a hospital. If it had, he wouldn't build it at the end of Madison. Even with the new road, it was too far out of town.

"It's where the town's moving," she said, as though she had read his mind.

Angela stopped to look at the hats in the window of Mademoiselle's Dress Shop. She never wore a hat, but always looked at them just the same. Standing as close to her as he could without their arms touching, Adam stared at her reflection. It was all he could do to keep from kissing the glass.

"Pretty girl! Pretty Girl!" Robert E. Lee cawed and whistled.

When Angela bent down to study a pocketbook in the window, Adam's eyes traced her hips. He imagined standing behind her, slipping his hands around her waist, kissing her neck. . . .

"It will be good for the town," she said, standing up and looking at him with those eyes.

"What?" He blinked.

"The hospital," she said patiently.

They walked side by side around the square. She always waved at the men whittling on the courthouse steps. When she smelled the roses at the Garden Club's flower garden, she closed her eyes. When she read the weekly platitude on the Baptist Church marquee, she smiled.

At the corner where they'd met, Angela always left Adam without saying good-bye. Hands stuffed in his pockets, he bowed his head and stared at the sidewalk. He was so deep in thought he didn't notice it had begun to rain.

"What you reckon's wrong with the Doc?" Ben Harrington asked, gazing out the diner window.

"Maybe he finally figured out he's married to a haint," Dot said, as she wiped the counter beside him. "How's that country ham?"

"Right good."

"Bought it from Reba Earhart."

"Well, it's still good," Ben said.

CHAPTER 22

"CLOSE THE DOOR," Adam said, when Lydia came into the library. "The room is too warm," she told him, and left the door open.

It was the first time Adam and Lydia had spoken since that night. They ate dinner in silence and slept in the same bed without touching.

There had never been a divorce in the Montgomery family. A divorce meant more than moral and personal failure. It meant social failure, which in Adam's mind was far worse. Montgomerys might not stay together—but they stayed married.

Adam was prepared to change all that.

"Lydia . . ." he began.

"I'm pregnant," she said.

They stared at each other for the longest time.

"Well, then," Adam said, turning to poke the fire, "there we are."

After the pregnancy was announced, Lydia saw no need to share her bed. Adam Montgomery arrived home one evening to find all his things had been moved to the room off the library. Everyone in town knew every detail before Adam walked through his own front door.

"Heard it from Mr. Garner, who heard it from Miz Meeks," Willie Wyatt said, leaning on his elbows in the service window at the diner. "Got him sleepin' in a room no bigger than a closet."

"Didn't even give the poor man the guest room," Dot tutted, as she refilled Charlotte's coffee cup.

"Knew the first time I laid eyes on that woman that she was salt-peter in a pretty package," the Sheriff said, shaking salt on everything on his plate before tasting it.

"Men who marry bitches," Charlotte said flatly, "shouldn't be surprised when they're treated like dogs."

Lydia's baby was born the day the Japanese bombed Pearl Harbor. Adam wasn't surprised that he came a month early, what with Lydia being so frail and all. Actually, it was a blessing. Adam Jackson Montgomery weighed seven pounds and four ounces as it was. The little fellow would have split her in half if he'd gone full term.

Normally, the women in town would have thrown Lydia a baby shower.

"But considering everything," Dot said, as she filled saltshakers, "maybe we should just drop the gifts off with Doc."

"Considering what?" Willie asked, from the window.

"Considering the fact that Lydia Montgomery is as cold as a witch's tit," Charlotte said, as she scanned the obituaries in the newspaper. "If she breast-feeds that poor baby, the milk will come out ice cream."

A hush fell over the diner as the men's thoughts filled with the image of a woman who could produce soft-serve.

"Believe I'll have a scoop of vanilla with my pie," Ben Harrington said.

"You barely got crust left," Dot said, staring at the crumbs on his plate.

"You want to sell me the ice cream or not?" Ben snapped.

Throwing open the freezer door with a bang, Dot dove down into the white fog, and reappeared with a large scoop.

"Use that tone with me again," she said, plopping the ice cream onto his plate, "and you won't have teeth to chew it with."

In the back of the restaurant, a dozen or so men huddled around the radio drinking coffee and listening to the news of the war. Someone had pinned a world map on the wall next to the poster of the smoking Uncle Sam so they could keep up with where the battles were taking place and who was winning them.

"Angela, you ought to go see her," Dot said, as she pulled an order from the serving window and lined the plates up on her arm. "It'd be bad luck if you don't. You know it would."

Angela acted as if she didn't hear Dot. Her eyes were fixed on Red McHenry, the florist's son. He was spinning her daughter around and around on one of the red vinyl stools at the counter, his hands on either side ready to catch her.

"Blow your uncle Willie a kiss," Willie called from the service window.

Pressing her lips to her palm, she blew a wet kiss in Willie's direction as she spun. Grinning from ear to ear, Willie blushed like a boy.

"That one's going to be a heartbreaker," the sheriff said.

"No doubt she's a Belle," Ben Harrington added, with a mouthful of ice cream.

Returning to the counter with a load of dirty plates, Dot picked up her campaign right where she'd left off.

"All I'm sayin' is, you'll feel real bad if you don't go and something happens to that child. Won't she, Charlotte?"

Charlotte raised her newspaper even higher, letting everyone know she didn't have a dog in this fight.

"You get prettier every day, don't you?" Red said, as he spun the stool.

No one called Angela's little girl by her real name. No one could spit it out. Angela had found the name in the family Bible. Apparently, it wanted to stay there.

"She's cute as a Dixie cup," Willie said from the service window.

"Are you my little Dixie cup?" Red asked, giving her nose a tap.

Clapping her hands, the child giggled and squealed.

And just like that, Aubrette Orianna Belle was christened Dixie.

Standing in front of the hall mirror, Angela studied her reflection. She was always a little surprised when she actually stopped and looked at herself. She was a mess. But she knew she would never do anything about it. There were too many other things on her mind.

Her hair would never look styled. Her clothes would never look chic. She would never be sophisticated or elegant. She would never be Lydia Montgomery.

"Well," Angela said to her reflection, "there you are."

Picking up the baby gift in one hand and the shopping bag of hand-me-down baby clothes in the other, she headed for the Montgomerys'. As she made her way across the Montgomerys' yard, she stopped at Lydia's flower garden. The trellis lay on the ground and weeds had taken over.

Sensing someone was watching her, Angela looked up at the Montgomerys' upstairs window. But no one was there.

The house sounded hollow when the door knocker hit the plate. When the housekeeper opened the door, cool damp air blew out.

"I'll tell Miz Montgomery you're here," Mrs. Meeks said, and left Angela waiting in the dark foyer.

The front foyer looked like a glossy page of a magazine. The Oriental rug looked as though no one ever walked on it, the furniture as though no one ever sat on it. Angela bent down to smell a vase of roses, then realized they were silk. The house was designed to look at, not touch—much like Lydia.

"Miz Montgomery ain't feelin' well," Mrs. Meeks said, as she came down the curving stairs. "She won't be takin' visitors today."

Glancing back over her shoulder, Mrs. Meeks put her finger to her lips and motioned for Angela to follow her.

"The nursery is downstairs?" Angela whispered, as she followed Mrs. Meeks down the hall.

"Dr. Montgomery keeps the boy close," Mrs. Meeks said.

The nanny looked up from her Bible when Mrs. Meeks opened the door. When she saw Angela Belle, her hand went to the cross at her throat.

Handing Mrs. Meeks the gifts, Angela walked across the room. Tilting her head, she looked down into the crib. The baby looked back solemnly, as though he'd been expecting her.

"He never cries," the nanny blurted, as though snitching on the child.

"He's not going to be a talker," Angela said.

Pulling the blanket back, she bent down over the child. He had a sturdy little body, with thick arms and legs. Reaching down, she placed her hand flat on his chest. His skin was warm and his tiny ribcage rose and fell under her palm. When she felt his heart beat, Angela gasped as though something had grabbed her. All a mother feels, she felt at that moment, no less than if he'd dropped from her own womb. With a single breath, she'd been stitched to the child like a piece of quilt, and it sucked the breath right out of her.

Mrs. Meeks stood frozen and the nanny clutched her Bible to her chest wide-eyed.

"You all right, Angela?" Mrs. Meeks finally asked quietly.

Gripping the crib with both hands, Angela nodded. When she finally tried to straighten up, the baby grabbed a fistful of her hair and held her.

"Not yet," Angela whispered, gently freeing his fingers.

CHAPTER 23

LYDIA WAS in Woolworth's the day she heard a local boy had been shot. She overheard Mrs. Smith tell Mrs. Madison, as the salesgirl measured out four yards of red-and-white linen for Mrs. Smith's Fourth of July dress.

"Shot," Lydia whispered, as though the bullet had passed right through her.

"Where'd they shoot him?" Mrs. Madison asked.

"Normandy," Mrs. Smith said.

"Who?" Lydia demanded.

"Boy from over in Stringtown," she said, surprised that Lydia Montgomery was taking any interest. "Boone Dickson."

Lydia collapsed to the floor like a puppet whose strings had been clipped.

Everyone thought it was anemia that sent Lydia to bed. She'd always been pale as porcelain. But after four months of not leaving her room, they began to fear it was something far worse.

"Never seemed all that right to begin with," Ben Harrington said.

"Always was a bit touched," the Sheriff said, tapping his temple.

"Hear Doc's thinkin' 'bout sendin' her away," Willie said from the service window, "to rest up at one of those sanitariums up in Boston."

"Hate to think of that little boy without a mother." Dot shook her head.

"Don't have that much of a mother as it is," Ben Harrington murmured into his cup.

The Montgomery house had taken on the atmosphere of a wake. No one spoke above a whisper or allowed their heels to click on the wooden floor. The curtains were always drawn. The rooms were so dark and damp that moss grew in the fireplace and it was not unusual for Mrs. Meeks to find a bat hanging on the curtain rod or a tree frog sticking to the window. The house had become a tomb. Only the humans didn't know it.

Every night Doc brought Lydia fresh flowers, trying to cheer her up. Her mother came from Boston to stay with them, and a psychiatrist drove down from Nashville to give her pills to make her sleep. But nothing lifted the fog that had settled over Lydia.

Knocking lightly on Lydia's bedroom door, Mrs. Meeks came in with fresh linens. Lydia's bed was covered in cool blue satin—blue satin bedspread, sheets, and pillowcases. Mrs. Meeks thought it looked just like the inside of a coffin.

Lydia sat in front of the window in her nightgown. Every day Mrs. Meeks found her there, staring out the window as lifeless as a china doll left forgotten in a chair.

Stripping the dirty linens off the bed, Mrs. Meeks rolled them into a wad and tied the corners like a hobo's sack. With a snap the clean sheet billowed in the air. For an instant, the room smelled like sunshine. Lydia was immune.

"You remember that boy who used to come 'round to fix things?" Mrs. Meeks asked casually, as she folded the corner of the sheet under the mattress and tucked it tight. "Boone Dickson?"

Lydia was so perfectly still, Mrs. Meeks wondered if she was breathing.

"Good-lookin' boy," Mrs. Meeks said, working her way around the bed. "Black hair. Black eyes."

Lydia's head tilted slightly her way.

"Word has it they shipped him to the V.A. hospital up in Nashville." Plumping a pillow, she smoothed the case. "They shot him up pretty bad, but they say he's going to make it."

Turning the bedspread down, Mrs. Meeks gathered up the dirty linens and started for the door.

"Mrs. Meeks . . ."

Mrs. Meeks stopped in the doorway.

"Thank you," Lydia whispered.

Nodding, Mrs. Meeks pulled the door closed behind her.

The lawn of the Veterans Hospital was scattered with broken and forgotten soldiers, like discarded toys no longer in favor. They hobbled along on crutches, or were pushed in wheelchairs by nurses in starched white uniforms. Some sat on benches under the trees, rocking back and forth, muttering to themselves. Some simply stared.

"You gettin' out?" the cabdriver asked, looking at her in his rearview mirror.

Lydia stared across the lawn at the damaged men. Then looking down at her gloved hands in her lap, slowly shook her head.

CHAPTER 24

WHEN ANGELA'S illegitimate daughter turned eight, it occurred to the child that most children had a mother and a father. And so she asked her great aunt about this. Taking Dixie by the hand, Charlotte marched her into the graveyard and pointed to a tombstone.

"There," she said, nodding to the grave, "that's your daddy."

Dixie Belle was born in 1937. According to the headstone, Colonel Elijah Mason died at the battle of Fort Donelson on February 16, 1862. Fortunately, along with history, Dixie was never that good at math.

Eli's grave was marked with the statue of a Confederate soldier—chin high, legs straight, and sword by his side. He stood under a post oak tree, boots mottled with moss and the ground in front of him slightly sunken. Lichens and time had pitted him, and black stains streaked down his face like tears, but judging by the hat on his head and the medals on his uniform, he was an officer and a gentleman.

Angela was just thankful Charlotte didn't choose the tombstone next to Colonel Mason. Having a long-haired androgynous angel with wings for a father could be very confusing to a child.

Every day after school, Dixie headed to the cemetery. Spreading a quilt on the ground, she carefully placed vanilla wafers on china plates, poured each of them a cup of milk from her china teapot and told Eli about her day.

"I don't know about this," Angela said, as they watched Dixie chattering away with the statue.

"Hell," Charlotte said, "Eli spends more time with the child than a real daddy would."

"And," Lettie added, "he has no bad habits to speak of."

Needless to say, having a cemetery monument for a father did not help Dixie's already rocky reputation. And so, when she wanted to have her birthday party in the graveyard, Angela balked.

"Since when have we given a rat's ass what people thought?" Charlotte said.

For herself, never. But Angela had, as all mothers do, wished for Dixie an easier life than her own.

Twenty-four invitations were sent. Three children showed up.

"Folks around here frown at celebrating a bastard's birth," Lettie said.

"Except, of course, at Christmas," Charlotte added.

Knowing the dual nature of man, Charlotte invited a few guests of her own. The fact that there were more adults than children at her party didn't seem to faze Dixie.

"That child is like a dandelion," Lettie said. "She could grow through concrete."

Dixie's birthday party had a combination Mardi Gras/funeral wake feel to it. Mr. Bennett and Digger looped and twirled pink crepe paper streamers all around the white graveside tent until it looked like a candy-cane castle. Leo Stinson scrubbed one of his ponies and gave pony rides. Red McHenry, the florist's son, made a unicorn's horn out of flower foam wrapped with gold foil, and strapped it to the horse's head.

"Had no idea that horse was white," Leo said, as they stood back and admired their work.

Angela, wearing an old, satin, off-the-shoulder hoop gown she'd found in the attic, greeted each guest with strings of beads, while Dixie, wearing peach-colored fairy wings, passed out velvet jester hats.

Charlotte, who never quite grasped the concept of eating while sitting on the ground, had her driver bring a rocking chair from the front porch. Mr. Nalls set the chair beside Eli's statue where Charlotte barked orders like a general.

"Don't put the food table under the oak tree!" she commanded, waving her arm. "We'll have acorns in the potato salad!"

Lettie kept the glasses full and between KyAnn Merriweather and Dot Wyatt there was enough food to have fed Eli's entire regiment. Potato salad, coleslaw, deviled eggs, bread and butter pickles, green beans, fried corn, spiced pears, apple dumplings, and one of every animal species, pork barbecue, fried chicken, beef ribs, and cold country ham stretched as far as the eye could see.

"You know," Willie said, as he watched people pile up their plates, "I'm thinking a man could make a little money with a lunch buffet."

Mouth full, the Sheriff nodded. There was certainly nothing he enjoyed more than a side of country ham with his fried chicken.

Reba Earhart and her five boys rattled up in their old farm truck, Reba's Country Ham hand-painted in pink on the rusty door. Throwing down the tailgate, her oldest son, Earl, who had moved back from Detroit after the war to help with the ham business, lifted six scrubbed piglets with starched lace collars from the back. Reba marked off a racetrack and gave each child a willow branch. Tapping the piglets on their fat haunches, the children laughed and squealed as they chased the bobbing corkscrew tails around the tombstones. When they got to the finish line, Reba's youngest, Booker, rewarded each piglet with a Fig Newton and a scratch behind the ear.

"Don't go gettin' attached," Reba warned, shaking her finger at him. "That pig ain't nuthin' but a pork chop on layaway!"

After the pig races, pony rides, and four solid hours of eating, they sang "Happy Birthday" and Dixie blew out her candles. Sprawled on quilts on the grass, they ate fresh-grated coconut cake and homemade peach ice cream while Mr. Bennett told stories. And the dead gathered 'round to listen.

"Tell us a war story," Booker said.

"During the War Between the States," Mr. Bennett began, as he tamped his pipe, "they used Bellereve as a hospital. My great-grand-mammy was just a girl at the time, but she could tell it like it was yesterday."

Mr. Bennett struck a match. Holding it down into the bowl of his pipe, he puffed until the tobacco glowed.

"Musette Belle, Miss Charlotte's great-great-grandma, had the gift, you know," he said, shaking out the match. "She could see things 'fore they got there. Six-months 'fore the Yankees floated down the Cumberland, she teared every sheet, slip and pillowcase in town into bandages."

They followed Mr. Bennett's gaze through the curl of pipe smoke to the white marble statue of Musette Belle, half hidden beside a weeping willow. She seemed to tilt her head at the mention of her name, and goosebumps ran up the children's arms.

"They brought the dead and the dying by the wagonload. Stretched them out on pallets along the porch and every flat spot in the house. The wood floors was so slick with blood the women threw down sand to keep from slippin'.

"They brought a young Yankee in and laid him on the dining-room table. Had a hole in his chest the size of my fist. Already had the death stare. Starin' straight up like he was lookin' at heaven's gate. Doctor took one look at him and said there weren't nothin' could be done.

"They told my grandmammy to sit with the soldier till the end. Nuthin' she could do but mop the sweat off his face. Even though he wuz a Yankee, he was so pretty, Mammy couldn't help but get attached. When she heered the death rattle, she put her hands to her face and wept.

"Musette Belle musta heard her and took pity. She walked over and laid her hand right on the hole on that Yankee's chest and whispered sumpthin'. Mammy couldn't understand a word. Musette was Cajun French, you know. Then she bent down and kissed that soldier right on his bloody mouth. Well, sir, that dead Yankee came off the table like God had grabbed him by the chest and was jerkin' him to attention."

"Did he live?" Booker Earhart asked, solemn as a preacher.

"I reckon he did," Mr. Bennett said, taking a puff on his pipe. "Grandmammy married him."

"I sees her, you know," Digger said, eyes round as saucers. "Ever times we's bury the dead, I sees Miz Musette awalkin' in the trees. Sees her like I's a-lookin' at you."

"Is she na-ked?" Booker asked.

Reba popped him on the mouth so fast no one saw her arm move.

"Some say Musette Belle was a witch," Mr. Bennett went on. "Some say—"

Pipe suspended in the air, Mr. Bennett stopped mid-sentence. Everyone turned to see what had grabbed his tongue. There walking across the graveyard toward them was Dr. Adam Montgomery, his son, Adam Jr., by his side.

"Good Lord," Dot muttered under her breath.

Sometime between Christmas and Easter, four-year-old A.J. had a growing spurt. The baby fat melted away and his features began to mold into the man he was going to be. He had a mop of black hair that wouldn't hold a part, full lips that never smiled, and black eyes like mercury moons. The women could not take their eyes off of him, and the child met their stare straight on.

While it was obvious to everyone that the boy was the spitting image of Boone Dickson, it was also obvious that the thought had never crossed Adam's mind. All the love Lydia shunned, Adam poured into the child, holding him as if it would tear his heart out to ever let him go.

The silence was as thick as fog. No one moved. No one said a thing. Nothing ties the tongue like knowing a secret that would hurt a man more than the lie he is living.

It was KyAnn Merriweather who finally broke the spell. In KyAnn's mind, white folks was always adding complicated sauces to things that should be plain and simple.

"Boy," she called out to the child, "you like ribs?"

A. J. nodded.

"Come to KyAnn," she purred, drawing him to her with her long brown finger.

Like all men, the boy flew to her like a bee to honey.

Ben Harrington picked up his fiddle, put it to his ear, and plucked a few strings to tune it. The man had the personality of a metal file, hard and grating, but when he tucked that violin under his chin, he was absolved. He played music fit for the graveyard, haunted with regrets and longing. When a man's wife runs off with the Porter Paint salesman leaving him with a four-year-old to raise, a part of him dies. Ben's music was the ghost of the man he once was.

While the grown-ups leaned back on their quilts and listened to Ben mourn, the children played hide-and-seek, crouching behind headstones, pressing flat against stone angels. Katydids whirred and bullfrogs croaked like a pipe organ. Lightning bugs were so thick it was like running through spilled glitter. When it was too dark to see, they found each other by running toward the jangle of bells on their jester hats. Eyes wide, breath hot and ragged, they ran screaming through the rock monuments as fast as they could, not only from the fear of being caught, but from the fear of what might be hiding in the shadows.

The darker it got, the closer Adam moved toward Angela. So close, he could smell her skin beneath the Ivory soap. But when she glanced back over her shoulder at him, the look that passed between them made him look away. Hands stuffed in his pockets, he wandered over to the tent where the other men were doctoring their lemonade with moonshine.

While Adam Senior was mesmerized by the younger Belle, A.J. was smitten with the older. Standing in front of Charlotte's rocker, he stared pensively up at her.

"What do you want?" Charlotte demanded.

The boy took a step closer.

"Scat!" Charlotte ordered, shooing him with her hands.

Lifting his hand in the air, he cautiously touched the arm of Charlotte's rocker.

"I said get the hell away!" she bellowed.

Slowly, he slid his slobbery fingers along the arm of the rocker until the tips touched hers. Drawing back from the little hand, Charlotte seemed temporarily struck mute by the boy's audacity.

"He's a persistent little cuss," Lettie said, knowing full well Charlotte's weakness for persistent men. "I'll give him that."

"Children are like cats," Reba said, as she picked through the fried chicken for a wing to get the sweet taste out of her mouth. "They always gravitate to the one who don't want um."

Arms crossed, Dot shook her head. "Poor child is starved for a woman's attention. Miz Meeks says a junkyard dog gets more affection from his mother than that little boy,"

"Well, sshe-it!" Charlotte hissed at them all.

Jerking the boy up, she plopped him onto her lap. Charlotte managed to maintain her indifference until he leaned back against her. Then slowly her arms wrapped around his small warm body.

"Do you know how they make the strongest sword?" Charlotte whispered in his ear, as she rocked him back and forth. "They hammer it flat, then hold it to the fire."

Perfectly still, the child listened with an intensity most men did not possess.

"What a brave boy you are. What a fine man you are going to be."

But only time would tell if Charlotte's spell would take.

Perched on top of Cleave Wilson's headstone, KyAnn Merriweather watched from a distance like a blue-black crow. She figured Cleave wouldn't mind her sitting on his grave, seeing as how he had forced her to sit on his lap when no one was looking until she was twelve.

A cemetery is like an orchard. Some lives were sweet. Some bitter as lemons. And some were rotten to the core.

Cleave Wilson had had an unnatural fondness for children, even his own. Probably still would have, if he hadn't up and died—despite the pot of homemade chicken soup Angela Belle brought him for his cold.

The Sheriff took one look at Cleave's black tongue, sniffed what was left of the soup, and knew exactly what had happened. When he returned the pot to the Belles and saw KyAnn standing behind Charlotte, mouth busted and eye swollen shut, he knew why.

"Suicide," he announced at the diner.

If there was one thing everyone knew about Cleave Wilson, it was that he didn't have the decency to kill himself.

"Well," Dot said, as she poured the Sheriff a cup of coffee, "we all saw it coming."

"Amen to that." Ben Harrington nodded.

The day before Wilson's death, when Charlotte had found KyAnn curled in a ball and bleeding on her back porch, she had gathered the child tightly into her arms and rocked her all night.

"What a brave girl you are," Charlotte whispered fiercely into her braided hair. "What a strong fine woman you are going to be."

CHAPTER 25

REVEREND THOMAS JONES'S wife always prayed before bed. Kneeling beside her husband she folded her hands over his and called out, "Lord, be present! Forgive my husband for his filthy disgusting desires and raise his thoughts to purer goals. . . ."

Needless to say, by the time she finished praying, Thomas had lost his focus. A religious man has trouble making love with a cat looking on, much less the Lord.

As the years went by and children did not come, the congregation's hearts went out to the minister and his wife. Prayer meetings were held and a laying on of hands. While Reverend Jones firmly believed in miracles, he seriously doubted that even Jesus Christ could get his wife to uncross her legs.

"What a good woman she is," people said, in a way that implied he wasn't a good man.

The Reverend had built his Lord's house on a foundation of guilt. He could give a sermon that made little old ladies, whose only sin was coveting their neighbor's fruitcake recipe, weep with remorse. He could make children have nightmares of hell.

But now, his sermons began to blaze with condemnation. He looked out at his congregation, and when his eyes landed on a man, the man froze with fear. Pointing his finger, the Reverend cried out, "Damned is the man who gives his soul to drink . . . gambling . . . lust . . . lying . . . stealing! Repent!"

And the man would. Until the next time.

Little by little, the Reverend's wife spent most of her days and all of her nights bent over her Bible, eyes red and fingers crawling across the page. She ate only bread and water and countered every comment with Scripture. Her eyes shined with suffering and the congregation went from feeling awe in her presence to feeling awkward.

"I wish my hands would bleed," she said, staring at her palms.

Thomas stared at her in horror. She smiled at him with pity because he did not have her devotion.

"My God! My God! Why hast thou forsaken us?" the Reverend thundered from the pulpit.

Filled with the fear of a vengeful God and eternal damnation, his congregation clasped their hands and pleaded for salvation. But the Reverend couldn't save himself, much less anyone else. On his way to finding religion, Thomas lost God.

Then one day his wife took to bed.

"I'm dying!" she declared joyfully, head resting on the starched white pillow.

The doctors could find nothing wrong with her. Thomas knew they were looking in the wrong places.

She lay in bed for two years before her prayers were finally answered. At the funeral, people could not conceal their relief.

"She was not of this earth," they said, as they offered him their condolences.

Thomas watched it all from a distance. He could feel nothing.

A year passed, maybe two. One day is the same as the next to a man at the bottom of a well.

"Start over," they urged. "A new town. A new church."

They sent him to a place he could not find on the map.

"I seem to be lost," he said to the gas station attendant.

"Where you headed?" the boy asked, as he pumped.

Thomas read the name off the paper they had given him. Lifting a greasy finger, the boy pointed to a peeling sign half hidden by vines and creeper not fifty feet away.

Welcome to Leaper's Fork, the sign said. *We Call It Home.*

CHAPTER 26

THE FIRST BAPTIST Church was the biggest church in the county. They knew this because Judge Lester kept a close eye on the numbers. Man creates God in his own image. Judge Lester's God wore a pocket protector.

Every Sunday Judge sent his only son around to the other churches on the square to take a census. Judge Jr. was a chip off the ol' banker's block. Face pressed against the window, he carefully wrote down the attendance numbers.

"The Methodists are down three percent from last week," Judge Jr. reported back to his father.

And Judge Lester said, "This is good."

The preacher at the First Baptist Church was Reverend Luther Lyle. Every preacher has his preferred sin. Reverend Lyle's favorite sin was dancing. He could give a sermon that made a woman's heels lift off the floor.

"Dance music," he declared with bravado, "is the devil's mating call!"

Back in the '20s Reverend Lyle was in his prime. The Charleston was a dance he could really sink his evangelical teeth into. Hands waving, knees flapping, and legs kicking, it had Satan written all over it.

"I'm not talking dance hall floozies! I'm not talking red-lipped hussies! I'm talking decent women! Young innocent fresh-faced girls sssh-shakin' their behinds and k-k-kickin' their legs over their heads in dresses no longer than shirts!" he bellowed, as he pounded the podium. "They open and close their knees like heathen whores! They show their most private garments!"

Every week the pews were packed.

But then the Lindy Hop came along and Reverend Lyle grew ambivalent. He was a huge fan of Charles Lindbergh. Always dreamed of being a pilot himself. By the time the Swing came into vogue, his heart just wasn't in it. Reverend Lyle's sermons, in the deacons' minds, had grown somewhat liberal.

Then Judge Jr. brought the bad news.

"The Episcopalians are building a new fellowship hall," he reported.

And the deacons were struck with fear.

"Those Whiskey-palians already have real wine in communion going for them!" Judge Lester declared. "A new fellowship hall could be the beginning of our end!"

That night the deacons lay in their beds, staring at the ceiling. In the morning they were in agreement. It was time for new blood.

They sent Reverend Lyle on his merry way with a slap on the back and a fully loaded tackle box. After fifty years as a fisher of men, he would become a fisher of the large mouth bass.

"Reverend Thomas Jones is your man," they were told. "He knows the Good Book and can preach a sermon that will light the fires of hell under your backside!"

And so, when Thomas walked into the church office, the church secretary was more than a little surprised. She had expected John the Baptist. Reverend Jones looked more like a beaten boxer.

"Where's my office?" he asked.

She pointed and Thomas walked inside and closed the door.

After he heard the church secretary leave for the day, Thomas forced himself out of the chair. On the floor outside his office door was a ring of keys and a note reeking of rosewater. The penmanship was so perfect, at first he thought it had been typed.

> *Dear Reverend Jones,*
> *Here are your keys.*
> *God Bless.*
> *Althea Nalls, Church Secretary*
> *P.S.—Don't forget to lock up.*

Wadding up the note, Thomas threw it into the waste can, which was otherwise empty. Reconsidering, he bent down to retrieve the note. That was when he caught the scent.

Under the church directory in Althea's middle desk drawer were a cigarette lighter, an ashtray, and a pack of Lucky Strike cigarettes. He found the Wrigley's Spearmint gum and a spray bottle of rosewater cologne in the top drawer.

Putting the church directory back where he'd found it, Thomas closed the drawer.

The children's Sunday school room smelled like paste and sticky fingers. The walls were papered with drawings of stick children walking hand in hand with a blue-eyed Jesus. The adults' room was empty except for the smell of Pine-Sol.

Thomas was always hopeful when he entered a sanctuary. Pushing open the heavy double doors, he took a deep breath, inhaling the stale stagnant air of a room kept locked most of the week. The afternoon sun passed through the stained glass window on the west wall and pinpoints of colored light spilled onto the altar like a broken necklace of glass beads. Slowly walking down the center aisle, Thomas took inventory: pews, pipe organ, pulpit, hymnals, Bibles, altar, cross. The only thing missing was God.

Standing outside the church, Thomas flipped through the keys on the ring, until he found the one marked Side Door. There was a time when there were no locks on the church doors. But then Judge Lester became a deacon. Now the pews were bolted to the floor and even the kitchen door was locked for fear someone might make off with the paper cups.

The parsonage was located on the street behind the church. Thomas stood on the sidewalk looking at the small brick Victorian. Turning away, he kept walking.

Leaper's Fork shut down at five. The merchants turned their signs around to Closed and flipped off the lights. There wasn't a car or person on the square. Thomas had the town all to himself.

He walked past Harrington's Hardware, the Feed Store, and the Kandy Kitchen. Hands in his pockets, he stood in front of Dot's and read the next day's specials on the chalkboard above the counter. In front of the courthouse, he checked his watch against the clock. He was running five minutes fast. He left it that way. At Mademoiselle's Dress Shop, a mynah bird in the window squawked, "Happy days are here again!" At the post office, he looked up at the clawed gargoyles and was reminded of a painting of hell in one of his seminary books.

He started to go down Monroe Street but something pulled him back. He turned toward the river instead. One by one he walked past old mansions tucked behind ivy-covered rock walls and wrought iron gates. At the end of the street he came to the cemetery. Closed at Dark, the sign said. Stepping over the chain, Thomas kept walking.

You can tell a lot about a town by the way they care for their dead. Some of the headstones were so old the corners were worn round and the names washed away, but the grass was carefully clipped.

The old trees, bent and twisted like elderly mourners, laced their limbs into praying fingers over his head. Hands in his pockets, he strolled through the stone angels and crosses, noting the names on the old markers, Fussell, Bellamy, Harrington, Wylie, Colston, Markam, Mann. The Stinson family plot had a wrought iron fence around it.

The Lesters' mausoleum had stained glass windows and a granite bench.

The mind plays tricks in a graveyard. Shadows move and the wind whispers. At first he thought the woman standing by the grave was a statue, she stood so still. But then she raised her head and looked straight at him. It was the look a woman gives a man, not a minister. Thomas did not correct her.

"You knew him?" she asked, nodding to the grave.

He shook his head.

"There wasn't that much to know," she said, staring down at the grave. "Even less to remember."

Pots of plants that the family couldn't fit into the trunk of their car sat around the freshly dug dirt, already starting to wither.

"You have to admire a business that convinces people to send gifts to the dead," she said.

Reaching down, she pulled a rose from an arrangement. Thomas shifted uncomfortably.

"If he were alive," she said, amused by his piety, "he'd give them to me."

Thomas didn't doubt that.

He tried to hold his focus on the grave, but couldn't. He couldn't take his eyes from her.

An owl hooted and Thomas jumped.

"You're afraid to meet your Maker," she said.

He couldn't argue with that.

The woman studied him for a long time.

"You from out of town?"

He nodded.

She liked men who were just passing through.

"You a salesman?"

Slowly, he nodded.

"What do you sell?"

"Salvation."

She laughed. She liked a man with a sense of humor.

"You married?" she asked, staring at the wedding band on his finger.

Thomas didn't say anything. He didn't know how to answer the question.

"She leave you?"

"She died."

"How long has she been dead?"

"Two years."

"You been with another woman since then?"

It took him a while to shake his head. The truth was, even when his wife was living, he hadn't been with a woman.

A breeze blew off the river and the smell of torn earth mingled with the death perfume of carnations and chrysanthemums. Closing her eyes, the woman took a deep breath.

"There is something about death that gives a person a love for life," she said.

Thomas had not loved anything for so long.

As she walked toward him, like an ember with the ash blown away, something inside him sparked.

It was the first time a woman knelt before him for anything but prayer. It was the first time he was truly humbled. He stood perfectly still as she loosened his belt. Then taking her head in both hands, he closed his eyes and pulled her to him. Thomas had devoted twenty-two years to life after death. For this brief moment, let him love this life.

Thomas sat at his desk and waited for the guilt to come.

Night passed and morning came.

Thomas looked out at the day, and the world was so beautiful it brought tears to his eyes.

*   *   *

By Friday, the church secretary was beside herself. The new minister had not left his office all week. As far as she could tell, he'd been sleeping there. Whenever one of the deacons showed up, she sternly told them that Reverend Jones was in prayer and could not to be disturbed. They were so stunned by a preacher who prayed in private, they backed away.

Sunday morning, Althea finally stormed the office. Using the master key she kept around her neck, she unlocked the door and found him standing at the window.

"Reverend Jones?"

Thomas turned around and the sight of him made her step back. He was either delirious or drunk. Maybe both.

"God is love," he said.

"Well," she frowned, "yes."

Thomas laughed.

"I never knew."

There wasn't time for Althea to shave him. She found one of Reverend Lyle's old ties, knotted it around Thomas's collar and threw a magenta robe on him. Unwrapping a stick of Wrigley's, she stuffed it in his mouth. Grabbing him by the arm, she dragged him down the hall and up the steps, and managed to shove him into the processional just as they were passing through the double doors.

The choir sang "Onward, Christian Soldiers," as they marched down the aisle. Thomas followed behind them, unshaven, eyes like two eggs floating in a bucket, and grinning like a fool.

Ed Wilson led the morning prayer, John Murphy gave the announcements, and Judge Lester gave the financial report. Then it was time for the sermon.

Pushing himself up from the chair, Thomas stepped up to the

pulpit. The bible was open to the Scripture he was to preach from. He could recite it with his eyes closed.

He stared down at the Scripture for what seemed like eternity. The congregation shifted uncomfortably in the pews.

Slowly, Thomas closed the Bible.

Gripping the lectern with both hands, he looked out at the congregation. Dressed in their Sunday best, they glared back, eyes hooded, arms crossed, and jaws locked like old maids' knees. It was a tough crowd.

"Faith . . . Hope . . . Love," Thomas called out, his voice echoing through the sanctuary. "Of these, the greatest is love."

Then turning his back to them, Thomas sat down.

Monday morning, the deacons gathered at the diner. Heads bowed over their coffee cups, they conspired to fire him.

"Heard 'bout that new preacher of yours," Ben Harrington called from the counter. "If anything could turn me into a Bible-thumping Baptist, a one-minute sermon just might do the trick."

"Amen to that," the Sheriff seconded.

The deacons decided to give Reverend Jones until the end of the month.

CHAPTER 27

IT DID NOT take long for Thomas to find out who the woman was. The church secretary was not surprised he was asking about Charlotte Belle. She naturally assumed he would be taking up the war against her where Reverend Lyle had left off.

"The Belles are earthy women," Althea said. "If you catch my drift."

Thomas caught it with both hands. He had spent half his life married to a woman not of this earth. He was more than ready for a woman with a little dirt on her.

When the new minister came calling, Lettie knew the minute she peeked out the curtain that Charlotte had already nailed him.

"You are going to straight to hell for messing with a preacher man!" Lettie declared, shaking her finger in Charlotte's face.

"He's a preacher?" Charlotte flared. "Why, that son of a bitch!"

Throwing the front door open, she glared at him.

"What the hell do you want?" she demanded, blocking the doorway.

"Charlotte Belle," Thomas said, "I love you."

Charlotte laughed in his face.

"You aren't the first man to say it, and you sure as hell won't be the last!"

"No," he said, taking a step toward her, "but I'll be the last man you say it to."

And he said it in a way that grabbed her right where it counts.

Charlotte slammed the door so hard, the knocker banged against the plate. She fell back against the door as if to keep the enemy out. Thomas, eyes closed, pressed his forehead against the other side. Each of them stood there, separated only by inches.

There was only one time when Charlotte Belle was vulnerable and now Thomas knew it.

"Death waits at the end of the road for all of us," Thomas said, when Althea brought the news that Martha Madison had died peacefully in her bed at the age of ninety-two. "Mourn for the man who is afraid to meet his Maker."

Althea went back to her desk, lit a Lucky Strike and gave this some thought.

As they were lowering Martha's casket into the earth, it occurred to Thomas that he was not the only man in Leaper's Fork. Charlotte stood by the graveside, a pallbearer staring at her as though there was nothing in the world he would rather do than lay her to rest.

As soon as Thomas said, "Amen," he charged.

"Reverend Thomas Jones," he said, shaking the man's hand until his whole body shook. "Son, have you been saved?"

As soon as the pallbearer could pull his hand free, he took off, boutonniere bouncing.

"I don't want you seeing other men," Thomas ordered, as he walked her to her car.

"I'm sorry," Charlotte said dryly. "Did I mistakenly give you the impression that I give a damn what you want?"

Three weeks passed before the next funeral. Thomas thought he was going to die.

"Marry me," Thomas ordered, as they stood side by side at the grave.

"What," Charlotte huffed, "and ruin my reputation?"

*   *   *

Thomas's new congregation quickly warmed to him. His faith gave them faith. His hope filled them with hope for themselves. Not to mention the fact that he always summed up his sermon five minutes early by the courthouse clock. Every Sunday he sent his congregation off with the same epistle.

"All things are possible for those who love the Lord!" he called out, and he said it as though it were a promise.

Thomas had been hammered flat and held to the fire. And the man who rose from the ashes burned with purpose.

His sermons were conspicuously low on hellfire and brimstone, and the deacons were a little worried that he was a Unitarian posing as a Baptist. But the offering was up twenty-five percent, and so they decided to turn the other cheek.

By the end of the year, people were driving across the county line to hear Reverend Jones. Church attendance had doubled and was growing. The deacons decided to add a ten o'clock service until a bigger sanctuary could be built.

On Sunday evenings they lined the banks of the river waiting to be baptized. Wet white robes clinging to their skin, they closed their eyes and folded their hands. Thomas leaned them back into the water, and when he lifted them up, they gasped as though they had been saved.

"Go forth and love the Lord!" Thomas commanded.

And they did.

CHAPTER 28

It was after dark when Boone Dickson stepped off the train in Leaper's Fork. The town had already closed up for the night. The porter handed him his duffel bag, and Boone hoisted it over his shoulder.

"Musta been hell," the porter said, staring at the empty shirt-sleeve rolled and pinned at Boone's elbow.

Boone wasn't sure if he meant the war, the year at the V.A. hospital, or coming back to Leaper's Fork.

"Yeah," he answered, to all of it.

Boone was well into his third month of drinking away the day when Mr. Nalls turned Charlotte's car down the dirt road to his house. The top was down and Charlotte wore a broad-brimmed hat held on with a silk scarf, sunglasses covering half her face.

"You lost?" Boone asked, as Charlotte climbed the steps.

"I'm never lost," she said.

Boone stiffened a little when Charlotte sat in his mother's rocker. The rocker was elegant in its simplicity, like his mother had been. He'd thought a lot about her since he'd been home. Once he thought he saw her sitting in the chair, rocking and stringing beans. He could hear the rhythmic snap, followed by the tap of her foot. He was sure it was just drunken delirium.

"Beauty fades, men lose interest and money comes and goes,"

Charlotte said, as she pushed the rocker, "but a rocking chair will always be there when you need it."

Boone had no doubt Charlotte Belle had never snapped a bean in her life.

"I take it the fix-it business is so good, you haven't had time to take care of things around the house," Charlotte said, fanning herself with her hat.

Boone followed her stare from the torn screen hanging off the door to the window with cardboard taped over the broken pane.

"Is this the tour of homes?" he asked.

"I'm looking for someone to help me with some land I own," she said. "I think you're the man I'm looking for."

Holding a beer bottle with two fingers, he tipped it back.

"I'm looking for a developer."

"A developer?" Boone scoffed.

"You manage the men. I manage the money."

Staring off the porch, Boone rubbed his hand up and down his leg. Through his pants he could feel the jagged scar the shrapnel had left.

"I handle the business," Charlotte went on. "You do the work. Partners, fifty-fifty."

Pulling a cigarette from behind his ear, he hung it on his lip. Lighting a match with his thumbnail, he took a ragged draw. Fixing a rotten floor or a leaking roof might not get a man a medal, but he'd been good at it. What if he wasn't good at developing? It was a distinct possibility, seeing as how he wasn't entirely sure what developing was.

"Not interested," he said.

Charlotte pushed herself out of the rocker.

"Then our business is over before it started."

As Boone watched her walk to her car he thought she'd given up awful easy. So easy, maybe "no" was the answer she'd come to hear.

"Don't treat me like a cripple!" Boone yelled fiercely off the porch, as Charlotte's car slowly pulled away.

"Then quit acting like one!" Charlotte yelled back.

It was around midnight when the truck turned down his road. Boone jerked awake in the rocking chair on his porch. Hand hovering over the shotgun on the floor next to him, he squinted across the yard. The truck door creaked open and slammed closed, but it wasn't until she stepped into the porch light that he could make out the tall black woman walking toward him carrying a picnic basket.

KyAnn Merriweather had heard that an arm wasn't the only thing Boone Dickson lost in the war. But the man she found sitting on the porch was a ghost. His cheeks were sunken and his skin was the color of flour. He was breathing, but the eyes were dead.

"I don't need your pity," he said, as KyAnn climbed the porch steps.

"Well, there's a good thing," KyAnn said, "bein' as I plum forgot tuh bring it."

She'd come straight from the Poor Man's. There were still drops of sweat in her cleavage and Boone could smell the hickory smoke on her skin. KyAnn pretended she didn't notice he was looking at her as she kneeled beside him and opened the basket.

Pouring a glass of sweet tea from a jar, she squeezed a lemon into it, licking her fingers before she set it on the floor beside his chair. Filling a plate with ribs, cornbread, and vinegar slaw, she held it out in front of him.

When Boone turned his head away, she set the plate in his lap.

Arms draped along the back of the swing, KyAnn stretched her long brown legs out in front of her. The old chains creaked and groaned as she pushed herself back and forth.

Women always complain that men don't talk. Most times it's

because they don't leave enough silence for a man to slip a word in. KyAnn was content with the sound of bugs hitting the screen door and katydids trilling.

"Charlotte Belle was by here," Boone said after a while. "Wants me to go into the developing business. Hell, what do I know about developing?"

"Charlotte Belle don't give you a dime if she don't know you'd make a dollar."

KyAnn stared off the porch, but she knew Boone's eyes were on her. Slowly, she ran her bare foot up and down the back of her calf. Boone sat up a little straighter in his chair.

"Don't get me wrong," he said, picking up a rib and staring at it, "I could build a house good as any man. I sure as hell could build one better than Joe Pegram. That fool don't know which end of the hammer hits the nail."

Boone tore a bite off the rib. The barbecue sauce burned his lips like liquid fire.

"Word is, Pegram can't build houses fast enough for all them men comin' home from war."

Boone picked up his fork and shoveled into the slaw.

"Always thought the old Madison farm would make a fine place for houses," he said, chewing. "Nice view of the river, but high enough it don't flood. Too hilly for farming. Nothing I hate more than houses planted like corn in a field."

The more Boone ate, the more he planned. When his glass was low, KyAnn filled it. When his plate was empty, she piled it up again.

The next morning Boone was up before sunrise. While the coffee pot perked, he stood on the back porch and shaved. Holding the shaving cup in his armpit, he whipped the cream into lather. Turning his face from side to side, he studied his reflection. The old mirror was so mottled he could barely see himself. It didn't matter. Every morning he'd watched his daddy stand at this mirror and shave. The way he brushed the foam on his face. The way he held the razor. For better or worse, a man does most things from habit. Rinsing the razor in the basin, he wiped his face with a towel. Slinging the soapy water off the porch, he hung the wash pan on a nail on the wall.

Coffee in hand, Boone leaned against the porch rail. While he was away his coon dog had gone blind in one eye, and his cat had gone half wild and wouldn't let him touch her. But the hills were just like he'd left them. Fog lay in the holler and he could smell Stinson's tobacco firing in the barn.

Through the cracks in the porch floor he could see the white feathers of chickens as they scratched for insects in the dirt under the house. And he thought about how hard his father had scratched to make a living, and his father's father before him. Dicksons had worked hard all their lives and ended up with nothing.

He rinsed his cup out under the pump on the porch and turned it upside down to dry. Then Boone made his way across the yard to the barn. Swinging the double doors open, he instinctively ducked as a guinea hen came flying out. The dust and chicken shit was so thick on his old truck he had to sweep it off with a broom. His brother had started her up from time to time and checked the antifreeze while he was gone. But since he'd been back, Boone hadn't touched her. Slipping the key out from under the front seat, he gave it some choke and pumped the gas pedal three times.

"Come on, girl," Boone soothed, until she finally turned over.

Easing the truck into reverse, Boone backed out of the barn. Steering with his knee while he shifted, he made a couple of loops around the pasture to get the feel back. Then he pointed her toward town.

"It's six-thirty in the morning!" Charlotte squinted as she wrapped the robe around herself.

"I start work at seven," Boone said, walking past her into the house.

CHAPTER 29

WHEN IT CAME to men, Charlotte strictly adhered to the law of catch and release. As soon as she could get them out of her bed, she threw them back into the stream. And so it came as quite a surprise to her that she could not stop thinking about Thomas.

Charlotte had never needed a man. She had money. She had Mr. Nalls for heavy lifting. And when it came to sex, her pond was well stocked. What else did a woman need a man for? And yet, she found herself thinking about Thomas. The way he smelled. The way his hair curled under his ear. The way he held the Bible in his left hand at the graveside during a funeral, leaving his right hand free to express himself. Charlotte found herself thinking about Thomas even when she didn't want to think about him. And it infuriated her.

"So," Adam said, positioning the stethoscope on Charlotte's chest, "you're going to the mountains."

Skipping town would be closer to the truth.

"The fresh mountain air will do you good."

"Is that the manure they're spreading at Harvard Medical School these days?" Charlotte huffed.

Every year Charlotte had an annual physical to keep Lettie from nagging her to death. As a rule, despite drinking, smoking, and carousing, Belles lived to be old women and died in their sleep—except for occasionally getting struck by lightning or shot by a jealous wife.

"Take a deep breath," Adam said, moving the instrument slightly on her chest. "And another . . . And another . . ."

Adam stole quick glances at Charlotte as he listened to her heart. She was an older version of Angela. Beautiful, although a man tended to forget it the minute she opened her mouth.

"When are you leaving?" he asked.

"Saturday."

"Really? Lydia is leaving to visit her mother in Boston on Saturday. Cough . . . and again . . ."

Hanging the stethoscope around his neck, he took her wrist and found the pulse.

When a woman was in his examination room she either chattered incessantly or never said a word. Adam made women nervous, some because they were uncomfortable being alone with him, some because they liked it.

"The mountains are beautiful this time of year," he said, scribbling a note in her file.

That Charlotte was not nervous made Adam nervous.

"In contemplation of created things, by steps we may ascend to God," he recited, as he tapped her knee with the rubber hammer.

"Quoting brilliant men doesn't make you brilliant." Charlotte said sharply, as her leg kicked the air. "Hattie Taylor's mynah bird quotes Milton."

As Adam examined Charlotte, Charlotte examined Adam. Most women hung on his blond hair and blue-eyed good looks. What Charlotte couldn't get past was that he was as prissy as a poodle. Adam Montgomery was not good enough for her niece. This made what she was about to say all the more painful.

"I want you to look in on Angela while I'm gone."

"Look in on her?"

"Keep an eye on her."

"Keep an eye on her?"

"Good God, man! Do I have to draw you a picture?"

Adam stepped back from the examination table. Quickly turning to the washbasin, he scrubbed his hands furiously under the gushing faucet.

"Why?" he finally asked.

"Because the pork chop sitting in the pan tastes better than the one sitting on the plate," Charlotte said plainly.

It had never occurred to Adam there might be another pork chop waiting on Angela's plate. His mind immediately took inventory of who the pig might be.

"I would never do anything to hurt Angela," he insisted.

"If I thought you had the mountain oysters to hurt her," Charlotte said, hopping off the examination table, "I'd have put a bullet between your eyes years ago."

All this talk about pork chops and oysters had made Charlotte hungry. Whether Adam was finished or not, she was.

Adam followed her down the hall. When they got to the waiting room, Charlotte stopped short. Patients lined the newly decorated room and leaned against the wall beside the split-leaf philodendron.

"I take it the doctoring business is doing well," she said.

"Up twenty-seven percent over last year," Adam answered automatically.

"It's comforting to know," Charlotte said dryly, on her way out the door, "that since you've taken up residence, illness is on the rise."

For the next week, Doc's mind was not on medicine. Twice he tried to take a patient's temperature with his fountain pen, and if Nurse Marshall hadn't stopped him, he would have put Booker Earhart's arm in a cast for poison oak. Word spread quickly that unless you were bleeding to death, your odds were greater surviving whatever ailed you than surviving a visit to Dr. Montgomery.

There was no doubt in anyone's mind what the problem was.

"Hard to do the two-step with the whole town keeping time," the Sheriff said, taking a bite of coconut cream pie.

"Just because you got a bucket," Willie said, from the service window, "don't mean the pump is primed."

While Charlie Earhart grunted through the door with a box of Reba's Country Ham, Reba casually spooned a cube of ice into her coffee. Knees bowed from the weight, Charlie shuffled up to the counter and waited to be told where to put it.

"Had a breed hog once couldn't perform if you watched," Reba said, slowly stirring her coffee. "He humped and he humped and that sow squealed and she squealed. But nuthin' happened. It was right pitiful."

Cheeks puffed, Charlie's face burned to a blister.

"Cain't have a breed hog that cain't breed," Reba said into her cup.

Charlie slammed the box of ham onto the counter next to her so hard the metal napkin holder jumped up and down.

Willie and the Sheriff eyed each other. For twenty-five years Charlie had treated Reba like a dog. When he said sit, she sat. When he said fetch, she fetched. When he threw her a bone, she chewed until he told her to stop.

But when Reba's ham business took off, the balance of power shifted. Reba had Charlie over the old pork barrel.

"If that ol' sow showed him a little affection," Charlie seethed, "that hog could be as passionate as the next."

Charlie had been a good-looking man when she married him. Reba had loved him so much it hurt. But twenty-five years of meanness and taking no notice of her had shriveled Charlie in Reba's eyes like a dried-apple doll.

"Unless passionate pork brings ten cents more on the pound," she said, studying her brand new gold tooth in the reflection on the napkin holder, "I'll take the hog that loves 'um and leaves 'um."

*   *   *

"There's fried chicken, deviled eggs, potato salad, loaf bread, pickles, ham, biscuits, pecan pie, and a jug of iced tea," Angela said, handing the picnic basket to Lettie.

"No cornbread?" Charlotte called out from the backseat of the Lincoln.

"You didn't tell me you wanted cornbread."

"In the event I forget to tell you," Charlotte grumbled, "bury me when I'm dead."

Lettie sat in the front next to Mr. Nalls, a wool shawl on the seat between them in case the mountain air was too cool for the knees, and a Bible on her lap in case Jesus came while they were in transit. Dixie sat in the backseat next to Charlotte.

Leaning through the window Angela situated a bag of books and toys on the floorboard, then brushed a kiss across Dixie's forehead. Before she could straighten up, Dixie caught Angela's face in both hands and held her.

"Kiss me like you mean it, Mama," the child said firmly.

Angela laughed. What had she done to deserve such a precious gift?

"A kiss for every hour of the day," Dixie insisted, as Angela covered her upturned face with kisses.

"And once on the nose for eternity," Angela said, kissing the tip of her nose.

Angela closed her eyes and pressed her forehead against Dixie's, memorizing the smell of her skin and the tide of her breath, marking her the way a cat marks her kitten. Maybe it was because she'd been born in a flower bed, or maybe it was because Angela dug her fingers into the dirt like roots, but Dixie was firmly planted. She would never know things beyond what she could see, touch, or hear. Her lust for life overshadowed all that. But she had a good heart, and that was worth more than all other things combined.

Reaching into her pocket, Angela pulled out a small, cloth, draw-string sack on a leather shoestring.

"Don't you take this off till you get home," Angela threatened, as she slipped it over Dixie's head.

"Smells like Martha White flour," Dixie said, rubbing her nose.

"You hear me?"

"I hear you, Mama."

"Enough! Enough!" Charlotte banged on the roof of the car with her fist. "Are you going to start this blasted automobile, Mr. Nalls, or do you plan for us to vacation in the driveway?"

Smiling pleasantly, Mr. Nalls shifted into gear.

Waving, Angela walked them to the gate. As the car disappeared down the street, she thought what incredible good luck it had been for Charlotte to find a driver who was not only good-natured, but also nearly stone-deaf.

A normal red-blooded male would have been waiting at Angela's back door as Charlotte walked out the front. It was three days after Charlotte's car pulled out of town before Adam climbed into Claude Wallace's barber chair for a trim and a shave.

"You want me to do sumptin' 'bout them nose hairs?" Claude asked, squinting down into Adam's nostrils as he wrapped the hot towel around his face. "Got one in there you could rope a calf with."

The Sheriff and Mr. Bennett, the graveyard caretaker, threw each other a grin, knowing Doc's temperature had gone up ten more degrees under the steaming towel.

It is the nature of men to pick on each other. Whether the purpose of this ritual is to toughen a man up or cause him to bleed to death is sometimes unclear.

"Heard Charlotte Belle's gone to the mountains," the Sheriff said, resting his hat on his knee.

"You don't say." Striking a wooden match, Mr. Bennett held it in the bowl of his pipe and took a few puffs. "How long she plan to stay?"

"Two weeks," Claude informed them, as he whipped his shaving cup into a lather.

"Two weeks." The way the Sheriff stretched out the words one expected Charlotte's Lincoln to pull back into town before he finished.

Mr. Bennett watched Claude lather Adam's face. There are those who might wonder about a man who has nothing better to do than watch another man get shaved. Compared to watching grass grow in a graveyard, it was fascinating.

"Heard she took Lettie and the Dixie cup with her," the Sheriff said nonchalantly. "Left Angela all alone in that big house."

Flipping open his razor, Claude tilted his head to study Adam's contours, then leaned over the chair like a Harvard surgeon.

"Beautiful woman, Angela Belle," Mr. Bennett said, tamping his pipe.

"Hurts to take your eyes off her."

"Smart as a whip, too."

Pinkie straight, Claude lifted the tip of Doc's nose and carefully shaved his stiff upper lip.

"Sharp as a Wilkinson blade," Claude said, as he slung shaving cream into the sink.

"And don't forget rich," the Sheriff added. "Money so old you have to blow the dust off."

Wiping his face clean, Claude turned Adam's head from side to side, then leveled his sideburns.

"Two weeks all alone in that big house." The Sheriff shook his head.

"Don't reckon Angela will be lonely long, if you know what I mean." Shaking aftershave in each palm, he slapped Adam's face with both hands. "That woman has more suitors than Carter has little pills."

*   *   *

Hair slicked down and face smooth as a baby's butt, Adam pulled open the door to McHenry's Florist. As it jangled closed behind him, the overwhelming smell of funeral wreaths mixed with after-shave just about made him swoon. Adam marveled at how one's sense of smell heightened with a hairless nose.

"What can we do you for, Doc?" Red McHenry asked, as he drove a white gladiola stem into a green frog.

The shop was a humid jungle. Waxy ornamental leaves and fra-grant flower petals carpeted the floor, and buckets of cut flowers lined the long wooden workbench where Red was working.

Hands in his pockets, Adam wandered aimlessly in the shop. Stopping at a shelf, he feigned interest in Red's number-one best-seller, a tiny ceramic coon dog barking up at a raccoon sitting on top of a twisted piece of driftwood. He couldn't make them fast enough on Father's Day.

"Personally," Red said, "I like a fresh arrangement."

Lifting a gladiola from the bucket, he cleanly clipped the end.

"But I have to say a silk flower never needs watering."

Red looked like his father, a Bantam rooster of a man with flam-ing red hair and the build of a featherweight boxer. Fortunately, Red did not inherit his father's disposition. Red Senior had a chip on his shoulder and a burning desire for someone to try and knock it off.

Plucking a wilted blossom off the glad, Red tucked it into the spray.

"Looking for anything in particular?"

Adam knew exactly what he wanted; a dozen white rosebuds tied with a satin ribbon. The card was already in his pocket, written and rewritten until flawless.

Adam wandered over to the sachets and lifted one to his nose.

"Just got a fresh shipment of calla lilies in," Red said, looping a white satin ribbon into a bow so fast and precise he reminded Adam of a sewing machine. "Want me to send a dozen over to Mrs. Montgomery?"

Adam's hand hung in midair over a pot of English gardener's cream. Recovering, he picked up the pot and pretended to read the label.

"Every woman has her flower," Red said. "Dot Wyatt's is a mum. Reba Earhart's is a daisy. Now, Mrs. Montgomery, she's a calla."

Adam was sincerely impressed. When he thought of calla lilies, he thought of a stiff corpse on a cold slab, which described his wife perfectly. Jerking a card from the holder, he mindlessly scribbled his name on it.

"Make it two dozen," he said, stuffing the card into an envelope.

"Anything else for you?" Red asked, wiping his hands on his apron.

Doc's eyes drifted over Red's shoulder to the bucket of tiny white rosebuds inside the glass cooler.

"That'll be all."

"By the way," Red said, as he wrote up the order, "when is Mrs. Montgomery due back from Boston?"

Doc's and Red's eyes locked.

"Any day now."

That night Adam lifted the brass door-knocker on the Belles' front door and let it fall. His shoes were shined, his underwear ironed, and his toothbrush was tucked into his inside coat pocket. He had no doubt how the night would go.

And so, when the door opened and he looked down at Dixie Belle, he was more than taken aback.

"What are you doing here?" he demanded.

"I live here," she said, looking up at him.

"But you're supposed to be in the mountains."

"Tire trouble," she said, scratching a chigger bite on the back of her leg.

"You had a flat tire?"

"Four," Dixie said, holding up four fingers. "Lettie said God didn't want Aunt Charlotte going to the mountain. He wanted to burn her butt right here."

Mind racing, Adam combed his fingers through his hair.

"Aunt Charlotte's mad as a hatter," Dixie chatted on. "What's a hatter?"

"Someone who is mad."

"You wanna come in?"

"No."

"Then whatdyu knock on the door for?"

"Where is your mother?"

"Out."

"Out?"

"With Red McHenry."

When Adam got home he grabbed the first thing he came to. Throwing back his arm, he smashed it into the fireplace. Unfortunately, it was Lydia's hand-painted porcelain swan from Egan Mercer.

CHAPTER 30

"YOU HAVE no idea how much this means to me," Adam said, as he carefully set the replacement swan on the mantel.

"Oh," Julia Mercer said, "I think I have some idea."

It was nothing short of a miracle that Julia not only knew where her brother Egan had purchased Lydia's porcelain swan, but was kind enough to hand deliver a new one on her way to Banyan Island.

"It's amazing you were able to find an exact copy."

"Actually," she said, as she strolled leisurely around Adam's library, "I send them to all the women Egan doesn't marry."

Adam had no idea if Julia was kidding, but laughed just the same.

Taking a cigar out of the humidor, Adam dropped into his chair. He was relieved to have the swan thing taken care of, and he was relieved to be in the company of a woman he understood. Julia was civilized, refined, and reserved—like himself. Absolutely nothing like Angela Belle.

"How long will Lydia be gone?" Julia asked, lifting a photo of Lydia from the bookshelf and holding it at arm's length.

Julia and Adam had run in the same circles all their lives. Adam's stepfather had been the Mercers' physician. But there had never been a hint of romance between them. As Adam watched Julia, he wondered why not.

"Another week," he answered.

Julia had been Lydia's maid of honor, and was as close a friend as Lydia was capable of having. Lydia chose her friends the way she chose everything in her life, by referral.

The two women were poured from the same mold, thin as whips and raised like thoroughbreds. The difference between them was kinetic. While Lydia's physical exertion rarely exceeded the lifting of a fork, Julia was a creature of motion. She was riding horses as soon as she could walk and could handle a sailboat as well as any man. They both suffered from terminal boredom, a common defect of their breed. But while Lydia wore her languor like a certificate of pedigree, Julia was forever on the lookout for a cure.

"Before the war, there was a handyman." Head tilted, Julia read the spine of a book on the shelf. "Black hair. Black eyes. Brooding sort."

"Boone Dickson."

"Boone Dickson," she said, as though committing the name to memory.

Puffing on the cigar until the end glowed, Adam shook the match out and dropped it into the ashtray.

"You need a handyman?"

"From time to time."

"Well, Dickson's not your man. Went into the construction business after the war. It was good timing. He's done quite well for himself."

Adam swirled the ice in his glass.

"But surely you have handymen on Banyan."

"Actually, I hadn't planned on using him at Banyan."

Adam looked up at her. "Surely, you can't be serious?"

Adam wasn't sure which irked him more, that Julia would lower herself to the likes of Boone Dickson, or that she would choose Dickson over him.

"He lost an arm in the war," Adam insisted, as though not only was the merchandise inferior, it was defective.

"Is that all he lost?"

The amused look on Julia's face pricked him like a thorn.

"You must come hunting on Banyan this year," Julia said, lightly tracing the stem of a calla lily with her finger. "Father stocked the game park with wild boar.

"They're wonderful to hunt," she said, eyes shining. "Charge like a rhino."

Julia turned down Adam's offer to stay at his house.

"You're staying next door?" Adam stuttered in disbelief.

Waving away his offer to carry her luggage, she hoisted the worn strap of her leather satchel onto her shoulder and headed for the front door. Julia migrated with the seasons. Like a bird that never landed, she traveled light.

"But I had no idea you and Angela Belle were friends," Adam stammered, as he followed her out the door.

"Darling," she said, brushing his cheek with a kiss, "there are so many things you have no idea about."

Julia pulled out the silk robe she kept hanging in the Belles' guest closet and slipped it on. Her skin was still damp from her bath and the robe stuck to her as she padded barefoot through the dark house into the kitchen. Filling two glasses with ice, she tucked a bottle of bourbon under her arm and backed through the screen door onto the porch. Angela was already sitting on the swing, her sleeping daughter's head in her lap. Julia handed Angela a glass, then stretched out on the divan. Sipping her drink, Julia watched Angela curl strands of Dixie's hair around her finger into corkscrew curls.

"Do you like him?" Angela asked after a while.

"Who?"

"Your new lover."

"Oh, God no. No one likes Crone Sewell."

During her first visit to Lydia and Adam's house, Julia had wandered, a little tipsy, onto Angela Belle's porch. The bond between the two women was immediate and effortless. They had nothing in common, but were exactly the same. Whenever Julia's battle against boredom seemed lost, a pilgrimage to the Belles' house inexplicably put the fight back in her.

"Why do you suppose rich men are so bad in bed?" Julia mused.

"Maybe it isn't the sport, but the arena you're playing in."

"Obviously, you've never made love to a rich man."

Angela's hand hesitated and her head turned ever so slightly toward the Montgomerys' house. When she caught Julia watching her, she went back to stroking Dixie's hair.

Rolling onto her back, Julia rested her head on her arm and stared up at the ceiling fan turning above her head.

"You should come to Banyan," she said after a while.

Angela laughed like a woman who had everything she desired within the radius of her own heartbeat.

"Adam Montgomery will be there."

It was the depth of Angela's silence that told Julia everything she wanted to know.

"No doubt he'll be coming alone. He and Lydia haven't traveled together since their honeymoon."

Angela traced her sleeping daughter's face with her finger as though she already missed her.

"They say there's a storm building off the coast," Julia said.

"I love storms."

"Yes," Julia said. "So do I."

CHAPTER 31

A T FIRST LYDIA did not recognize the woman calling her name at the opposite end of the Leaper's Fork train station. After eight weeks in Boston, she had barely recognized her own husband.

"Adam! Lydia!" Julia Mercer called again, waving to get their attention.

Julia looked as though she had been jumping her horse, hair blown, cheeks flushed. All around her, people were fanning themselves with their hats, wilting from the heat. Julia seemed personally air-conditioned.

Lydia had not been caught off guard this time. After a summer in Boston, her fashion sense, as well as her aloofness, had been fully restored.

"Julia!" Adam called back, waving.

When the man standing next to Julia turned around, the world rolled under Lydia. Grabbing one of the trunks stacked behind her, she gripped the metal hinge until her knuckles turned white.

Lydia had not seen Boone in five years. As Julia and Boone walked toward them, she was struck by how right they looked together, like a matched set. A simple change of clothes had outwardly put Boone Dickson on equal standing with Julia Mercer.

"Dickson," Adam said, reaching out his hand, "prosperity looks good on you."

It was when Boone extended one hand that Lydia realized the other was missing. When she looked up from the rolled sleeve, Boone was staring at her.

"What a shame," Julia said, brushing cheeks with Lydia, "crossing paths like this."

Julia had the vague blurry look of a woman fully satisfied. Lydia recognized the look. She had seen it once in the mirror years ago.

"But we'll have plenty of time to catch up on Banyan," Julia went on. "I've already spoken to Adam and it's all settled. Isn't it, Adam?"

"Julia has invited us to Banyan," Adam explained to Lydia.

Julia and Adam seemed very far away to Lydia. The sounds of the train station were muted. The only thing clear to her was that time and distance had not dulled her desire for Boone.

Lydia's trunks and cases were stacked two and three deep, and so Boone did not notice the boy until the nanny led him around by the hand. Adam Jr. was wearing short pants and held a painted tin airplane, the propeller whirling as he swooped it through the air. Boone's eyes dropped from Lydia to the boy and stayed there.

The warning whistle blew. Passengers standing on the platform finished their good-byes and hurried to climb on board.

"Well, it's time," Julia said, glancing past them to the porter.

Pressing against Boone, Julia kissed him good-bye on the mouth, in full view of everyone at the station.

"Please, come to Banyan," she whispered to Boone urgently. Then boarded the train.

Adam was opening the car door for Lydia when he noticed the blood.

"Good Lord," he said, taking her hand. "You're bleeding."

Pulling a handkerchief out of his pocket, he wiped her hand. The cut ran all the way across her palm, the imprint of the trunk hinge sliced into the skin. Deciding it wouldn't need stitches, he wrapped the handkerchief around and tied the ends.

"We'll give you a tetanus shot when we get home," he said, as he closed her hand tightly around the handkerchief to stop the bleeding.

Holding her elbow, Adam helped her into the car.

"Can you believe Julia and Dickson?" he asked, as though this was where his mind had been all along. "What could they possibly have in common?"

Lydia didn't answer. Opening her hand, she stared vacantly at the bloody handkerchief. The inside of the car was stifling hot and smelled like leather and cigar smoke. Lydia didn't roll down the window. She needed the silence.

CHAPTER 32

BANYAN ISLAND wasn't really an island. It was a pinkie finger of land off the gulf coast separated from the mainland by marsh. The Mercers called it an island because island had a much nicer ring than swamp.

Spanish moss draped the cypress trees, flamingos stood motionless in the dark water, and crocodiles sunned on the muddy banks. Strewn across the coast like a giant shipwreck was the Mercers' "cottage," a sprawling hodgepodge of a complex with a footprint like something a giant bird had splattered from above.

Each generation of Mercers, lacking the gene that distinguished bigger from better, had the overwhelming urge to expand. They would add a porch, a wing, or a conservatory with no attention to the lay of the land or the original architecture. Tudor turrets jutted above Corinthian columns. Art Deco sconces snickered at Louis XIV armoires. There were rooms the Mercers hadn't seen in years. Occasionally, a guest they didn't know they had wandered in for dinner.

"I say," Egan would ponder, popping a martini olive into his mouth, "how long do you suppose Collis Taylor has been here?"

"Haven't a clue," Julia would answer, as their guest helped himself to a second serving of pork loin.

Despite the fact that the Mercers spent a small fortune maintaining it, the place had a ravaged appearance, which gave the guests the illusion of roughing it. While the ocean tried to blow the mansion

back to the mainland, the swamp patiently took back its own from
the rear. Paint weathered and peeled as fast as it was applied, salty sea
spray made the nails rust and bleed, and tree roots pushed up through
the clay tennis courts. During the rainy season, swamp water the
consistency of thick roux gurgled up through the storm drains and
into the sinks and tubs. Add to this what the elder Mercer referred to
as "the difference in aesthetics" with the locals hired to take care of
the place, and maintenance was a futile battle.

Depending on one's perspective, the locals were either lazy
good-for-nothings, or people who knew how to pace themselves.
When you complained about bullfrogs breeding in the swimming
pool, salamanders swimming in the bathtub, or snakes curled under
the cool sheets of your bed, they simply stared at you as though they
didn't understand the problem—or English. From their point of
view, you build in the swamp, you live with the swamp.

Still, the Mercers managed to make some headway over the
years. They cleared the sea grass to expand the beach and leveled the
land to improve the view. They cut down the Banyan trees to build
the golf course, then drained parts of the swamp to add another room
or two. If they continued to build, in a few years, Egan would be able
to dock his yacht off one of the kitchens.

The young Mercers and their friends saw Banyan as a respite
from the unbearable burden of being the children of rich men. On
the island there was no pressure to uphold the family name. There
was no one staring at you across the room whispering behind a liver-
spotted hand that you were certainly not made of the stuff Great-
granddaddy was made of.

And so, after the first frost in Boston they fluttered to the island
like monarch butterflies flying south for the winter. They might
muster up enough energy to play tennis or golf, stroll along the
beach, or sail. But mostly they preferred to sit and stare, transfixed

by seagulls riding the wind like stringless kites. From time to time a crocodile wandered onto the lawn and gobbled up a poodle. Other than that, the main entertainment was adultery.

Of course, Adam thought he was there to hunt wild boar.

"I hear they keep charging even after they've been shot," Adam said.

"Fight to the bitter end," Collis Taylor declared, despite the fact that he wouldn't know a wild boar from a borer bee.

A dozen or so guests gathered in the conservatory for breakfast. The sweet scent of jasmine perfumed the air and an aviary of lemon yellow canaries sang for them. They drank fresh-squeezed juice that smelled like orange blossoms and spooned perfect bites of soft-boiled egg from fragile shells. White sunlight poured through the glass dome above their heads like an affirmation from heaven, and a constant breeze blew over them as though fanned by invisible servants.

Beyond the open doors stretched emerald lawn. Beyond the lawn, the ocean, blue as a robin's egg. And presiding over it all was their golden host, Egan Mercer.

Egan was more than the sum of his perfect parts. He was a gilded-haired, blue-eyed god in the making. The guests tilted toward him like plants to the sun, their every word and action aimed at his approval. Egan hardly noticed. Preoccupied with peeling an orange, he anointed them with a mist of citrus.

"Are we *still* talking about the Germans?"

Jane Field was always irritated by discussions that were not about her. She was as frothy as meringue, but had the physical attributes to make a man forget and forgive.

"Boars," Collis explained. "We're talking about wild boars."

"Boars are boring," Jane pouted.

Drunk from the moment, everyone thought this hilarious and their laughter filled the room like a Handel chorus.

Introductions had not been necessary. They all knew each other's pedigree and net worth, eliminating the vulgar need of pointing it out or rubbing it in. Everyone knew that *his* family owned the coal mines that fueled *her* family's trains that moved *their* family's steel to *his* family's factory that built the battleships that won the war. Exhilarated by the eliteness of their gathering, the tiresome fact that Granddaddy had paid their admission fee dissipated like steam.

"It's a shame Lydia couldn't make it," Julia Mercer said, as she selected a sausage from the servant's tray.

"Yes." Adam delicately touched the corners of his mouth with his napkin. "Truly a shame."

He said it in a way that let everyone know it wasn't a shame, and they all burst out laughing in a naughty collaboration.

Adam could not remember the last time he felt so good. It was as if he'd been rescued after years of captivity from socially ignorant savages. Taking a deep breath, he looked around the elegant table. Not one man—or woman—was chewing tobacco or scratching himself, at least overtly.

He hadn't realized how stressful living in Leaper's Fork had been on him. How exhausting. Now, sitting among his equals, he was euphoric.

And so, when Julia's guest appeared in the doorway, Adam nearly spit coffee across the table.

"There you are!" Collis exclaimed, jumping up from his chair.

While the rest of the women could have been dining on the Riviera, Angela Belle looked as though she had just washed ashore. She wore a man's wrinkled linen shirt tied in the front and a pair of scavenged men's white trousers cinched at the waist and rolled to the knee. One imagined she found them in a pile at the bottom a closet. Her tangled black hair dripped seawater down her back and she left a trail of wet footprints on the slate floor as she padded barefoot to the table.

Adam saw Angela through the eyes of the others and his face flared. Didn't she at least have the sense to dress for breakfast?

"I was starting to worry," Collis said, pulling out her chair. "Where did you get off to?"

"I went for a swim." Angela said.

"A swim?" Jane Field blinked blankly. "But where is your swimsuit?"

"Swimsuit?"

While Adam contemplated crawling under the table, the other men grew silent as they envisioned Angela Belle's slick naked body bobbing in the ocean like a mermaid.

Angela's presence disrupted their harmony like a blues rift in the middle of Mozart. No one knew quite what to think of her. Collis Taylor lingered faithfully at the back of her chair, while she filled her plate as though she'd been adrift for days. But the Taylor fortune came from cheap imports, so his alliance carried very little weight. And so they turned to Egan for the thumbs-up or thumbs-down, but his detached demeanor offered them no moral bearing.

"I don't believe we've been introduced."

Crone Sewell was rich in almost every way a man could be. He had good looks and more money than God. It was the worst hand a man like Crone could have been dealt. Leisure had left him bored, and boredom had left him lethal.

"Angela Belle," she said, extending her hand across the table.

"Yes," he said, taking her hand lightly. "I've heard a great deal about you."

Crone's blue blood was as icy as Angela's was red hot. Like a cold front running into a warm front, their meeting was destined to be stormy.

"I'm sorry," Angela said, "and you are?"

The twitch of his upper lip was almost undetectable. Crone could sooner do without air than without deference.

"Darling," Julia said, "this is *Crone Sewell.*"

"Ahhh," Angela said, nodding as the name slowly came back to her.

Crone glanced from Angela to Julia. Conspiracy between women always makes a man raise his defenses. In this case, Crone had no doubt he was justified.

"And what do you do, Mr. Sewell?"

The contempt in Crone's stare would have mortally wounded one of his own.

"Do?"

"Crone's family is *the* Sewell of Sewell Shipping," Collis explained with a clipped laugh.

"Ahhh," Angela said.

Angela might as well have slapped Crone across the face.

"And what exactly do *you* . . . do, Miss Belle?"

Picking up a piece of bacon with her fingers, Angela took a bite. "No doubt nothing that will ever make it into the history books."

"Yes, well, I suspect rearing a child without a father is all-consuming."

Angela and Crone's eyes locked across the table like two fighters squaring off.

"I suspect not as consumin' as raisin' a child *and* takin' care of a no-good husband," she said, slipping into her native tongue.

The room held its breath, and Julia decided to change the subject before they all turned even bluer.

"How do you like Banyan?" she asked, turning to Angela.

"I love the ocean," Angela said. "It's the only thing missing in Leaper's Fork."

Before he could stop himself, Adam let out a sharp laugh. "Of all the things missing in Leaper's Fork," he assured his peers, "the ocean is not the first thing that comes to mind!"

Adam didn't mean to cast the first stone. But once his blow struck home, Crone eagerly hurled the next.

"We are, after all, talking about a town where pig races in the cemetery are the highlight of the social calendar," Crone informed them.

Adam's face went pale. He'd had a little too much to drink the night before, and in his eagerness to entertain old friends might have said a few things he wished he hadn't.

"Some might say racing a pig is far more civilized than shooting one from a distance," Angela said.

"I believe, Miss Belle," Crone said sharply, "the word 'pig' has one syllable, not two."

"I believe, Mr. Sewell," Angela replied, "that one of the more admirable qualities of a pig is, he don't give a shit what you call him."

Throwing her hand to her mouth, Jane Field let out a shocked laugh.

"I take it, Miss Belle," Crone said, "you know a great deal about pigs."

"I say, Sewell," Collis sputtered indignantly. "Did you leave your manners in Boston?"

"Collis, old boy, you're wasting your time. Miss Belle's taste leans toward the common man. Apparently, she not only charms their pants off, she wears them."

The room shifted uncomfortably—all except Adam, who had lost all the feeling in his extremities and couldn't move.

"It's been my experience, Mr. Sewell," Angela said, "that the best way to cull the common man from the uncommon is with his clothes off."

"No doubt, Miss Belle, the number you've culled would boggle the mind."

The look on Angela's face was one of curiosity and mirth. She seemed bemused by a man who considered experience in a woman a flaw.

"Unfortunately, Mr. Sewell, " she said, "I've been credited with far more than I've enjoyed."

Pushing her chair back, Angela excused herself from the table. Adam thought her exit might have seemed stately, even noble, if she hadn't looked like she'd just fallen off a shrimp boat.

"Really, Crone!" Julia threw her napkin onto her plate. "Why didn't you just pull out your John Thomas and bludgeon her with it?"

Glances were exchanged and eyebrows lifted. After tallying the direct hits, everyone seemed quite certain that Crone Sewell had permanently shot down Angela Belle.

Everyone except Egan Mercer, who always held out a little hope that the wild boar would win.

CHAPTER 33

Egan and Julia were actually half brother and sister, the products of Egan Senior's first and second marriages. No one was quite sure what the old man's third marriage had produced, but they called it Teddy.

"Teddy!"

Jumping up from the lounge chair on the veranda, Jane Field waved wildly.

"Good lord," Adam said, hand shielding his eyes and squinting toward the lawn, "he looks like he just crawled out of the Bowery."

"You know a man has real money," Jane said, "when he doesn't have to flaunt it."

Smoothing her hair and licking her lips, Jane ran down the steps to meet Teddy.

"What on earth is that all about?" Adam frowned.

Being a permanent guest at Banyan, Collis Taylor knew the skinny.

"She's given up on snagging Egan," he said, feet kicked up in the lounge chair and hat tilted over his eyes. "Now, she's baiting her hook for Teddy."

Egan Mercer Sr. had gone about acquiring wives much like stock. His first wife, Egan's mother, was blue chip. Julia's mother, while a moderate risk, had been a quality producer. His marriage to Teddy's mother was a purely passionate venture, highly speculative and extremely volatile. That the dividend from this investment had been Teddy was not a surprise.

"Marry Teddy?" Adam stared at Collis incredulously. "Surely, you can't be serious?"

"You know what they say," Collis said, lifting a drink off the servant's tray. "A third of a trust fund is better than none."

One month after graduating from Harvard law school, Teddy moved to Banyan and went native. His uniform was a rumpled white linen suit, sweaty straw fedora, and ratty espadrilles worn sockless. His hair was untrimmed, his face unshaven, and he wore rum for cologne. While his official address was Mercer Mansion, rumor was that he spent most nights at the shantytown across the swamp.

"But Teddy?" Adam insisted, as they watched Jane throw her arms around Teddy's neck.

"The odds are good," Collis said, stirring his drink with a finger and sucking it dry, "but the goods are odd."

Something happened to a man when he crossed the Mason-Dixon Line. The heat and the humidity melted the morals and the southern whiskey seeped into the pores, rusting the ethical compass. A sweet, caramel-colored woman, damp as dew and half-naked in a dress worn thin as curtain sheer, could do more to a man with a glance than a refined lady could do with her entire cultural repertoire.

Still, one has responsibilities. No matter how bored you are, no matter how miserable, you have absolutely no right to go your own way. Put a bullet through your head, jump out of a window, but for God's sake don't throw in the towel.

"Appalling," Adam muttered, as though Teddy had let them all down.

As Teddy and Jane ascended the steps, Julia appeared in the doorway in her riding clothes. She had mud on her boots, cockleburs caught on her pants, and strands of Spanish moss stuck in her hair. Julia was not known for staying on the beaten path. Even when she wasn't straddling a horse, she had the air of a woman accustomed to having something strong and sweaty beneath her.

"Teddy," she called out, as she peeled off a riding glove, "there's a toothless man with a fish here to see you."

"That would be a client," Teddy said.

"But why does he have a fish?" Jane frowned.

"That," Teddy answered, slipping his arm from hers and kissing her hand, "would be my retainer."

"So, Montgomery, what have you been up to?"

It took a while for Adam to realize that all the men in the library were staring at him. Cigars suspended in the air, they waited for an answer.

"Up to?"

"In Liar's Fort."

"Leaper's Fork," Adam corrected.

"Ah, yes."

Adam's life in Leaper's Fork flashed before his eyes—and it was a boring blank. He could not think of a single accomplishment worth mentioning. Cauterizing a boil and delivering a breech were not the sort of things that would bowl these men over. Until that moment Adam had not realized how small his life had become.

"He's building a hospital," Crone said, dropping a cube of ice into a glass.

Egan Mercer looked up from his newspaper.

"A hospital?" Collis echoed.

"It would be the only hospital in four counties," Crone said in a bored drawl. "Good for the community and all that."

"My, my," Collis said, puffing on his cigar. "Turning into a phi-lanthropist, are we?"

"Disease is good business," Crone said, reminding them all that, along with shipping, his family had made a fortune in pharmaceuticals.

The truth was that Adam had no intention of building a hospital.

Never had. He was on the verge of setting the record straight when he suddenly sensed the mood in the room. They were all jealous as hell.

Build a hospital in the middle of nowhere. Why hadn't any of them thought of it? It had everything a man trying to make his mark could possibly hope for. Damn the symphony and art museums. How in the world do you top healing poor white trash and little brown babies?

"Benevolence and profit," Collis said absently, "always a winning combination."

"He's breaking ground in the spring," Crone said, as he selected a cigar from the humidor and ran it under his nose.

Adam flashed him a bewildered look.

"Julia told me." Crone shrugged.

"Julia?"

"We've been seeing quite a lot of each other."

There was the awkward silence that occurs when a man is making a complete fool of himself and no one knows exactly what to do about it.

"It's quite serious, actually."

Dropping their heads, the men stared into their glasses.

"Dickson here is Julia's guest for the week," Teddy said straight out.

Crone followed Teddy's nod to a dark corner of the room. He hadn't noticed Boone before. But then, Crone made a habit of overlooking the unimportant. Dickson was dressed more or less like the rest of them. His hair was styled the same. There was nothing about him that appeared significantly different. Yet, instinctively Crone knew he was not one of theirs.

Boone made no effort to win him over. Taking a long draw on his cigarette, he returned Crone's glare with indifference.

Crone's laugh was sharp and bitter. They thought he was laughing at the absurdity of Julia being with this man. The truth was, Crone was laughing at himself. He had thought his competition on the island was Angela.

"Don't ever ask my advice on women," he said, with a wave of the hand.

One of the markers of class is the ability to deflect humiliation. In that department, Crone was bulletproof.

"Well," Collis said quickly, "you certainly wouldn't be the first man to let a good woman slip away."

Everyone pretended it was friendship that brought Collis to Sewell's defense and that it had absolutely nothing to do with the fact that Collis Imports depended almost entirely on Sewell Shipping.

"Even the great Egan Mercer let Lydia Jackson slip through his fingers," Collis went on.

Egan looked at him blankly. "Lydia Jackson?" he echoed, as though he couldn't quite place the name.

Everyone could tell by the look on Egan's face that he had no idea what Collis was talking about.

"Lydia married Montgomery here," Collis insisted, awkwardly trying to clean up the mess he'd made.

"Oh, yes," Egan said slowly. "Yes, of course. The best man won."

There wasn't the slightest bit of sarcasm in Egan's voice. No hint of the truth. Yet there was no doubt in anyone's mind that Lydia had not turned Egan down to marry Adam, as they had been led to believe. Egan had never asked Lydia to marry him. He had never even considered it.

Adam's humiliation was palpable.

Something outside the window caught Egan's attention and brought him to his feet.

"Gentlemen," he said, grinding his cigar out in the ashtray, "if you will excuse me."

The room seemed empty after Egan left them. The men didn't

quite know what to do with themselves. Clearing their throats, they smoked their cigars and drummed their fingers on the arms of the leather chairs.

"Anyone for billiards?" Collis finally asked.

As the men chalked their cues and laid their money on the table, Adam stood at the window watching Egan jog down the steps and across the lawn.

Suddenly everything was crystal clear for Adam. There was nothing original about him. Nothing authentic. The clothes he wore, the car he drove, the books he read, the philosophy he espoused were all the ideals of others. He was a doctor because other men thought highly of doctors. He married a woman because he thought a better man had wanted her.

Adam was a hermit crab, inhabiting the dreams of others. This is what he realized as Egan jogged down the sandy path that led to the beach. This is what settled inside him, cold and heavy, as he watched Egan Mercer run to catch up with Angela Belle.

CHAPTER 34

Egan Mercer was a hero who had never done anything heroic. What kept him from being arrogant was that he knew it. What kept him from being humble was he knew he was meant to do great things. He just didn't know what they were.

"You should run for office," Angela said, as they walked along the beach.

Julia had warned him that Angela Belle was a woman who cut to the chase. This was either a relief or an anxiety depending on a man's level of security.

"Office?"

"Politics."

Bending down, he picked up a rock and skipped it into the ocean.

"Politics," he echoed.

His white trousers were rolled above the ankle, his sweater tied around the neck. His hair was as attractive windblown as neatly parted. Egan was the poster boy for the American dream.

"The Senate," she decided.

"The Senate? Why?"

"To make the world a better place."

He laughed. He was amused at her sincerity, then ashamed of his cynicism. If he ran for office, that would have to go.

The sound of the others setting up on the beach drew their attention. Hands shielding her eyes from the sun, Angela turned to watch. Egan followed her gaze to Adam.

"He'll never divorce her," he felt free to say, since she had set the rules.

"It doesn't matter," she said, pushing her hair from her face. "I was meant to be the spice in a man's life, not the main course."

Egan had no doubt she was telling the truth. He wondered what it would be like to have a woman want him without motive.

"He isn't good enough for you."

"He has potential."

"Potential," Egan said, "doesn't carve stone."

Slipping her arm through his, they continued walking.

"You're going to make a wonderful senator," she told him.

Angela looked up at him with complete satisfaction. It was the most contented moment Egan would ever know.

CHAPTER 35

"ONE'S REPUTATION is not a title one is given for life. It is a fragile thing that must be carefully maintained. Once lost, it can never be recovered."

Elbow resting on the mantel, Crone addressed them from the fireplace. One had the impression that he had his personality starched along with his shirts.

"Women like Angela Belle have their affairs in public," Crone said. "Women like Julia Mercer do not."

Julia sat on the couch, legs crossed, and arms draped languidly along the back. Egan absently turned a pen from tip to end at his desk, while Teddy strolled around the billiard table studying his next shot. The chair Boone Dickson had occupied earlier was vacant, but there was no doubt his presence lingered.

"Julia, you're making a fool out of yourself," Crone said simply.

Crone was having this conversation in front of Egan and Teddy in an effort to form an alliance between the three men. He assumed that together they could reason, or humiliate if need be, Julia into appropriate behavior.

"It's one thing to amuse yourself with this man," Crone went on. "It's quite another to bring him to Banyan."

Julia said nothing, prompting him to continue.

"Teddy has his little brown woman," Crone drawled on, "but you never see her agonizing over which fork to use at our dinner table."

"For the record," Teddy said, leaning low to line up a shot, "it's not the little brown woman I'm ashamed of."

Smoothly sliding the cue stick through his finger, Teddy hit the ball solidly. There was a crack followed by a muted rumble as the ball rolled down the felt and dropped into the leather pocket.

Crone knew instantly the battle had been lost. The Mercers moved as one.

"Well," Julia said, pushing herself off the couch, "I think I'll grab a swim before dinner."

As she passed him, Crone grabbed her arm.

"I don't understand," he said quietly.

Reaching up, Julia touched his face.

"Neither do I," she said.

Then freeing herself, Julia hurried to find her lover.

Julia found Boone sitting alone on a side porch smoking a cigarette. Kneeling beside his chair, she draped her arms over his knees and looked up at him. She could stare at him forever, she thought.

"Are you completely miserable?" she asked.

When Julia was eighteen she became obsessed with a wild horse. The family was hunting elk in Montana when she saw it and knew she had to have it. Never having said the word "no" to his daughter, Egan Mercer Sr. had the stallion caught, broken, and brought to her. Julia immediately climbed on and rode off.

"Take me," she whispered, as she unbuttoned her blouse. "Right here. Right now."

That night, just before her father sent the search party, she rode back up. Sliding off the horse, she pulled the saddle off. The stallion stood perfectly still as she stroked him and whispered into his neck. Then slipping the bridle over his head, she yelled "Ya!" and slapped him on the haunch. He never looked back.

Grabbing her by the hair, Boone pulled her head back and kissed her savagely. Even as he made love to her, Julia could feel him pulling away. There was nothing she could do to keep Boone, if he didn't choose to stay. Knowing this thrilled her.

The truth was, Julia Mercer was a woman who knew how to set things free.

The next morning Collis got up before the others and made his way down to an isolated stretch of beach. When he was sure no one was looking, he stripped off his clothes and ran bare-assed naked into the incoming tide. He hit the gray foam running, and the cold nearly stopped his heart. Gasping, he took a few stiff strokes just to be able to say he had, then clawed his way back to the beach. Shivering, he ran to his clothes and jerked them on so fast he caught the material in the zipper of his pants.

"She was speaking allegorically, you know."

Startled, Collis stumbled backward, with his pants around his knees.

"Egan! Jesus!"

Propped on an elbow in the sand, Egan Mercer chewed the end of a blade of sea grass.

"Damn!" Collis grumbled, pulling and jerking at his zipper. "Now I've gone and broken the blasted thing,"

"The only way to cull the uncommon man from the common is with his clothes off," Egan mused.

"How long have you been hiding there?" Collis demanded.

"I hate to break it to you, my friend, but even with your tailored shirts and starched boxers, you're common. As are we all."

"I have no idea what you're talking about."

"That's because you're ordinary. An extraordinary man would understand perfectly."

Head down, Collis walked in a circle searching the sand for a shoe while Egan stared thoughtfully at the ocean.

"We will build schools, museums, and parks. We will collect great art and mingle with great men, but when we die, all that will remain of us will be a short inscription on a granite stone. Do you know why?"

Huffing, Collis rolled his eyes at him.

"Because we do it to make ourselves extraordinary—and that's what makes us ordinary."

"You're an idiot."

"I'm not the one freezing my balls off at sunrise."

"I was in the mood for a swim," Collis insisted.

"Of course you were."

Standing up, Egan dusted himself off. The sky had suddenly grown dark and the ocean was starting to white cap. Reaching down he picked up Collis's towel and threw it over his shoulder. He was halfway down the beach before Collis looked up and realized he was alone.

"I'm not ordinary," Collis insisted, as he jogged to keep up.

"A hawk doesn't wear a sign that says hawk."

"Buddha?" Collis asked.

"Boone Dickson."

"Dear God, you're quoting rednecks now?"

"Actually, his neck is more of an olive color."

"I worry about a man who studies another man's skin tone."

"If it's any consolation, I've never had the least inclination to study yours."

Collis was on the verge of being insulted when a bolt of lightning jagged across the sky, immediately followed by an explosion of thunder that shook the ground. Collis nearly jumped into Egan's arms.

"I don't know why we're friends," Collis grumbled, as he pulled himself together.

"Supply and demand would be my guess," Egan answered.

Another boom and they scurried down the beach like crabs, their footprints washed away as quickly as they made them.

Running across the yard, Collis and Egan bounded up the steps just as the sky cracked wide open. The other guests, china cups and saucers in hand, had gathered on the porch to watch the storm move in. The servants, who had a sixth sense about these things, had long ago closed and fastened the shutters.

"Where have you been?" Jane Fields demanded, indignant that she might have missed something.

"Collis decided to take a sunrise swim," Egan said, as he dried his hair with a towel a servant handed him.

"Reeal-ly?" she said, stretching the word like chewing gum. Then, leaning close, she whispered, "Did he wear a swimsuit?"

"Not even his skivvies," Egan whispered back.

"Reeal-ly," Jane drawled deliciously, her eyes following Collis across the porch.

The storm moved toward them ominously. The ocean churned and black clouds bled across the sky like spilled ink. A sudden bolt of lightning sent a shiver of anticipation through them.

"One, two, three, four . . ." Julia counted until they heard the crack of thunder.

When the wind picked up, one by one the guests moved inside until the only two people left standing by the porch rail were Adam and Angela.

Another ragged flash of lightning scarred the sky and Adam, whose income was built on accidents, flinched as if he'd been hit with a cattle prod. But the storm seemed calm next to the tempest growing in Angela. Eyes shining and hair whipping her face, she leaned into the coming squall like the figurehead at the bow of a ship. It occurred to Adam that a man's ability to become aroused while standing in the middle of a typhoon was truly a biological marvel. Clearing his throat, he shored himself up for what he had to say.

"I'm not going to build a hospital," he blurted.

Angela's silence prompted him to continue. Nothing ignites a coward's courage like meeting with no resistance.

"It's a huge undertaking," he hurried on. "Enormous! The whole idea is overwhelming."

Angela stood perfectly still. The wind ripped at her hair while sea spray and rain turned her linen shirt transparent. He could see the curve of her breasts and the dark peak of her nipples as clearly as if she were naked. Like a guilty voyeur, Adam dropped his eyes, only to have them involuntarily buoy back to the surface.

"I never said I was going to build a hospital. I don't know where you got the idea."

Turning to face him, Angela placed her fingers on his lips to silence him. Slowly, her hand slid inside his open collar and down his chest until it came to rest on his racing heart.

"You can do this," she whispered. "I know you can do this."

It was all Adam could do to keep from bawling like a baby.

"I can't," the butcher's son insisted, shaking his head. "I simply can't."

"Adam Montgomery," Angela said, eyes shining like mercury, "I have no doubt you could walk through fire if you set your mind to it."

The blessing and the bane of man is the woman who makes him rise to the occasion.

Adam reached for her hungrily, and Angela stepped back.

"A great hospital," she said, in a tone that offered no compromise.

Rain blowing in his face, Adam had to wipe his eyes to watch her walk away.

CHAPTER 36

THE PHONES DIED before noon. The electricity blinked off shortly after. They ate canned smoked oysters and martini onions by candlelight for supper. After drinking far too much, they stumbled off to their beds, or someone else's. They'd sort it all out in the morning.

The only people left sitting in the dark were the two men who couldn't sleep, or more accurately, had no one to sleep with.

"I should think you'd be fucking Miss Belle by now," Crone said casually.

Crone was the only man Adam knew whose diction sharpened along with his disposition when he drank.

"I don't know what you're talking about," Adam said, staring at the fire.

"Oh, please."

"I'm married. Being as you were my best man, you shouldn't need reminding."

"Married?" Crone laughed into his whiskey. "If what you and Lydia have is a marriage, then Stalin and Churchill were blissfully wed."

Throwing back his drink, Crone stared at his empty glass. Steadying himself on the back of Adam's chair, he staggered to the bar to pour another. Pulling the glass stopper out of the decanter, he waved the whiskey under his nose, then topped off the tumbler. Glass sloshing, he weaved back across the room, the candles wafting in his breeze as he passed.

"I've seen loveless marriages—most marriages, actually," Crone said, dropping into his chair. "Yours is not only loveless, it isn't even good business."

Repeatedly flicking his lighter, Crone managed to light a cigarette and take a deep draw.

"Of course, you had to marry her. You wouldn't be here if it weren't for that, now would you? It was the right move for a man like you to make."

Dropping his head back, Crone exhaled to the ceiling.

"And I must say Lydia makes a very nice accessory. The problem is, not only is she broke, she's a bit of a frigid bitch. There's nothing more irritating than an ungrateful whore with a wedding band."

After a while Crone turned to him.

"I'm sorry, old boy. Which part of the conversation didn't sit well?"

"Everyone knows?"

"Dear God!" Crone nearly choked on the laugh. "Of course everyone knows. Everyone has always known."

Upstairs, Collis Taylor was having a nightmare. At least once a week, for as far back as he could remember, he dreamed he was drowning. Kicking, choking, and beating the mattress, he tried to swim to shore in his linen sheets to no avail. But that night, as he sank in the cold murky water, he floated past Angela Belle, her black hair wavering around her face like a mermaid's.

"Take off your clothes," she said in a watery whisper. "Take them off, and you'll rise."

"I can't!" he cried, clinging to his favorite pair of silk pajamas. "I can't! I can't!"

"Darling! Darling, wake up!"

"What? What?"

Drenched with sweat and gasping for breath, Collis sat straight up in bed.

"You were having a nasty nightmare."

"I dreamed I was drowning," he muttered, half asleep, the other half drunk.

"That means you're trying to be something you're not."

Somehow the notion that he was not destined to drown, but was merely a fake comforted Collis enormously. As he was breathing a sigh of relief, it occurred to him that he had gone to bed alone that night and had no idea who he was talking to.

Jumping up, he clicked on the lamp on the nightstand and squinted down at the woman lying in his bed. It was Jane Fields. A wave of defeat flooded over him like the nausea he had felt when he finally crawled into the family business after his humiliating fling at professional tennis. Jane was exactly the kind of woman he was supposed to end up with.

"I hate my life," he said, dropping onto the side of the bed. "I hate myself."

"Oh, darling, all men do," Jane said simply. "Except, of course, Egan."

"Screw Egan!"

"Believe me, darling, I've tried."

Even in his foggy inebriated despair, it occurred to Collis that he didn't know a single woman Egan had slept with.

"Come back to bed," Jane said, patting the pillow.

Collis could only assume Jane was in his bed because she had struck out with Teddy. He did not appreciate being her third swing at the plate, and was about to let her know this, when she threw back the covers. The sight of her splendid naked body stretched on Irish linen shocked him into judiciousness. In all fairness, he decided, he had never fully explored Jane Fields's bountiful assets.

Clicking out the light, he crawled back into the bed beside her. Snuggling his face into her warm breasts, Collis wrapped his arms around her waist.

"Don't worry, darling," she soothed, stroking his hair. "Jane is going to make it all better."

Hugging her like a life preserver, Collis floated into sleep as hopeful as a baby.

In a weather-beaten shack hanging on the edge of the swamp, Teddy pulled the woman he loved close. Curling to fit his body, she sighed contentedly. The wind whistled through the walls and the yellowed lace curtains whipped as if the windows were wide open. Rain beat on the tin roof, dripping through the rusty cracks into a bucket on the dresser. The mattress was as lumpy as a sack of rolled socks. She couldn't sleep in the big house, she said. She needed to be close to the ground. As she slept in his arms, Teddy thought about the law. How white men used it. How coloreds had it used against them. How he was going to change all that.

At Mercer Mansion, Adam paced the floor, agonizing over hospitals. Egan sat at his desk in the candlelight, contemplating his political platform. On the balcony of Julia's bedroom, Boone sat in the dark smoking a cigarette. He thought about Lydia and the boy he knew was his son. He thought about the business he was going to build to make him worthy of both.

Around them, the storm raged furiously. The wind howled, lightning cracked open heaven and thunder shook the earth. The sky filled with water and the old mansion creaked and groaned like a wooden ship. A jealous God was not happy that the drive of man was being steered by the dreams of women. Torn between baptizing and drowning them, he brooded over when exactly he lost control of his creation and why he had created women in the first place.

"What was I thinking?" he thundered.

His Son, being celibate, could only shrug.

CHAPTER 37

"You don't hunt, Dickson?" Crone asked, shoving a shell into his gun.

Boone had grown up with a rifle in his hand. In Stringtown you killed to eat. But after four years watching men hunt men, he had lost the taste for killing. He figured this information would be wasted on Crone, and so said nothing.

"Probably just as well," Crone said, resting the rifle on his shoulder. "Hard enough to handle this cannon with two arms, much less one."

"Really, Crone!" Collis insisted, as he rubbed his throbbing temples. "He lost it in the war!"

"And grateful we are!" Crone declared loudly.

After the storm broke midmorning, the men set out, trudging along the muddy path to the edge of the swamp. Using a croquet mallet as a walking stick, Teddy led the way. A white tent had been set up with all the amenities—dining table, buffet, and bar. While the men nursed their hangovers with Bloody Marys and cursed their discomfort, white-gloved servants stood perfectly still as the mosquitoes ate them alive.

In Argentina, men hunt wild boar on horseback with knives and Dogos. The American industrialists considered this highly inefficient. On Banyan, the prey was driven to the hunter. In the distance, colored men beating metal pans with sticks slowly waded through the muddy thicket toward the tent. It was not so much hunting as shooting boar in a barrel.

The sun simmered white hot, and the scalding heat slowed their already dulled senses. Alcohol sweating from their pores, they slumped in the tent as if in a stagnant steam bath. The air pressed down on them heavy as loam and they sensed the denouement extended beyond the day. Mouths bitter, they licked their crusty lips and could taste the decay.

"Where is Egan?" Adam asked, as he halfheartedly helped himself to poached oysters.

"He'll join us later." Stirring his drink with the stalk of celery, Teddy tapped it on the rim of his glass, then tossed it into the brush. "He doesn't hunt."

"Doesn't hunt?" Adam looked betrayed. "Then what the hell are we doing here?"

The drumming grew louder and faster and Collis's head began to throb in time with the hypnotic beat. Insects whirred and rattled their waxed paper wings, cursing him. And the day drifted into a dream.

When the drummers were in sight, Crone walked into the clearing in front of the tent. Spreading his legs, he threw the gun to his shoulder.

"There!" Adam cried, pointing to where the tall grass was parting like a zipper.

The squeal brought the men in the tent to a stand. The hair on the back of their necks bristled and their hearts begin to race.

Suddenly, the boar thundered out of the palmettos. She was around 200 pounds and still nursing, judging by the heaviness of her udders. Spotting Crone, she hesitated. Running left, then right, she could find no way around him. Behind her, the drummers were closing in. Turning back to Crone, she squealed hideously. Then dropping her head, she charged.

The sow was scarcely in range when Crone squeezed the trigger. The shot grazed the gristle on her back and passed right through.

She barely blinked. Pulling the gun tighter to his shoulder, he took aim and pulled the trigger again. This time he caught her in the chest. She screamed, and her legs folded. A flock of squawking black crows filled the air as she fell to her side in what seemed like slow motion.

A heavy silence fell over the party. Even the insects grew still. Adam waved his plate away.

Momentarily made stupid by the thrill of the kill, Crone strutted around the dying boar, emptying his gun into the air, then shaking it over his head.

"I suppose we should go watch him gloat," Teddy finally said, throwing the croquet mallet to his shoulder.

Dragging themselves to where Crone was posing to have his picture taken, they stared down at the wheezing sow. Her black eye looked up at them, and her blood was pulsing onto the mud.

"Aren't you supposed to put it out of its misery, or something?" Adam demanded.

Grabbing a knife from a drummer's belt, Crone squatted down and slit the sow's throat.

Swooning, Collis began to gag. Turning away from them, he threw his fist to his mouth and ran to the edge of the clearing. Dropping to his hands and knees in the mud, he bowed his head and retched. It was when he came up for air that he saw the second boar.

He was huge, even by Banyan standards—maybe 500 pounds, black, with stained yellow tusks at least eight inches long. Standing at the edge of the palmettos, he stared at his dying mate. Then slowly, he turned his massive head to Collis.

Collis opened his mouth to scream, but nothing came out. Mired since birth, the option of saving himself eluded him. As if to accept his fate, Collis closed his eyes. The wild boar dropped his head and charged.

"Boar!" a drummer yelled, pointing toward Collis.

While Crone fumbled, trying to spill his spent shells and reload, Boone grabbed the first thing he could use as a weapon, Teddy's croquet mallet.

Frozen by the inevitable, the men watched Boone run between Collis and the boar. When the charging animal was in range, Boone threw back his arm and swung the mallet with everything he had. The blow struck the boar solidly on the snout. There was a loud crack as wood met bone, and the head of the mallet snapped off and spun into the air.

Shaking his head, the boar stumbled backward.

"Get him out of here!" Boone ordered.

Running across the clearing, Teddy and Adam grabbed Collis under the arms and tried to drag him back to the tent. Another cartridge flipped from Crone's shaking fingers and dropped into the mud.

Snorting and pawing, the wild boar dropped his shoulders and charged again.

Gripping the splintered handle over his head like a spear, Boone braced himself. The hog was barely ten feet away when the shot rang out. Jerking, he temporarily veered to the left. Then righting his path, he kept charging. The second shot hit home. The wild boar didn't make a sound as he slammed into the mud at Boone's feet.

There were tears running down his muddy face when Collis looked up and saw Egan standing on the rise, legs spread and rifle still firmly planted in his shoulder.

"In the future, Mr. Dickson," Egan called out, "may I suggest you keep your head down during your swing."

"Oh, my poor, poor darling!" Jane cried, as she helped Adam lower Collis onto a lounge chair on the porch.

Teddy and Adam had more or less carried Collis back to the

house. Collis was speckled with vomit, covered in mud, and Adam strongly suspected he'd peed on himself.

"Dear Lord," Jane fretted, as she patted Collis's hand, "he's white as brie!"

Mouth gaping and hair sticking up like a rooster, Collis stared vacantly off the porch.

"You're a doctor!" She looked back at Adam over her shoulder. "Do something!"

"There isn't a scratch on him," Adam insisted.

"Well, nothing you can see!"

Walking over to Collis, Adam jerked up his limp wrist and rolled his eyes to his watch.

"Is it normal?" Jane demanded, wringing her diamond covered hands. "Is he in shock? His face looks numb to me. Dear God, please don't let it be a stroke!"

Dropping Collis's hand, Adam threw his finger toward the door. "Go get my bag!" he ordered, for no other reason than to get rid of her.

Jane took off like a bloodhound.

"Well?" Teddy asked, dropping onto a lounger beside Collis and throwing his hands behind his head.

Adam studied Collis's face carefully and diagnosed, "a severe case of scared shitless."

"Thank God. I thought it might be terminal humiliation."

Gasping, Collis suddenly sat straight up. He looked from Adam to Teddy, then lurching over the side of his chair, promptly deposited the remains of his dignity on the flagstone.

"It would have been much tidier," Teddy noted, "if we'd rescued the pig."

Teddy was still waxing eloquent about the swine's contribution to civilization, when Jane suddenly burst onto the porch with two servants carrying trays.

"I couldn't find your doctor's bag," she said breathless, "but I brought steamed towels, fresh clothes and martinis."

"Did you look in the boathouse?" Adam demanded, lifting a martini from the tray.

"No." She frowned, biting her lip.

"Well?"

Feet kicked up, the three men watched Jane, bodacious breasts bouncing, sprint across the lawn toward the dock.

"You know," Collis said, taking a sip of his martini, "I believe I'm going to marry that girl."

"How he did it was nothing short of a miracle!"

Crone told the story again and again. Each time the boar and the story grew bigger.

"The beast topped six hundred pounds and was charging like a rhino. There isn't another man alive who could have dropped it from that angle at that distance! Collis Taylor wouldn't be alive today if it weren't for Egan Mercer. . . ."

Crone told and retold the story until everyone who wasn't there, and most who were, believed it. He told it until Egan Mercer emerged the hero and Boone Dickson totally disappeared from the day.

CHAPTER 38

"ABOUT THIS hospital you're building," Collis said, as he and Jane, arms linked, walked Adam to the train. "Jane thinks we should . . ."

Collis searched for the right word. "Invest" seemed mercenary. "Donate" seemed dishonest. Not that he had a problem with dishonesty. He just hated wasting a sin on minutiae.

Opening her purse, Jane slipped out a check and handed it to Adam. He looked down at the amount and stopped walking. Jane assumed he was overwhelmed by their generosity. The truth was he was irritated beyond words. Now, he had no excuses.

"I can't accept this," Adam said, handing it back.

"That," Collis said, pushing his hand away, "and ten times more, if you need it."

Squeezing his arm, Jane looked at Collis with complete adoration. If you can't be extraordinary, Collis decided, then the next best thing is to ride the coattails of the man who might be. When they reached his railcar, Adam kissed Jane's cheeks and shook Collis's hand. Down the way he could see Julia seeing Dickson and Angela off.

"By the way," Collis called out, as Adam boarded the train, "do you have any idea how to build a hospital?"

"Not a clue."

"Wonderful!" Jane clapped her hands under her chin. "You won't be distracted by other men's mistakes."

*　　*　　*

Adam swayed back and forth with the rhythm of the train as he walked down the car. When he got to Angela's door, he raised his hand to knock.

"Something I can help you with, Dr. Montgomery?"

The train attendant seemed to appear out of nowhere.

"No. No," Adam said, jerking his hand down.

He found Boone sitting alone in the smoking car, a bottle of whiskey on the table in front of him. While Adam took a seat, Boone motioned for the bartender to bring another glass.

"I can never sleep on trains," Adam said, staring out the window. "It's all the noise. Clack. Clack. Clack. Nothing like a ship."

The only ship Boone had ever been on had German artillery firing at it. It wasn't all that quiet.

The countryside was dark outside the window. Adam was glad they were traveling at night and couldn't see the shacks along the track. Nothing like poverty to ruin a man's mood.

"It will be good to get home," Adam said, turning his head from the window.

Reaching into his breast pocket, he pulled out his wallet. Flipping it open, he stared down at A.J.

"He's going to put us all to shame," Adam said, passing the photo to Boone. "Sharp as a tack and already has the women wrapped around his fingers."

Boone stared at the photo of the boy and saw his mother's smile.

"I always said I'd never force my son to follow me into medicine. But he will go to Harvard. There won't be any discussion about that."

"Harvard," Boone said quietly.

Adam held out his hand and Boone handed the photo back.

"You should think about settling down," Adam said, tucking the wallet back in his coat. "Nothing like a son to make a man whole."

They rode in silence for a while. The darkness and the rhythm of the train seemed to rush the effects of the whiskey along. Adam looked over at Boone and felt such admiration his eyes welled up.

"It was the bravest thing I've ever seen," Adam said, leaning toward him, "facing that boar with nothing but a stick."

Adam looked at him with such awe Boone had to drop his eyes.

"It's only brave," Boone said into his glass, "if you stop and think about it."

Adam wasn't sure what Boone meant, but assumed he would never need to know.

"Crone isn't really a bad sort," Adam said. "It's Julia, you see. Unrequited love does funny things to a man."

Boone threw back his drink and poured another.

"He comes from good stock. Family owns the shipping business." Adam swirled his drink. "Of course, it takes more than old money to be old money."

Boone Dickson knew exactly what Adam meant.

"So . . . " Clearing his throat, Adam leaned back in his chair. "What do you know about building hospitals?"

"Not a thing."

"Then you're exactly the man I'm looking for."

CHAPTER 39

"WHICH DO you think?" Lydia slurred slightly.

Lydia was an exquisite drunk. Soft and blurred like a watercolor.

"Well?"

She held one dress up against her body for Mrs. Meeks to see, then another.

"Where you plannin' on wearin' it?" Mrs. Meeks asked, as she picked up discarded clothes from around the bedroom and draped them over her arm.

"My funeral," Lydia said, turning to face the mirror.

"You plannin' on dyin' soon?"

"A lady should have an ensemble planned for every occasion."

Since Mrs. Meeks had only one dress for church, weddings, and funerals, she felt she had the situation covered.

"En-sem-ble," Lydia said again, having a little trouble with the word. "En-sem-ble, on-sem-ble, onsombal," she said, over and over until it was completely unrecognizable.

She sighed.

"I hate foreign words. I think they should be sent back to wherever they came from, like the Japanese and the Germans and . . . Who else were we at war with?"

"The Italians."

"Yes, them too," she said. "Although, I'm very fond of Italian shoes."

The day Adam left for Banyan, Lydia started drinking. There are four kinds of drunks: mean, weepy, happy, and horny. Lydia was a happy drunk. If Mrs. Meeks had known, she would have started spiking Lydia's tea the day she arrived.

"Where exactly is Normandy?" Lydia called from her closet.

As Lydia pushed coat hangers across the rod in her closet, her hand suddenly hung on the rod. The longing for Boone always came in waves. The craving so sharp and intense she thought she could not bear it. Arms wrapped around her waist, she bent double, shoulders shaking.

"France," Mrs. Meeks called from the bedroom. "Normandy is in France."

Holding on to the rod, Lydia wiped her eyes with the back of her hand.

"France? We were at war with France too?"

Standing straight, she took deep breaths until all expression was gone from her face. Then lifting a dress from the rod, she dragged it into the bedroom. The silk was the color of torn peach and sheer as sunshine. It was as if Lydia were pulling the sunset behind her. Letting it slide over her head, the material poured over her slender body like spilled shimmering color.

"Promise me you'll bury me in this dress," Lydia said, turning from side to side in front of the mirror. "I bought it in Milan. I really think we should forgive the Italians. Don't you?"

Charlotte woke up to Lettie shaking her. Mrs. Meeks was standing at the foot of her bed, wringing her hands and pale as a ghost, while Mr. Nalls twisted his hat out in the hall.

"What?" Charlotte demanded, reaching for her robe.

"It's Miz Montgomery," Lettie said gravely.

"I only left her for a second," Mrs. Meeks insisted.

"Dammit! What's happened?"

"Miz Montgomery's runnin' bare-ass naked in the graveyard," Mr. Nalls called loudly from the hall.

"Except," Mrs. Meeks added quickly, "for her Italian shoes."

"People are always making messes for the rest of us to clean up," Charlotte complained, as she loaded her .45.

"It's not like you haven't been naked in the cemetery a time or two," Lettie said, handing her a kerosene lantern. "Everybody figures you're the most qualified for the job."

As she walked past the kitchen window, Charlotte could see Mr. Nalls contentedly sitting at the kitchen table while Mrs. Meeks and Lettie fawned and fussed over him. One cut pie, the other poured coffee, and Mr. Nalls smiled from ear to ear. Charlotte hated to think how much that slice of pie and cup of coffee was going to cost the poor bastard in the long run.

Lantern swinging and the .45 in her pocket, Charlotte made her way across the damp grass and into the cemetery. The full moon lit the night with cool white light. She could have found her way without the lantern, but wasn't so sure the snakes could.

On the other side of the old dry-stacked stone wall that separated the old part of the cemetery from the new, a pale streak flashed behind a monument.

"Lydia Montgomery!" Charlotte called out.

Eyes wide, Lydia peeked around the tombstone. Spotting Charlotte, she took off like a deer.

"Only a male god would give beauty to a brainless woman," Charlotte grumbled.

Hanging the lantern on an angel's praying hands, Charlotte situated herself on the Marable sisters and waited for Lydia's battery to run down.

The Marable sisters' tombstone was carved like a bench. No one knew which function came first, to mark the resting place, or a place to rest at the marker. Regardless, the gray granite bench sat in the

Marable's rose garden until the last sister, Posy, died at the age of ninety-seven. Up until then, every time one of the old maid sisters passed away, Posy drove a little brass herb marker into the ground with a name on it, Alpha, Estolene, and Edris.

When they moved the bench from the garden, a bit of mint must have stuck to it. Now, despite all of Mr. Bennett's efforts to get rid of the invasive vine, the sisters are covered in it. Whenever Digger mows, the air smells of mint julep.

Charlotte was thinking about mint juleps when the flashlight beam scanned the horizon. Slipping her gun out of her pocket, she cocked it.

"Take your finger off that trigger, Charlotte Belle," a voice called out, "or you'll be shootin' two of your pallbearers!"

Dot Wyatt and Reba Earhart came stumbling out of the darkness, clinging to each other.

"Lettie thought you could use some company," Reba said, feeling her head to make sure none of her curlers had popped loose under her hairnet during the transit.

"I brought coffee." Dot held up a thermos.

"Well, that's all I need," Charlotte said, "to be even more awake."

"Never thought I'd have the old woman's walk," Reba said, lowering herself onto the bench with a groan. "Back hurts. Knees hurt. Hell, the soles of my feet hurt when they hit the floor in the morning. This growin' old is shit."

"Your problem is you don't have a man who keeps you lubricated," Dot said, passing Charlotte a cup of coffee.

"I don't wanna hear 'bout you and Willie in the storeroom. Might as well wave a porterhouse in front of a junkyard dog."

Slipping a pint of whiskey from her sweater pocket, Reba poured a shot into her cup and passed the bottle. Taking a sip of coffee, Reba stomped the ground.

"Anyway, I'd rather spend the night with Jack Daniel's than any man I know."

"If I was married to Charlie Earhart," Dot said, "I'd be spooning with the Reverend J.D. myself. Speaking of reverends . . ."

Dot and Reba turned their heads toward Charlotte.

"Mind your own damn business," Charlotte said.

Somewhere out in the darkness Lydia laughed.

"What do you suppose got into her?" Reba asked.

"You mean besides the pitcher of gin and tonic?" Dot sniffed.

About this time, Lydia floated past them. Silk scarf fluttering behind her like butterfly wings, she pointed her Italian shoes as she twirled.

"Good Lord," Dot said, "she's wearing pearls."

"Dancing buck naked in a graveyard, and the woman is still perfectly accessorized," Reba said with the utmost admiration.

"Now, there's something to carve on her tombstone," Charlotte said into her cup.

Skin smooth as white marble, Lydia glowed luminescent in the moonlight like a beautiful ghost.

"Were we ever that young?" Dot mused.

Reba sighed long and hard.

"I wuz young and pretty once. But I wasted it. Had a pot of gold between these legs and spilled it."

"Jesus Christ!" Dot snapped at her. "We've been listening to you moan and groan about Charlie Earhart since high school! First you couldn't live without him! Now you can't live with him!"

Arms crossed and legs locked, Reba pouted.

"Dot Wyatt, you always were a mean drunk."

"Charlie Earhart doesn't have you chained to the porch! Love him! Leave him! Or shut up!"

Dabbing her eyes with the hem of her dress, Reba whimpered. The last thing a woman wants to hear is that she's made her own bed.

"What's that?" Charlotte suddenly asked, tilting her head.

Lydia's singing floated in the night air, sad and sweet as the scent of honeysuckle. It was song about lost love and lost youth. Reba knew both well. Tears ran down her cheeks as she croaked the alto to Lydia's soprano. And just like that, she was young again, sweaty skin sticking to the backseat of Charlie's Ford as he frantically pulled her panties to her knees.

"Goddammit!" Dot cursed, for no apparent reason.

Lydia danced, Reba cried, and Dot cursed. Now Charlotte had three drunk women in the graveyard to take care of—Happy, Weepy and Bitchy.

It was long after midnight when Lydia finally wore out. They found her in front of the Manns' mausoleum wrapped in her silk shawl on the dewy grass, surrounded by stolen funeral flowers.

"He loves me . . . He loves me not . . . ," Lydia slurred, as she picked petals off a mum.

Draping her arms over their shoulders, Dot and Reba carried Lydia back to the house and up the curving stairs to her bedroom, leaving Charlotte to finish it. Lydia sat on the edge of the bed as Charlotte threw back the satin comforter. Plucking petals off a red rose, she dropped them on the rug at her feet.

" . . . He loves me . . . He loves me not."

The last petal floated to the floor and Lydia stared at the thorny stem.

"He doesn't love me," she said numbly. "He doesn't love me."

"Why the hell should he?" Charlotte asked. "What have you done to deserve it?"

Lydia looked up at Charlotte, stunned. Men had always loved her. Worshipped her. It had never occurred to Lydia that she should do something to deserve it.

Dropping onto the chair next to the bed, Charlotte studied Lydia, searching for even one redeeming quality. But Lydia was nothing but a beautiful ornament, as useless as a porcelain knickknack. For Charlotte, beauty without purpose was just taking up space. Pulling a cigar out of her pocket, Charlotte ran a match under Lydia's night table.

"Now," she said, leaning back in the chair, "have you been to Stringtown lately? Children with no shoes. Playing in abandoned cars. You can't tell where the dump begins and where it ends."

There were few things Charlotte thought less of than a woman who devoted her days to committee meetings for fund-raisers that cost as much as the money they raised. But she could think of absolutely nothing else Lydia Montgomery was good for.

"It's three in the morning," Thomas said, squinting in the yellow porch light.

"Indeed it is," Charlotte said, pushing past him into the parsonage kitchen.

"And you've been drinking."

"Indeed I have."

Standing in the middle of the kitchen, Charlotte swung around to face him. But when she got a good look at him under the light, she couldn't say what she'd come to say. Turning away, she looked around his kitchen. The counter, stovetop, and kitchen table were covered with pies, cakes, and boxes of cookies. The top of the refrigerator was piled high with homemade yeast rolls and loaves of bread.

"Is the church having another damn bake sale?" she asked.

Then Charlotte remembered why she came.

"You'd have fallen in love with Lizzie Borden if she'd screwed you in the graveyard," she said flatly.

"Only," Thomas said, raking his fingers through his hair, "if she had your modest manner and pious personality."

"You don't know me. And you can't love what you don't know."

Resting his hands on the back of a chair, Thomas held her with his eyes.

"I know you have the personality of broken glass. I know you couldn't boil water with directions or find a broom with a map. I know you smoke, drink, and curse. I know you're rich as Midas but would sooner burn your money as give it to the church.

"I know that you took in your sister's child and reared her as your own. I know that whenever anyone in this town needs help, you're the one they turn to. I know that you give more of yourself to a total stranger than most wives give their own husbands.

"I know," Thomas said, "that you brought a dead man back to life in that graveyard."

And he said it in a way that made Charlotte want him inside her.

"Turn off the light," she said.

Reaching behind him, Thomas flipped the switch. He was blind in the dark, and so it caught him by surprise when he felt her press against him.

"I love you, Charlotte," he whispered into her hair.

"Shut up," she said, "and show me."

That Sunday, Thomas's sermon was on love.

"May we live in a world where love need not be spoken," Thomas preached, "but rather lived."

Eyes straight ahead, Reba Earhart slowly rested her hand on top of her husband's. Charlie stared at it for the longest time. Then lifting his wife's fingers to his lips, he kissed them.

Adam arrived home from Banyan Island to a driveway full of cars and a living room full of chattering women balancing china plates on their tightly squeezed knees.

"It's the Christian Women's Charity," Mrs. Meeks explained, as she took his coat and hat. "Miz Montgomery has become a do-gooder."

"But I was only gone a week," he stammered in disbelief.

"Miracles happen," Mrs. Meeks said, "when you're filled with the spirits."

CHAPTER 40

WHEN THE GYPSIES came to town that year, a well-dressed lady came to call on Charlotte Belle. Lettie showed her to Charlotte's office and was about to pull the sliding double doors closed when she noticed the wolf tooth hanging around the lady's neck. Lettie left the doors wide open.

The lady was standing in front of the French doors when Charlotte walked into the room.

"You didn't warn me that being rich was such hard work," Mila said, without turning around.

"What would life be without surprises?" Charlotte answered.

They sat in Charlotte's office. As Charlotte poured them each a whiskey, Mila sank comfortably back in the chair and told her story.

After they buried Emil Mazursky, her *kumpania* left Leaper's Fork. And Mila went back to being a thief. She was in the process of stealing a family's silver knives, when she realized the *W* engraved in the handles matched the initial on the silverware she had stolen from the Lesters'. She still had the Lesters' silverware. They had not traveled a safe enough distance for her to sell it.

At first Mila thought it was great luck. The whole set would bring far more than bits and pieces. But as she was stashing the knives in her skirt, she felt a weight on her chest. It wasn't guilt.

She asked herself, "What would the rich Charlotte Belle do?"

Mila didn't steal the knives. Instead, the next day, she brought the rest of the silverware to the Ware family and told them she suspected it might belong to them. Indeed, it did.

During the Depression, Mr. Ware nearly went under when the bank unexpectedly called in a loan. He was forced to sell almost everything he owned to save his business. The banker who did this to him, one Judge Lester, was kind enough to buy his possessions for pennies on the dollar. The loss of the silverware, a family heirloom, was especially bitter for Mr. Ware.

Then came the war. Mr. Ware's fortune not only bounced back, it catapulted. Long story short, he didn't care how Mila had *acquired* his silverware, since in his mind it had been stolen from him in the first place. He gave Mila twice what the silverware was worth and sent her on her way.

"It was so much money." Mila shook her head at the thought of it. "More money than I had ever held in my hand. It called to me. All I could think was what to buy, a new dress, real gold bracelets, French perfume. . . ." She was about to fritter it all away when again she felt the weight on her chest.

Mila asked herself, "What would the rich Charlotte Belle do?"

She loaned the money to a man who bred horses so that he could buy a new stallion. Some might think lending money to a Gypsy horse trader is a risky business venture. Mila promised him, if he did not honor the deal, he would be rolling dice with Emil Mazursky.

The horse trader did pay her back—with interest. And Mila discovered the first rule of wealth. Money makes money.

She continued to make loans and her *kumpania* began to prosper. Other Gypsy tribes began to notice that while they were still bumping around in wood wagons, Mila's tribe was driving pickup trucks. Soon, men from other tribes came to her with business propositions. And so it went.

The Gypsy thief became a banker. It was a natural evolution.

"Did you ever buy your gold bracelets?" Charlotte asked.

"Truthfully," Mila said, "I lost my lust for them."

Charlotte held the humidor open for Mila, then chose a cigar for herself.

"And what of you?" Mila asked, running the cigar under her nose. "Did you find your lifeguard?"

"You didn't warn me he was a preacher."

"Ah." Mila smiled. "What would life be without surprises?"

Striking a match, Mila puffed on the cigar as she studied Charlotte over the flame. "He has your heart," she said, shaking out the match.

"I will never be any man's wife," Charlotte said firmly.

"We are what we are," Mila said, "until we decide to be different."

The day the Gypsies pulled out of town, Ann Lester found a package on her front porch. Inside was a velvet-lined leather box of silverware so stunning her hands shook as she ran her finger over the *L* engraved in the handles.

Ripping open the card, she quickly read the inscription.

"Kintala," was all it said. *"A favor for a favor."*

CHAPTER 41

THERE ARE many things that divide people. In Leaper's Fork, it was elevation. Those living on high ground were high society. Those living down by the river were the bottom dwellers.

Then they built the dam. While it didn't completely stop the annual floods, as the Corps of Engineers had solemnly promised, it did make them biannual. Suddenly, land on the river became choice. This gave the mayor, Joe Pegram of Pegram's Construction, just enough time to throw up a neighborhood and sell it before the home owners figured out that every other spring they could gig bullfrogs in their basements.

A Pegram house looked like a boxcar with windows, three bedrooms, one bath, and a five-by-five concrete porch just big enough for two Jehovah's Witnesses to teeter on while you hid in the hall closet.

Except for the various shades of watery thin paint, they were identical. It was not the least bit unusual for a man to coast into the wrong driveway after pulling the evening shift at the meatpacking plant and not know he was lost until his neighbor's wife met him at the front door in her bathrobe. Some might say the Pegram home was the beginning of the fall of family values.

The rain came down and floods came up, and the poor fools living in a house built by Pegram watched their worldly goods float to the lake.

People whose heads are barely above water are always looking to move up. It didn't take long for word to get out that Boone Dickson built a house that would weather a family through any storm. A Dickson house had a kitchen big enough to eat in, a bathroom you could actually turn around in, and a backyard wide enough for a man to toss his boy a football. There was a window over the kitchen sink and a fireplace in the living room. There was a swing on every front porch. Most important, during the rainy season you didn't need a bass boat to get home from work.

Pegram boasted he could throw up a row of houses before Dickson got out of his truck.

"He'll be flat broke in two years," Pegram claimed, every morning at the diner.

It didn't quite work out that way.

Boone knew nothing about money. Charlotte Belle knew everything.

"It's not what you make," Charlotte told Boone. "It's what you keep."

Boone made a lot of money and Charlotte taught him how to make it multiply. Within five years, he was a rich man. So rich Talker's Building Supply sent him a presliced Reba's Country Ham every Christmas, and Judge Lester sought him out after church to shake his hand and try to lend him more money.

Despite the fact that Boone could have bought or built just about any house in Leaper's Fork, he still went home every night to his mother's place in Stringtown. Granted, it wasn't the house it had been. After the "restoration," his workers joked that the only thing original was the half-blind coon dog sleeping under the swing. Regardless, everyone knew that sooner or later Boone would move up.

In Leaper's Fork, you could not climb higher than Belle's Bluff without a hot-air balloon. And the highest point on the Bluff was the Hilliard House.

Hilliard House looked down on the town like a Baptist on a Unitarian. The old place reeked of southern nobility and Adam

Montgomery had desperately tried to buy it when he first moved to Leaper's Fork.

"This house has been in the Hilliard family for five generations," Mrs. Hilliard told him flatly. "And I intend for it to stay in the family."

Things change. Mrs. Hilliard was still living when her children started looting the old place. They threw up the For Sale sign the day after her funeral.

When Boone bought the house, rumors began to fly. Some said he was trying to buy his way into old money. Others claimed he was going to tear the old house down and build a modern mansion out of glass and steel, like those monstrosities in New York City.

The truth was, Boone didn't change a thing. He kept the grass mowed and the trim painted, and once a month a woman came in to knock the cobwebs down. Every night he stopped by for a few hours. Otherwise, the old place just sat there.

The inside of the house was cool, even in August. The old-timers knew porches weren't just for looks. The empty rooms smelled like Olde English furniture polish, fresh paint, and floor wax. The scent of Mrs. Hilliard's perfume was gone forever. The only furniture was a beat-up kitchen table Mrs. Hilliard's children didn't think they could sell and a single ladder-back chair in the guest bedroom. From time to time a door opened by itself or the floor creaked where no one stood. The woman who cleaned swore old Mrs. Hilliard was trying to find her furniture.

Boone ran his hand along the banister as he slowly climbed the stairway. He made a mental note of any new cracks in the plaster or creaks in the stairs. His footsteps echoed in the cool hollow house as he slowly walked from room to room, studying the ceiling for watermarks and the walls for peeling wallpaper.

In the guest room, he pulled the curtain back with his finger and looked directly down at the Montgomerys' yard. Lydia was on her knees in her flower garden. A.J. was throwing a wooden glider. Swinging the window open halfway, he could just make out the boy buzzing his lips together to make the sound of the engine.

Pulling the ladder-back chair up to the window, Boone sat down to watch his son grow.

CHAPTER 42

I N THE FALL of 1946 a black man came to teach in Stringtown. He was a spindly thing with twisted legs and glasses that made him look like a fly.

"Beer?" KyAnn asked, wiping her hands on her sauce-stained apron.

"Iced tea," he said.

All the men looked up from their barbecued ribs.

"Whatyu need that for?" KyAnn nodded to his crutch on his arm.

"Polio."

She handed him his tea.

Levon Sevier was a creature of habit. Three nights a week he ate supper at the Poor Man's Country Club—pork barbecue sandwich, slaw, and tea. On payday he had the smoked chicken platter with a slice of pecan pie. He always had a book tucked in his coat pocket, always ate alone at a picnic table under the trees next to the river, always spread his napkin in his lap, not tucked in his collar, always cleared the table when he was through, always read until it was too dark to see the words.

But the thing that KyAnn noticed most about Levon Sevier was that he didn't notice her at all.

"You gots yourself a education?" KyAnn asked, as she wiped the picnic table next to him off with a rag.

"I teach English literature at the high school," he said, not looking up from his book.

It was the way he said literature that got her, crisp and effortless as if he'd plucked each syllable on a banjo.

From then on KyAnn's eyes were fixed on Levon Sevier. She was struck by the way he cleaned his glasses, unhooking the wires from the backs of his ears, meticulously buffing the lens with a white handkerchief, then holding them up to the light and buffing them again. She was struck by how children, no matter how shy or rambunctious, found their way to him. She was struck by how, next to Levon, other men seemed crippled.

"Whatsat you readin'?" KyAnn asked, nodding to his book. "Is it a love story?"

"That would depend on your definition of love."

KyAnn slid onto the bench across from him.

"Tell it to me, that story," she said, with a lift of her chin. "And I'll tell you if it be love."

If God spoke he would sound like Levon Sevier. It was impossible to believe such a voice could come from such a frail and twisted instrument.

"Once there was a young sculptor who disliked women," Levon began. "He detested a woman's nature and resolved to never marry."

KyAnn crossed her arms.

"Baffled by other men's obsession with such flawed creatures, the sculptor set out to carve a statue so virtuous it would show the world the inadequacy and weakness of actual women.

"The young man worked incessantly, day after day, night after night, focusing on the smallest detail, the arch of her brow, the curve of her hip, her placid expression. He poured all his energy into the statue, imbuing her with such flawless perfection that she did not appear to be made of stone at all.

"When the statue was finally finished, a cruel fate befell its creator. The young sculptor fell in love, deeply, passionately, eternally in love with his own creation. But when he kissed her perfect lips, she did not kiss him back. When he rested his cheek against her breast, she was cold as stone. No love was ever so unrequited. No man so unhappy. He loved a woman who could not love him back."

KyAnn leaned back from the table.

"Fool," she said. "That sculpture man, he ain't nuthin' but a fool."

"And why is that?"

"Love ain't 'bout how a person look. It about how they feels in the dark."

KyAnn leaned across the picnic table toward Levon. Her amber eyes held him as firm as if she'd put both hands on the sides of his face.

"How you feel in the dark, Mr. Sevier?"

Levon, who words had never failed, was speechless.

From that night on, Levon's book was open on the table, but his attention was focused on KyAnn Merriweather. There was a small white girl with long black hair who seemed always underfoot. KyAnn treated the child as her own and kept her busy cleaning tables and washing glasses. When business was slow, she lifted the child onto a wooden crate and taught her how to cook.

"You gots to hold the bowl with one hand," KyAnn instructed gently, as she held Dixie's hand and turned it around the large wooden bowl, "and stirs with the other."

"This is very good cornbread," Levon said quickly, when they caught him staring at them.

"The secret to good cornbread is," KyAnn said, taking his empty plate, "you wants your batter smooth and your grease hot."

And she said it in a way that made Levon's face burn.

Levon was struck by how KyAnn knew each and every customer by name and could keep orders in her head without writing them down. He was struck by how she sashayed around the tables, both arms lined with plates, as light as a dancer. He was struck by how she had a tongue as sharp as a razor.

Levon saw what men blinded by their desire for her did not see.

KyAnn Merriweather, in her sauce-stained apron and red bandana twisted around her head, carried herself like a queen.

On Monday nights, after the tables had been cleared and the sign on the door turned to Closed, KyAnn sat down at the picnic table across from Levon. All week he studied on the story he would tell her. She would listen with the wonder of a child, then respond with the wisdom of a woman. It never ceased to amaze Levon how he had failed to see in the story what KyAnn saw so clearly.

"There'll be frost on the ground in d'mornin'," she said one night, as they watched a barge full of sand pass on the river.

"Yes," he said. He could feel it in the air.

"Mr. Sevier, I would make you a good wife."

It was his silence that set her back.

"I knows I ain't educated."

"It isn't that."

"And I ain't been no angel."

"I never expected to marry an angel, Miss Merriweather."

Levon had seen the way men looked at her.

"Could you be content . . ."

He could not look at her.

" . . . with this?"

"Mr. Sevier, I ain't never been content 'cept with this."

Levon slid his hand across the table until the tips of his fingers touched hers. It was the first time skin met skin, and the thrill of it made them both tremble.

Levon's mother and sister took one look at KyAnn and passed judgment. His brother-in-law was still in deliberation when his wife slapped him on the back of the head.

"Son," Mrs. Sevier said, lips tight as the seams she had sewn to put him through school, "I did not raise you to marry trash."

The Seviers sat at Levon's usual picnic table by the river, their barbecue growing cold on their plates. Stiff-backed and dressed for a funeral, Mrs. Sevier disapproved of everything she saw. Her grandson reached for a potato chip and she popped his hand.

KyAnn and Bush Hog watched it all from the pit. Lifting the brush from a pan of sauce, Bush Hog swabbed a rack of ribs and hot peppery steam hissed and spit on the hot hickory coals.

"If them chins get any higher," he said, "they'll be lookin' back-wards."

Wiping her hands on her apron, KyAnn made her way to Levon's family. Laying a large manila envelope on the table, she pushed it toward Mrs. Sevier.

"These here is my business papers," KyAnn said. "I owns fifty percent of this here barbecue. I owns fifty percent of the building it sits in. I owns fifty percent of the land it sits on, from that road there to the river. See's them three houses over there? I rents them out. Gots me one bad tenant, but he's fixin' tuh go. See that little house over there?"

The Seviers followed KyAnn's finger to a small white house sit-ting off to itself, neat as a pin with red geraniums on the porch and peach trees in the yard.

"That's my house," she said, resting her hand on her chest. "I's owns it free and clear."

Levon's brother-in-law flipped through the papers in the enve-lope, his eyes chewing from left to right. He was a lawyer, and there-fore something of a crook, but he knew what he was looking at.

"Who's this Charlotte Belle?" he asked, without looking up.

"We's a partnership. Fifty-fifty. She puts up the money. I puts up the work."

"Is this Charlotte Belle white?"

KyAnn nodded.

"Why would a white woman go into business with you?"

"I's a magician with money. You give me a dime . . ." KyAnn rubbed her fingers together in the air, "I turns it into a dollar."

Levon's brother-in-law read every page from top to bottom. When he got to the end, he turned back and read it again. Looking up at Mrs. Sevier, he nodded.

Mrs. Sevier estimated the number of customers, multiplied it by the price of a barbecue sandwich, slaw, and beer, then multiplied that by six days per week.

"Paydays and Sata-days we does even better," KyAnn said, reading her mind.

Mrs. Sevier was not a woman who enjoyed the success of others, even if her son stood to benefit from marrying it. In her mind there was a finite amount of happiness. Those who had it took from those who didn't.

"My ice has melted," she said, holding up her glass.

Taking the glass, KyAnn left them to talk about her.

"Why didn't you tell me she had money?" Mrs. Sevier demanded.

"Because I didn't know she had money," Levon answered.

"What else don't you know about this woman? What she want with a man like you?"

Carefully unhooking his glasses from behind his ears, Levon polished them, rubbing the lens until his thumb burned. A mother can cripple her son far worse than any disease.

"Son," she said gently, sliding her hand across the table so that her fingertips touched his, "I'm only telling you this because I love you."

Levon looked at his mother's hand, knuckles knobby and fingers bent like a spider's legs. Laying both his hands over hers, he sighed.

"Mama, I would have you be happy for me. But if it isn't in you, so be it."

Pushing himself up from the table, Levon slid his arm into his crutch and left his mother behind forever.

"Why didn't you tell me you own all this?" he demanded, as KyAnn scooped ice from the chest into his mother's glass.

"I don't want you marryin' me fer my money."

"I would never marry you for your money."

"Well, I knows it now." KyAnn shrugged. "But I don't knows it then."

Levon watched KyAnn sashay across the grass, chin high, hips swinging from side to side as if she were dancing. Glancing back over her shoulder, KyAnn gave him a look that made his face hot.

If Levon had carved his ideal woman from stone, she would have been nothing like KyAnn Merriweather. She would have been demure with light skin and perfect diction. She would have worn tailored suits and sat with her knees held tight together. She would have given him no surprises.

What a fool he would have been.

KyAnn and Levon were married at the courthouse. It was the first time Levon had ever seen KyAnn without her sauce-stained apron and kerchief.

"I cleans up pretty good, don't I?" KyAnn said, running her hand down the pale yellow dress.

Levon could only nod.

The judge took one look at the couple and shook his head. He had no doubt KyAnn Merriweather was going to chew the poor boy up and spit him out.

Staring sternly at them over his reading glasses, the judge gave them their vows, lectured them on the binding obligations of marriage, and instructed the groom to kiss his bride. If he'd been a priest, he would have given Levon his last rites.

KyAnn went to kiss Levon, but he held her back. She was surprised by this and slightly perturbed. A man had never pushed her away. Holding her firmly by the arms, Levon gave KyAnn a look that slowly made her mouth soften and her bones as malleable as biscuit dough. When she understood his terms, he pulled her to him and kissed her as though they were alone in the room.

All the judge's fears flew out the window.

The old men whittling on the benches in front of the courthouse clapped as the couple walked through the double doors, and Ben Harrington broke into "Happy Days Are Here Again" on his fiddle. After his wife ran off with the Porter Paint salesman, he swore he'd never again play the wedding march—or sell Porter Paint.

Dixie Belle and Levon's nephew threw rice as they made their way down the courthouse steps. And the mayor's secretary threw a hissy.

"Someone is going to have to clean this mess up!" Clara fussed.

"Now, now, Clara," the Sheriff said, in the same voice he used to sooth drunks and cornered criminals. "It's a wedding, not a vandalism."

Bush Hog and some of the regulars had scrawled Just Married! with white shoe polish across the rear window of Levon's Chevy and strung old boots and tomato sauce cans from the bumper. In the backseat was a picnic basket from Angela, and a white lace gown wrapped in tissue paper from Lettie for the honeymoon night.

While Levon told his family good-bye, Charlotte and KyAnn talked a little business.

"I've been thinking we could use a barbecue pit on this side of the river," Charlotte said, leaning against the car. "What do you think?"

"Women cook," KyAnn said, nodding. "Men eat."

As the car slowly pulled away, everyone waved and wished them well. Everyone except Mrs. Sevier who watched, her lips drawn tight.

"She will humiliate him and ruin his life," she cursed under her breath.

Suddenly, Angela slapped her hands together in the air and Levon's mother jumped like a cat. Black eyes flashing, Angela gave Mrs. Sevier a look that made the old woman's breath freeze.

"They will be happy," Angela swore.

Then Angela spit on the sidewalk in front of Mrs. Sevier and dragged the toe of her shoe through it. Eyes wide and clutching her pocketbook, Mrs. Sevier shrank back. And her words fell to the ground dead as dust.

Standing shoulder to shoulder on the sidewalk, the Belle women watched Levon's brother-in-law help a severely shaken Mrs. Sevier to their car.

"Where in the hell did that come from?" Charlotte asked.

"Just made it up as I went along," Angela said.

"Have I ever told you how proud I am of you?" Charlotte asked.

"I know," Angela said.

They honeymooned at the lake. Levon read and KyAnn fished. When he looked up from his book, she was watching him.

"You need sumpthin'?" she asked, reaching for the picnic basket.

He shook his head.

"You want sumpthin'?"

And his face grew hot like a boy's.

Every morning an old white man in a boat puttered past them on the bank. "The Lord bless you!" he called across the water. And every evening, as he puttered home, the old man held up a string of bass and called out, "Thanks be to God!"

Levon, who had never before believed in such things, took this as a sign.

CHAPTER 43

THE FORMER minister of the First Baptist Church had ruled his flock with a firm fist and a closed mind. While Reverend Lyle was all in favor of breeding baby Baptists, recreational sex sent him into a fury.

"A good woman," Reverend Lyle declared from the pulpit, "does not paint her mouth like the whore of Babylon!"

While there was some question as to whether whores in Babylon wore Revlon, Mary Louise Binkley dropped her face into her pocketbook and scrubbed her lips with her handkerchief until they were raw—just to be on the safe side.

Thirty years of Reverend Lyle had just about neutered the good women of the First Baptist Church. They hid their hair under hats and wore shapeless dresses that looked like couch throws. They kept their eyes down, their hands folded in their laps, and their thoughts on *Good Housekeeping*. Unnoticed and undesired, they shriveled like grapes drying into raisins.

But the day Reverend Thomas Jones stepped up to the pulpit all that changed.

His clothes were wrinkled, his hair was sticking up like a rooster, and his face was covered with stubble—but they knew. They leaned forward in their pews, scrubbed faces tilted up like sunflowers to the sun. Reverend Jones smiled down on them, and they sighed as though awakening from a deep sleep. Color rose in their cheeks, their eyelashes involuntarily fluttered, and their starched white blouses billowed like sails.

"Ed Binkley, you are a lucky man," Reverend Jones said, slapping him on the back. And Mary Louise blushed like a rose.

"Why, Miss Clara," he said, cupping his hand over her bony fingers, "you're looking absolutely radiant this morning."

The Sheriff, who passed Clara every day in the courthouse but never paid her any mind, leaned sideways in the receiving line to get a better look at her. He wouldn't exactly call her radiant, but he had to admit she wasn't as dull as usual.

It temporarily escaped the Sheriff's mind that Clara was a nit-picking, bossy busybody. He invited her to have Sunday buffet with him at the lake. Clara was so surprised by the invitation she forgot to mention that he'd filled out his weekly time sheet wrong.

Monday morning, Clara sharpened a brand new number 2 pencil and made the corrections on the Sheriff's time sheet herself. She was so overwhelmed by her anonymous act a kind of glow came over her.

"Why, Miss Clara," the Sheriff said, taking off his hat, "you are absolutely radiant this morning."

After the Sheriff left, Clara walked down the hall of the courthouse to the ladies' restroom. Locking herself in a stall, she lowered the lid on the toilet, wiped it with a paper towel, then sat down and cried.

Like rain after a thirty-year drought, the barren desert began to bloom.

Six months after Thomas arrived in Leaper's Fork, half the women in the congregation were expecting, including Mary Louise Binkley, who'd been trying for twelve years. Sunday morning, they waddled out of the church, hands resting on their swollen stomachs and smiling with a peace that passeth understanding.

While they could never say it out loud, they knew it was Thomas who had broken the spell that bound them. And they longed for his happiness, which in a woman's mind only comes in pairs.

And so the call went out. Old maids, widows, and unwed women half his age flocked to the church like moths to the eternal flame. Mademoiselle's Dress Shop could not keep enough perfume and stockings on the shelf. And on Saturdays the Beauty Barn Hair Salon had them lined up, wet hair twisted tight on pink plastic rollers, waiting for a dryer.

There is something irresistible about a man of God. Maybe it's the job security. But Thomas raised the bar. Not only was he good-looking and charismatic, he had a way about him that made a woman want to whip things up.

The more his sermons stirred them, the more feverishly they stirred. Cakes and pies lined the parsonage countertop and the church refrigerator was stacked with casseroles.

They baked spicy apple harvest cakes and angel biscuits so light they seemed to hover above the pan. They brought him jars of homemade bread and butter pickles, plum preserves, and chow-chow. Every morning cars lined the sidewalk in front of the church, and ladies bearing gifts of honey buns and banana bread still warm from the oven filed into the church. After a particularly moving sermon on "Faith, Fishes, and Loaves," they whipped up enough salmon croquettes and tuna casseroles to feed the masses.

But despite all their efforts, Thomas could not be snagged. Of course, this did not deter them. There is nothing a woman wants more than a man who can't be had.

CHAPTER 44

O N FRIDAYS, Thomas always rehearsed his sermon at the pulpit. On that particular Friday, when he walked into the sanctuary, an old man was standing in his place. His hair was white, his face looked like weathered wood, and he smelled like fish and lake water.

"Reverend Lyle," Thomas said, "it is good to finally meet you."

"Are you a man of faith?" Reverend Lyle called out, his voice booming through the empty hall. "A preacher without faith is like a car salesman with no cars on the lot. You can't sell what you don't got!"

"Yes, sir," Thomas called back. "I am a man of faith."

"Are you a man of God?"

"Yes, sir. I am a man of God."

Gripping the pulpit with both hands, Reverend Lyle stared down at Thomas with watery blue eyes.

"Reverend Jones," he said quietly, "are you a moral man?"

Thomas said nothing. And Reverend Lyle had his answer.

"End it!" the old preacher ordered.

"I love her."

"What man ever hated his sin?" the old man thundered.

Reverend Lyle did not tolerate wayward preachers. But he had seen the church attendance numbers and had walked through the new sanctuary still under construction. Reverend Lyle was, above all else, a company man.

"Ninety days," he said, stepping down from the pulpit. "End it, or leave my church."

"She'll marry me," Thomas said resolutely.

"Son," Reverend Lyle said, resting his hand on Thomas's shoulder, "the day Charlotte Belle agrees to be any man's wife, hell will freeze over."

When the sanctuary door swung closed behind him, Reverend Lyle stood alone in the foyer of the church he had built. He left his ministry with only one piece of unfinished business. Now he had the means to tie up his one loose end—and his one loose woman.

Thomas was standing at the window in his office when Althea brought the mail. His lunch from the day before was still sitting on his desk. Thomas hadn't eaten in three days and the casseroles were starting to pile up.

Of course, Althea knew about Charlotte Belle and Reverend Jones. She wouldn't have been much of a church secretary if she hadn't. She also knew about Reverend Lyle's ultimatum.

Every preacher has a thorn in his side. The Presbyterian minister dipped his hand in the till. The Catholic priest tipped the bottle. Stand too close to the Methodist minister and you'd be pinched black and blue. And somewhere along the line, the Episcopal priest had misplaced God.

Althea did not see it as her job to judge.

Some preachers lead by example. Some stand at the pulpit and tell you where to go. In Althea's book, no preacher gave directions better than the one who had been there.

Thomas, she knew, had been to hell and back.

Leaving the mail on his desk, Althea quietly pulled the office door closed behind her. Pulling on her coat and hat, she jotted a note in perfect handwriting and laid it on the floor in front of his door. Opening her bottom desk drawer, she grabbed her Lucky Strikes. Then, for the first time in twenty years, Althea left work early.

*   *   *

"They're up to no good," Ben Harrington said, glancing back over his shoulder.

Hands wrapped around coffee cups and heads together, Althea and Lettie huddled at a table in the corner.

"There ought to be a law against women congregating," the Sheriff said, taking a sip of coffee.

"There's whispering," Willie said from the service window, eyes fixed on Dot's hips as she bent down to pick up a tray, "and then there's *whispering.*"

"Well, as far as I'm concerned, all women should have their vocal chords snipped like Ann Lester's cocker spaniel," the Sheriff sniffed.

"Amen to that." Ben nodded.

It was clear to Willie why neither man was married.

CHAPTER 45

Every day Adam and A.J. drove out to the construction site to take a look at the progress on the hospital. And every day Boone was waiting for them with two hard hats, one for Adam and one small enough for the boy.

As they walked through the hammering and sawing, Boone pointed and shouted over the noise. Adam nodded as though he understood. When they came to a ditch, Boone instinctively grabbed the boy under the arm and swung him across to the other side. When they walked below men hammering, he gently held the boy's face down.

"Didn't know Mr. Dickson had a son," a framer said, as they passed.

"He don't," his partner said, taking a nail from his mouth and driving it flush. "Ain't even married."

The framer looked at the boy again, mop of black hair, black eyes, the body of a tiny boxer.

"Well, you coulda fooled me," he said.

"You want my advice," his partner said, "you'll stay fooled."

While Adam occupied himself with the hospital, Lydia threw herself into the Christian Women's Charity. She had found her calling.

It was Lydia's idea to cut out the bake sale and go straight to the source.

"You mean we should just ask men to give us money?" Ann Lester asked incredulously.

"Where's the fun in that?" Clara grumbled into her cup.

When Lydia showed up with a check from Charlotte Belle for more money than the ladies had raised at the annual bake sale in five years, Clara missed her mouth and poured spiced tea into her lap. Charlotte Belle had never so much as bought a cookie at their bake sales.

Not to be outdone, Ann Lester showed up with a check from Judge. And so it went.

By the time it was all said and done, the ladies not only had raised enough money to build a park in Stringtown with swings, teeter-totters, and a merry-go-round, but to pave the abandoned lot next to it and put up basketball goals.

Then Lydia came up with the idea that they should go to all the churches in town and get them to buy new school clothes for the children in Stringtown.

"But the First Baptist Church has a used clothes drive ever year," Ann Lester insisted.

"If the Baptists can send missionaries to Africa," Lydia said flatly, "they can buy new shoes for the children in Stringtown."

Lydia personally made a visit to Baker Shoe Store to promote her cause. John Baker was so smitten by her, he not only sold the CWC shoes at cost, but threw in a dozen pairs for free.

Then Lydia came up with the idea that instead of giving money to the poor, they should lend it to them.

"Lend poor people money?" Ann Lester echoed incredulously.

"Give a man a fish, he'll eat for a day," Lydia explained. "Lend him start up capital for a Catfish House, he'll not only eat for the rest of his life—so will his ten employees."

The ladies couldn't quite put their fingers on it, but they were starting to suspect that Lydia was not working alone.

In the afternoons, when Adam and Adam Jr. were at the hospital construction site, Lydia would drive across the river to Stringtown.

She parked her car at the edge of the playground and rolled down her window. She liked to watch the children swing. Jaws set with determination, they leaned back, throwing their legs above their heads, pushing higher and higher until they rose above the top of the frame. For a split second they seemed to defy gravity, suspended in the air, eyes bright, faces full of hope, as if the wind might lift them up and take them away. Knuckles white on the steering wheel, Lydia held her breath for them. She hadn't expected that.

CHAPTER 46

M ONTGOMERY Memorial Hospital opened its doors in the fall of 1947. While a reporter from the Nashville newspaper took pictures of the governor cutting the ribbon, a baby was being delivered in the new delivery room.

KyAnn and Levon Sevier's son weighed seven pounds, eight ounces. He had a mat of soft black hair and lashes that curled like springs from a pocket watch. He came into the world with his eyes wide open and his hands reaching for the light.

"You is goin' to be a educated man," KyAnn said, kissing her baby's tiny fingers, "jest like your daddy."

Standing beside the hospital bed, Levon looked down at his wife. He was so proud he thought his heart would burst.

Half of Massachusetts showed up at the hospital ribbon cutting. Jane Fields-Taylor even charmed a *Boston Globe* reporter into making the trip. To the locals, it seemed that the Yankees had invaded again.

"Collis Taylor, my husband, was the first and largest contributor, you know," Jane Fields told a group of reporters. "That's Taylor, as in Taylor Imports."

The names under the photos of the board of directors in the lobby read like a list of Boston's *Who's Who*. Along with Taylor and Montgomery, there was Lyons, Mercer, Sewell, Dugan, Nash, and the list went on.

"Quite a list," the Boston reporter said, as he jotted down the names.

"Indeed," the man standing next to him said.

"Heard the first baby born was a Negro," the reporter went on. "I guess some people down here might be a little uneasy about a hospital that doesn't have a segregated area for coloreds."

"I guess those people will have to drive to a Nashville hospital or, depending on the severity of their illness, straight to hell."

"May I quote you on that?"

"Indeed, you may," the man said, spelling his name.

The reporter looked up from his pad. "There's a Mercer running for the U.S. Senate in Massachusetts."

"My brother."

"You don't say."

The reporter flipped the page on his pad.

"You involved in the campaign?"

"Campaign manager."

"As campaign manager, do you speak for your brother?"

"No man speaks for Egan Mercer except Egan Mercer."

"But can I safely say that racial integration will be on Mr. Mercer's campaign platform?"

"You can carve it in stone," Teddy said.

It was after visiting hours when Angela came to see KyAnn's baby. The nurses sent Levon home at suppertime and the room was quiet and dark.

Gently pulling her baby off her breast, KyAnn laid him on the bed, fists clenched and lips still smacking.

"He's as fine a boy as I've ever seen," Angela said, looking down at the baby. "He'll lead with his mind, like his daddy."

Folding back the flannel blanket, Angela laid her hand on his tiny chest. Her hand had barely come to rest on his warm skin when stifling a scream, she jerked away.

"What?" KyAnn demanded. "Whaddyu see?"

Angela's jaw was set as she slipped her hand into her pocket.

"Angela, you got tuh tell me. I got tuh know."

Some things, Angela never told. Knowing can speed bad news along. Then again, some things she had no right to hide.

Angela held her friend with her eyes, as if to steady her.

"He'll walk through fire."

Dropping her head, KyAnn nodded. She knew about walking through fire. But like every mother, she had wished for her son a life easier than her own.

"You don't say nuthin' 'bout this to Levon," KyAnn ordered, as she gathered her son into her arms.

Some things men are not strong enough to know.

Walking to the window, KyAnn looked down at Leaper's Fork. Night was falling. Gas streetlights glowed in the haze and church steeples pierced through the fog settling on the town like the masts of sinking ships.

Holding her son tightly, KyAnn rocked back and forth.

"You know how they makes the strongest sword?" she whispered into his soft hair. "They hammers it flat, then holds it tuh the fire. What a brave boy you are. What a fine man you goin' tuh be."

Alone in the hall, Angela leaned her back against the freshly painted wall. She held her breath as she lifted her hand from her pocket and slowly opened it. The skin on her palm was blistered and burned as if she'd held it to the red-hot eye of a stove.

CHAPTER 47

LYDIA WAS waiting for Adam when he arrived home from the hospital.

"What's wrong?" he asked.

In the twelve years that they had been married, Lydia had never once waited up for him. Not even when he was on top of her making love.

Lydia was sitting on the stairway in her dressing gown, arms wrapped around her knees. Her platinum hair was down and the light from the chandelier lit her from behind. Most men would have taken one look at Lydia and all would have been forgiven. Adam had stopped looking at Lydia years ago.

"I wanted to congratulate you," she said.

"For what?" he asked, laying his hat on the table.

On top of his mail was an open manila envelope from Jane and Collis. Inside was a newspaper clipping from the *Boston Globe* about the hospital. Above the article was a picture of Adam standing next to the governor at the ribbon-cutting.

"You've become the man you always wanted to be," Lydia said, as he scanned the article.

It hadn't occurred to Adam, but yes, he had the life he had asked for.

Lydia stood up and slowly climbed the stairs. At the landing, she stopped and looked down at him.

"Adam . . ."

He looked up from the newspaper.

"I'm very happy for you."

Nodding, he looked back at the article. They had been at war so long he didn't recognize her offer of peace.

CHAPTER 48

"Today's sermon was from Matthew. When you give, don't blow your horn. When you pray, go into your room and close the door." Lettie began, as she lowered herself into the rocker. "Reverend Jones says we should take Jesus off our sleeve and put him in our hearts. . . ."

Leaning back in her chair, Charlotte stared off the porch as she listened. She would never admit it, but hearing her words echoed in Thomas's sermons filled her with more satisfaction than any business deal she'd ever made.

"How many were in church today?" she asked.

"Filled to the rafters," Lettie said, as she unpinned her hat. "Had 'um sitting in the aisles in folding chairs."

"We were up ten percent last week," Charlotte told her.

"He's a popular preacher, all right. Especially with the women. Every hussy in a fifty-mile radius is limbering up that ring finger like a piano player."

Charlotte smiled like a woman who not only had the superior product, but held the patent.

"He's pulling them in. . . ." Lettie said, and left the sentence hanging.

Charlotte turned her head to look at her.

"But what?"

"Oh," Lettie shrugged, "some say he's not the preacher Reverend Lyle was."

"Ssshe-it! Tommy preaches circles around Lyle!"

"It's not his sermons. . . ."

"What?" Charlotte demanded.

"Well, some say he's just not the businessman Lyle was."

"Who says?"

"Judge Lester, for one."

"What the hell does that fool know about business? He's nothing but a glorified loan shark."

"I have to admit," Lettie said slowly, "when Reverend Jones calls for the offering . . ."

"What?" Charlotte demanded, leaning forward in her rocker.

"Well, he just doesn't seem to know how to . . ."

Forehead furled, Lettie searched for the words.

"Close the sale?" Charlotte asked.

"He can fill the pews," Lettie said. "He just can't seem to fill the collection plates."

Dropping back in her chair, Charlotte crossed her arms defiantly.

"Don't think I don't know what you're doing, old woman."

Lettie pushed herself out of the rocker with a groan and tottered toward the door.

"All I'm saying is, a successful church is like any other successful business. It isn't enough to have a good product and pretty packaging. You need someone who knows how to manage the money."

Having stirred the pot, Lettie left Charlotte on the porch to simmer.

At the early service on Sunday morning, Ben Harrington dropped his Bible on the floor when he saw Charlotte Belle standing by his pew. Glancing around, he checked to see if he'd wandered into the Poor Man's Country Club by mistake.

"Charlotte, are you lost?"

"I'm never lost!" Charlotte said. "Now, scoot over!"

Knowing the Belles' standing with the Almighty, Ben gave Charlotte a wide berth.

It was the hottest August anyone could remember. Children lay wilted on their mother's laps, hair pasted to their foreheads and tiny pearls of sweat on their upper lips. Robes hiked up and knees spread, the choir blew down into their collars trying to get a draft going. Jesus fans flapped so hard in the pews the candles flickered and the pages of the hymnals turned themselves. It would be their last Sunday in the old sanctuary, and their last Sunday sweating. The new sanctuary had air conditioning.

In the small white room beside the baptistery, old Reverend Lyle sat on a wooden chair, jaw set and gripping his Bible. Through the sheer curtains he watched Thomas. The day of reckoning had arrived.

Thomas had tried everything in his power to get Charlotte to marry him. He had reasoned, ordered, and begged. But nothing would change her mind. Charlotte wasn't in the market for anything Thomas had to sell.

Ed Wilson led the Morning Prayer, John Murphy gave the announcements, and Judge Lester gave the financial report. Then it was time for the sermon.

If Thomas had known Charlotte was sitting in the church, he would have given a different sermon. Gripping the pulpit, he looked out at his congregation.

"I once knew a man who never sinned," Thomas began. "He never lied. He never stole. He never took the Lord's name in vain. He never once coveted his neighbor's wife.

"People said, 'What a good man he is.'

"But I want you to know he was not a good man. He was merely a man who did not sin. He was merely a man who loved the law. A man who loved the law—but not the Lord.

"What good is the garden where the weeds are pulled, but the seeds are never planted? What good is the life that has no stain, but leaves no mark?

"Who among us will make our mark? And who will leave nothing but a rock to mark where our bones are buried?

"Goodness is not the absence of sin. Goodness is the presence of God. And God, my friends, is love.

"I once was a man who did not sin. I did not lie. I did not steal. I did not commit adultery. And I was cold and lonely, and my bitterness made everything I touched shrivel and turn to dust.

"Hear it from a man who knows. You will not be saved by what you do not do."

Slowly, Thomas weaved his web. It was not a web to trap the guilty, but to catch the falling. Charlotte was mesmerized by the beauty, humbled by the design, and challenged by the example. But mostly, she was in awe of the architect.

Drawn forward, Charlotte gripped the pew in front of her. She looked around at people she had known all her life and was filled with such love for them it brought tears to her eyes. They were still complete fools, of course, but she loved them just the same.

Charlotte Belle was first and foremost a businesswoman. If ever there was a man for her to invest in, it was the man who could perform miracles.

"What's that?" Ben whispered.

It took Charlotte a moment to hear the tapping on the roof. Leaning her head back, she looked up at the rafters above them.

"Hail," she whispered.

Suddenly, the double doors of the sanctuary slammed open. Judge Lester Junior, back from his reconnaissance mission, ran breathless into the church.

"Tornado!" he yelled, running down the center aisle. "Tornado!"

Through the open doors they saw white icy hail the size of baseballs hurling from the sky. Pelting cars and street signs, it dented the metal like tinfoil. On the horizon a sinister red gleam was growing in the sooty sky as if Satan were opening his eye.

"Single file to the basement!" Thomas ordered from the pulpit, as the deacons rushed them out a pew at a time.

Never in the history of the Main Street First Baptist Church had the congregation been so enthusiastic or undivided in a mission. Women clutching their babies and men pushing the elderly along ran out of the sanctuary and down the hall to the basement stairs like soldiers in retreat.

Charlotte and Althea Nalls were helping the last of them down the basement stairwell when Charlotte sensed something was missing.

"Where's Thomas?" she demanded, frantically searching the huddled crowd below them.

"He went to save Judge Lester!" Althea Nalls yelled over the crying and praying.

"Where did Judge Lester go?"

"To save the collection plates!"

Before anyone could stop her, Charlotte ran back up the stairs.

The wind turned solid as it shoved its way through town. Wood splintered, metal twisted, and concrete crumbled. Hundred-year-old trees ripped out of the ground like green onions. Electric poles were mowed down like grass. At the post office, the claw-footed gargoyles broke free and swirled in the debris-filled sky like bronze bats.

Snapping off the of steeple of the Presbyterian church, the storm hurled it into the Episcopalians' bell tower like a javelin. At the courthouse, the wind crushed through the west wall like a wrecking ball.

As if to savor the moment, the twister hovered over the First Baptist Church, then slammed down like the wrathful fist of God. The old sanctuary groaned as the roof peeled back. Hymnals flapped into the air and candlesticks twirled like batons. Everything not bolted down was sucked spinning into the sky. Then the windows shattered and the air was filled with stained glass glitter.

Down in the basement, it sounded as if a freight train was roaring over their heads. The beams shook violently and planks pulled free as the nails were sipped away. Tears running down their faces and fingers laced bone-knuckle white, they bartered with their Maker, calling out all the things they would give up in exchange for life.

While his former congregation cowered on their knees with their eyes squeezed shut, Reverend Lyle stood in the middle of the room looking up. Over the roar and the crying, he thought he heard the faint sound of Charlotte Belle's laugh, as thrilled as a child on a roller coaster.

Even if the streets hadn't been blocked with shattered trees and upside down cars, the fire engines could not have gotten to the fire in time. When the electric line hit the broken gas main, the explosion rocked the new hospital.

Adam was one of the last out. He stood with the others on the front lawn and watched the hospital burn. The fire was so hot he held his hand up to shield his face. As the flames blew out the fourth floor windows, two nurses held KyAnn back. Twisting and fighting, she screamed like a wounded animal.

"My baby! My baby! Sweet Jesus, my baby!"

Adam turned to KyAnn. And when she saw the look on his face, she grew perfectly still. Slowly, he turned back to look at the burning hospital. Then, before anyone could stop him, Adam jumped across the crackling electric line and ran back into the burning building.

CHAPTER 49

IT TOOK TWO DAYS to dig the bodies out. Miraculously, there was hardly a scratch on them.

"It was an easy death," Mr. Foster said. "When the air gave out, they just went to sleep."

Digger said he saw Boone's truck fly past the cemetery right before the tornado touched down on Franklin Street.

"Musta seen it a–comin' from the big house on the hill," Digger said.

After the fireplace fell, taking the curving stairway with it, Boone and Lydia managed to throw a mattress out the French doors of her bedroom. They dropped A.J. to safety right before the house collapsed like a deck of cards.

The rescue team found them in a closet off the bedroom. Lydia leaned against Boone's chest as if sleeping, and Boone had his arm wrapped around her as though this time he would never let her go.

The smile on Lydia's face was so peaceful the rescue workers laid their hats over their hearts and cried.

CHAPTER 50

ON WEDNESDAY, Angela Belle went to town, or what was left of if. Most of the windows had been boarded up. Where the Feed Store used to stand, there was now a black gaping hole.

The fact that Adam was sitting by the diner window waiting for Angela, when the flowers on his wife's grave had barely withered, did not go unnoticed.

"Some might say it's a little soon to come courting," Dot said, as she refilled his cup.

"Do I look like a man who gives a damn what people think?"

"Son," Dot said, resting her hand on his shoulder, "it's about time. We'd just about give up on you."

Angela was standing in front of Mademoiselle's when his reflection appeared on the window beside her. The burn that ran down the side of his face made his eyes seem even bluer. But it was the burn beneath his skin that made her lips part.

Turning away, Angela continued walking down the sidewalk. Hands in his pockets, Adam followed.

"After you rebuild the hospital," she said, as they strolled by what was left of the Kandy Kitchen, "you should build a school."

Grabbing her roughly, Adam pulled her to him. Right there on the sidewalk, in front of God and everybody, he smashed his mouth against hers as if he were suffocating and she was air. For the first time in his life he was oblivious to himself and to the crowd that had gathered in the shop windows to watch. For the first time, Adam

Montgomery was not thinking about his past or his future, but only the moment he held in his hand.

As his mouth moved down her neck, Angela laughed. It was more of a cackle really—one of those laughs that promised Adam he was in for the ride of his life.

CHAPTER 51

CHARLOTTE AND THOMAS stood at the altar of the new sanc-tuary. The pews were packed. Charlotte's first time in church had resulted in a tornado. No one was about to miss her second.

Ironically, Judge Lester was the best man. Thomas figured if Judge hadn't bolted the pews to the floor of the old sanctuary, none of them would have been standing there. Charlotte figured if the idiot hadn't gone back for the collection plates, they wouldn't have been clinging for their lives underneath the pews in the first place. But she was feeling altruistic on her wedding day and let it pass.

KyAnn and Levon sat at the front of the church, their baby peacefully sucking on his fist. They named their first son after the man who saved him. Adam Montgomery Sevier was so plump and healthy every time Levon looked down at him he'd swear the boy had grown.

"We are gathered this day to join together Charlotte Belle and Thomas Jones in the bonds of holy matrimony. . . ."

Worried Charlotte might still back out, Reverend Lyle read the marriage vows so fast, the congregation thought he was speaking in tongues.

"Do you, Charlotte, take this man, Thomas, for richer or for poorer, in sickness, and in health . . ."

When Reverend Lyle got to the part about "honor and obey," there was a pause in the ceremony. Everyone held their breath, sens-ing the merger had definitely hit a potential deal killer.

"Obey?" Charlotte echoed. "The hell I will."

Reverend Lyle rocked backward on his heels.

"Charlotte Belle!" Lettie hollered from the front pew. "You marry that man, or so help me, I'll lay you over my knee!"

Turning to face Charlotte, Thomas took her hands in his.

"Charlotte Belle, do you want to be my partner?"

"Equal partners," she countered.

"Fifty-fifty," he agreed.

And Charlotte said, "I do."

The
ROCK
ORCHARD

PAULA WALL

A Readers Club Guide

About This Guide

The suggested questions are intended to help your reading group find new and interesting angles and topics for discussion for Paula Wall's *The Rock Orchard*. We hope that these ideas will enrich your conversation and increase your enjoyment of the book.

Many fine books from Washington Square Press feature Readers Club Guides. For a complete listing, or to read the guides online, visit www.BookClubReader.com.

A Conversation with Paula Wall

1. This is your first novel. What inspired you to write *The Rock Orchard?*

   A million snapshots in life just came together.

   How did you stay focused and motivated?

   Focus and motivation are not my problem. I loved living in Leaper's Fork with these people. I still wake up there.

   What was the most difficult part of writing it?

   Sometimes the images I could see in my mind wouldn't bleed onto the page.

2. You grew up in the South, and still reside there. How much did you draw on your hometown to create Leaper's Fork and its residents?

   I blurred the line between fact and fiction quite a bit. My great-aunt Hattie worked at Mademoiselle's dress shop and they had a mynah bird. We played hide-n-seek in the graveyard, running through lightning bugs and hiding behind tombstones. One tombstone was an anchor with two children sitting on it like a swing. Both children had drowned. My great-aunt Birdie lived in an antebellum house that was used as a hospital during the Civil War. There were rust-colored watermarks on the living room ceiling. My cousin, Earl, told me they were Yankee blood stains to scare me. Earl lives in the house now. I'm sure those Yankee ghosts are praying he'll die while away on vacation and haunt a Holiday Inn.

3. The Belles are a distinct breed of seductive, strong-headed, big-hearted women. Was there a Musette, a Charlotte, or an Angela in your life that you drew from to create these characters?

I wasn't aware of it while writing, but my mother, as a young woman, was a lot like Angela, a dark, beautiful, bleeding heart with "the gift."

What role did these kind of women play in your life?

I spent my childhood in church bazaars and making cakes for bake sales. Some of the things we made could have ten dollars' worth of materials and a hundred hours in labor and they'd sell it for a dollar. I'd look around at those wonderful women and think they have absolutely no idea what they're worth.

How did your characters come to you?

I have no idea. Writing, at its best, is like channeling music. You rest your fingers on the keys and hope they play.

4. Charlotte is, quite literally, a force of nature, exerting a gravitational pull on those around her. She is bawdy and tough, but

ultimately a deeply caring person. What qualities do you share with her?

Charlotte dropped out of the writer's womb with some qualities I had to work on. Probably the quality we have most in common is we're both businesswomen.

Which of her qualities do you *wish* you shared with her?

The hardest thing to do in life is to let someone you love make a mistake. Charlotte has a handle on this.

5. On Banyan Island, the subject of ordinary versus extraordinary, common versus uncommon is discussed on several occasions. What do you think makes a person extraordinary and uncommon?

   They both move mountains, but the ordinary person uses a pick and shovel.

   How do you nurture those qualities in yourself?

   One shovel at a time.

6. Many of your characters feel tied or bound to their background and upbringing, whether it be one of wealth and privilege or poverty and abuse—until they are inspired to change. What are some things or people that have inspired you to make a change in your life?

   The ideal is to be self-inspiring. The love of my life taught me that—and if the person you live with doesn't inspire you, you're probably living with the wrong person. I've also been known to find inspiration in a fortune cookie.

7. What lessons would you ideally like the reader to walk away with?

   Whatever lessons they can carry. And that's the lesson I walked away with when writing the book.

8. When you write, do you find yourself writing to inspire, to educate, or to entertain?

   When the stars are aligned, all of the above.

   What type of books are you drawn to?

   I choose books like I choose friends. After an evening with them, I don't want to feel like sticking my head in the oven.

9. The residents of Leaper's Fork are truly endearing and make the reader want to check in on them long after the last page has been turned. Do these characters and this town have more stories in them?

   Maybe.

   Do you think you will write about them again?

   Truthfully, I never know what will end up on the page until the end of the day.

10. What are you working on now?

My mother used to say, "The person who talks about it the most is doing it the least." That said, I don't talk about my work. But to keep my publisher from smothering me with a pillow, I will say The Rock Orchard *will not be my last book.*

Questions and Topics for Discussion

1. In the preface we are introduced to Musette Belle and her ability to "read the future." Most Belle women have retained this gift of "sight." In what other ways do the Belle women see differently? How do they use this gift to enrich their community?

2. What similarities do Angela and Charlotte share? What makes them distinctly different? What do you think these characters learn from each other?

3. *The Rock Orchard* of the title is a reference to a cemetery. "A cemetery is like an orchard. Some lives were sweet. Some bitter as lemons. And some were rotten to the core." The cemetery in Leaper's Fork is practically a character in itself—a place that figures especially in the lives of the Belle women, often in unexpected ways. In this way the cemetery sheds its stigma as a place of sadness and death. Discuss the cemetery as a place of happiness and rebirth. How does the cemetery serve as a turning point for Charlotte? For Lydia? For Reverend Thomas?

4. Reba Earhart and Mila are just two of the many people Charlotte inspires. "You are what you are, till you decide to be different," she says. Compare and contrast these two women—how did they both succumb to the initial lots they had drawn in life? What patterns of behavior did they share? How did they go about changing those patterns? How did they perpetuate the chain of inspiration in others around them?

5. Empowerment is an important factor throughout the novel. How do various characters overcome their circumstances? Does empowerment always come in the form of financial wealth? Where else do these characters find power?

6. What was the significance of Levon Sevier initiating the kiss at his and KyAnn's wedding?

7. Charlotte is described as having "a man's mind" and frequently engages in behaviors stereotypically reserved for men, such as drinking and smoking cigars. Discuss the reversal of gender stereotypes found throughout the novel. How does it change the reader's point of view on gender roles in society? Are the characters who adhere to the classic gender stereotypes viewed differently from those who break out of their gender roles?

8. The Belles, KyAnn Merriweather, and Julia Mercer are independent women who take ownership of their sexuality. This intimidates some, and inspires others. By the end of the novel, both KyAnn and Charlotte are married. Does this in any way undermine their independence? Why or why not?

9. Throughout the novel we see a variety of partnerships—business, friendship, marriage, religious, and sometimes a blend of two or more. Discuss some of the partnerships found in *The Rock Orchard*. Which were most successful? Which surprised you most?

10. While national and world events are occasionally mentioned in *The Rock Orchard*, much of the story seems to take place in a suspended space and time. Why do you think this is? How does it help the plot? Does it hurt the story in any way?

11. Where do you see Charlotte, Angela, and Dixie in the next five years? In what ways will they have changed? In what ways will they remain the same?

12. Just for fun, imagine you are a casting director working on a film version of *The Rock Orchard*. Discuss whom you would cast to play some of the main characters and why. Who would you cast for Charlotte? Angela? KyAnn? Adam? Lydia? Boone?